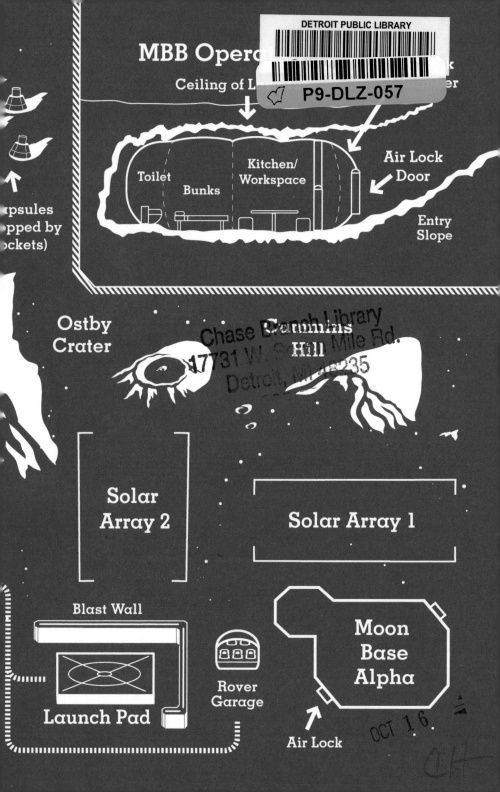

MBB Opera___

Ceiling of L_____er

Toilet
Bunks
Kitchen/
Workspace

Air Lock
Door

Entry
Slope

___psules
___pped by
___ckets)

Ostby
Crater

Brummins
Hill

Solar
Array 2

Solar Array 1

Blast Wall

Rover
Garage

Moon
Base
Alpha

Launch Pad

Air Lock

spaced out

Also by Stuart Gibbs

The FunJungle series
Belly Up
Poached
Big Game

The Spy School series
Spy School
Spy Camp
Evil Spy School

The Moon Base Alpha series
Space Case

The Last Musketeer

STUART GIBBS

spaced out

A **moon base alpha** NOVEL

Simon & Schuster Books for Young Readers

New York London Toronto Sydney New Delhi

SIMON & SCHUSTER BOOKS FOR YOUNG READERS
An imprint of Simon & Schuster Children's Publishing Division
1230 Avenue of the Americas, New York, New York 10020

For information about special discounts for bulk purchases, please contact Simon & Schuster Special Sales at 1-866-506-1949 or business@simonandschuster.com.
The Simon & Schuster Speakers Bureau can bring authors to your live event. For more information or to book an event, contact the Simon & Schuster Speakers Bureau at 1-866-248-3049 or visit our website at www.simonspeakers.com.
Book design and principal jacket illustration by Lucy Ruth Cummins
Map art by Ryan Thompson
The text for this book was set in Adobe Garamond.
Manufactured in the United States of America
0216 FFG
First Edition
10 9 8 7 6 5 4 3 2 1
Library of Congress Cataloging-in-Publication Data
Gibbs, Stuart, 1969– author.
Spaced out / Stuart Gibbs.—First edition.
pages cm
Summary: In 2041 twelve-year-old Dashiell Gibson is a resident of Moon Base Alpha, and at the moment he is faced with a number of problems: coping with the nasty Sjoberg twins, finding out how the commander of the base has managed to disappear from a facility no bigger than a soccer field, and dealing with the alien Zan who communicates with him telepathically from afar—and who is hiding a secret which may threaten the whole Earth.
ISBN 978-1-4814-2336-6 (hardcover)—ISBN 978-1-4814-2338-0 (eBook)
1. Space colonies—Juvenile fiction. 2. Extraterrestrial beings—Juvenile fiction. 3. Human-alien encounters—Juvenile fiction. 4. Telepathy—Juvenile fiction. 5. Secrecy—Juvenile fiction. 6. Moon—Juvenile fiction. [1. Mystery and detective stories. 2. Space colonies—Fiction. 3. Extraterrestrial beings—Fiction. 4. Human-alien encounters—Fiction. 5. Telepathy—Fiction. 6. Secrets—Fiction. 7. Moon—Fiction. 8. Science fiction.] I. Title.
PZ7.G339236Sl 2016
813.6—dc23
[Fic]
2015004025

For Barry, Carole, Alan, and Bobbe Patmore

acknowledgments

In writing the Moon Base Alpha books, I do my
best to be as realistic as possible in describing the future of
space travel (and yes, that even applies to the possible way
alien contact might eventually happen). I continue to be
indebted to my good friend, Garrett Reisman, former astro-
naut and current director of crew operations at SpaceX, who
was always available to answer any questions I had. I'd also
like to thank Dr. Angel Abbud-Madrid, director of the Center for Space Resources at the Colorado School of Mines,
and Joel G. Duncan, PhD, senior lecturer in the Department of Geology and Geological Engineering at the School
of Mines, for their help in figuring out how construction
of a moon base might proceed. My intern, Caroline Yost,
did some exceptionally good research for me. And finally, I'd
also like to thank my junior research team, my children, the
original Dashiell and Violet, for being such good sports on
my fact-finding trips, whether they be to the Kennedy Space
Center to learn about spaceflight, the Griffith Observatory
to learn about moon rocks, or Hawaii Volcanoes National
Park to study lava tubes. I love you guys!

contents

1: EXTRATERRESTRIAL MOVIE NIGHT 3

2: SELF-DEFENSE WITH PLUMBING 16

3: THE SPACE TOILET INCIDENT
   INVESTIGATION   26

4: MALICIOUS BLUEBERRIES   37

5: STEALING JULIET   51

6: FRUITLESS SEARCHING   65

7: DIRE WARNING   82

8: DEAD ENDS   95

9: SENTIENT NANOBOTS   108

10: BREAKING AND ENTERING   121

11: ILLEGAL CONTRABAND   137

12: SPACE JERK REBELLION   155

13: DESPERATE TIMES   173

14: MOONLIGHT RIDE   193

15: DEATH FROM ABOVE   205

16: VIDEO TRANSMISSION   218

17: FRAYED NERVES   232

18: HYPOTHETICAL SPACE SNAKES 253

19: IMAGINARY FRIENDS   265

20: BIG REVELATION   279

21: RACING THE CLOCK   287

22: SECRET IDENTITY   307

23: THE ASTEROID   322

Moon Base Alpha Resident Directory

Upper floor:

Residence 1 *(base commander's quarters and office)*
Nina Stack, moon-base commander

Residence 2
Harris-Gibson residence
Dr. Rose Harris, lunar geologist
Dr. Stephen Gibson, mining specialist
Dashiell Gibson (12)
Violet Gibson (6)

Residence 3
Dr. Maxwell Howard, lunar-engineering specialist for
Moon Base Beta
Kira Howard (12)

Residence 4
Brahmaputra-Marquez residence
Dr. Ilina Brahmaputra-Marquez, astrophysicist
Dr. Timothy Marquez, psychiatrist
Cesar Marquez (16)
Rodrigo Marquez (13)
Inez Marquez (7)

Tourist Suite

currently occupied by the Sjoberg family:

Lars Sjoberg, industrialist

Sonja Sjoberg, his wife

Patton Sjoberg (16)

Lily Sjoberg (16)

Residence 5 *reserved for temporary base residents (female)*

Residence 6 *reserved for temporary base residents (male)*

Residence 7

Former residence of Dr. Ronald Holtz. Currently
reserved for new moon-base doctor. *(Note: Selection still
in process; not due to arrive until Mission 8.)*

Lower floor:

Residence 8
Former residence of Garth Grisan. Reserved for new moon-base maintenance specialist. *(Note: Selection still in process; not due to arrive until Mission 8.)*

Residence 9
Dr. Wilbur Janke, astrobiologist

Residence 10
Dr. Daphne Merritt, base roboticist

Residence 11
Dr. Chang Kowalski, geochemist

Residence 12
Goldstein-Iwanyi residence
Dr. Shari Goldstein, lunar-agriculture specialist
Dr. Mfuzi Iwanyi, astronomer
Kamoze Iwanyi (7)

Residence 13
Kim-Alvarez residence
Dr. Jennifer Kim, seismic geologist
Dr. Shenzu Alvarez, water-extraction specialist

Residence 14

Dr. Viktor Balnikov, astrophysicist

Residence 15

Chen-Patucket residence

Dr. Jasmine Chen, senior engineering coordinator for Moon Base Beta

Dr. Seth Patucket, astrobiologist

Holly Patucket (13)

(Note: Arrival has been pushed back until Mission 9. This residence will be used as housing for temporary base workers until then.)

Excerpt from *The Official Residents' Guide to Moon Base Alpha*,
© 2040 by National Aeronautics and Space Administration:

APPENDIX A
POTENTIAL HEALTH AND SAFETY HAZARDS

Although every effort has been taken to make Moon Base Alpha the safest human habitat ever built, we still urge you to be extremely careful and vigilant for your own well-being. MBA's medical bay has been stocked with plenty of emergency supplies and the latest medical technology* so that the doctor on staff can handle even extreme medical emergencies, but all lunarnauts should bear in mind that life on the moon is inherently dangerous and that the closest hospital is back on earth, more than 250,000 miles away. Thus, you are advised to exercise extreme caution at all times and take great care to avoid risks.

To that end, we have compiled the following catalog of potentially dangerous areas, facilities, objects, and situations. Bear in mind this is by no means meant to be a complete list, but rather a guide to provide for better safety. There may be many other hazards at MBA not included below. Please do your best to be safe and alert to danger at all times while you are on the moon. Remember: The best way to avoid trouble is to not get into trouble in the first place!

---

* At the time of printing. Because of the difficult nature of replacing technology on the moon, some tech may be slightly out-of-date by the time you read this.

EXTRATERRESTRIAL MOVIE NIGHT

Earth year 2041
Lunar day 216
Bedtime

If I hadn't made the mistake of showing *Star Wars*
to an alien life form, I never would have ended up fighting
Patton Sjoberg with the space toilet.

But then, being friends with an alien had been one problem
after another. It was far more difficult than I had ever imagined.
For starters, there was no end of things I had to explain.

Every single aspect of my life was strange and unusual to
Zan Perfonic. She wanted to know the reasons for everything
I did. But it turns out, there's not much reason behind half
the things we humans do.

For example, blessing someone after they sneeze.

One day, Zan overheard me do this for my sister, and later she asked why I'd said it.

I had to think for a moment before admitting, "I have no idea. It's just something we humans do. It's supposed to be good manners."

"Like when you use napkins to blot partially eaten food off your faces?"

"Kind of."

"What does 'bless you' mean?"

"Um . . . that you want good things to happen for someone. I think."

"So every time someone involuntarily blasts snot out of their nose, you humans tell them you want good things to happen to them?"

"Er . . . yes."

"Do you say 'bless you' for other involuntary actions? Like when someone burps?"

"No."

"Or farts?"

"Definitely not."

"Why not?"

"I guess because farting is considered rude."

"And yet, is also considered funny?"

"Not by everyone."

"Your sister seems to think it's funny."

"Well, she's six."

"Your father does too. He's not six."

"Good point."

"So why do some people find involuntary emissions of noxious gases from their rectums funny while other people find it rude?"

"I don't know."

"Do you think it has something to do with the sound?"

It went on like that for twenty minutes, with Zan asking me to try to explain everything from whoopee cushions to "pull my finger" until I was mentally exhausted. For this reason, I'd taken to showing Zan movies whenever I could. They made life easier. I'd used them to help explain everything from dinosaurs to World War II to professional sports.

I know I sound like a crazy person with all this talking-to-an-alien stuff. Like the kind of lunatic who stumbles through the streets babbling gibberish and wearing a tinfoil hat.

But I'm not crazy. My name's Dashiell Gibson and I'm a totally sane twelve-year-old boy who happens to live on the moon. You've probably heard of me. All of us up here are pretty famous, seeing as we're the first families to colonize someplace that isn't earth. There's so much coverage of us down there, you might think you know everything about us.

But you don't. You only know what the government wants

you to know. And a lot of that is lies. Like when you hear that Moon Base Alpha is a really amazing, incredible place? Or that we're all getting along great up here and having the time of our lives? That's all a big, steaming pile of garbage.

Plus, there are things we all keep to ourselves. Like being in contact with aliens from the planet Bosco.

Zan's planet wasn't really called Bosco. But I couldn't pronounce its real name. When Zan said it in her native language, it sounded like a bunch of dolphins who'd sucked the helium out of a Macy's balloon. It was so high-pitched it made my ears hurt. So we went with "Bosco" instead.

No one else at MBA knew I was in contact with Zan. I was the only one who could see her. Or hear her. Or speak to her.

There was a perfectly good reason for this: Zan wasn't really there. You see, her species hadn't mastered interstellar travel yet. (Not that we humans have come anywhere close to figuring it out ourselves.) Zan's species had found a short-cut, though. They could *think* themselves to other places.

I had no idea how it worked. Zan had been doing her best to explain it to me, and it always left me feeling like I was an idiot. But then, even Albert Einstein would have looked like an idiot to Zan.

The point being, I wasn't really seeing Zan with my eyes. Instead she was connecting directly with my mind, inserting herself into my thoughts. I didn't even see the *real* Zan. Instead I saw an image of her that she wanted me to see: a beautiful, dark-haired thirty-year-old female human with startlingly blue eyes. In truth, I didn't know what Zan really looked like, because she hadn't shown me yet.

Communicating with Zan wasn't actually that difficult. She had learned English and could speak it better than half the humans I'd met. The hard part was that she insisted our friendship remain a secret. However, she had a very good reason for this:

Zan had befriended only one human before me, Dr. Ronald Holtz, who had been the doctor at Moon Base Alpha. Dr. Holtz had wanted to reveal Zan's existence to all humanity, but he never got the chance. Because the second person who learned about Zan was another Moonie named Garth Grisan, a whacked-out, ultra-paranoid spy for the military who believed humanity wasn't ready to learn we're not alone in the universe. Garth killed Dr. Holtz to keep the secret safe, but he made it look like an accident. I'd figured it out with Zan's help, though, and Garth had been shipped back to earth to stand trial for murder.

So Zan wasn't in any rush to reveal her existence this time. I understood. Frankly, I was surprised she was willing to give humanity another try. And it was absolutely thrilling to get to talk to an alien.

It just wasn't easy.

Maybe things wouldn't have been so much trouble if I still lived on earth. Back there, if I wanted to spend some private time with Zan, I could simply go to my room and lock the door. But on the moon, I don't have my own room. I share a cramped one-room residence with my parents and my little sister, Violet, and my "bedroom" is a niche built into the wall. On earth, I could go for a walk around the neighborhood. On the moon, I can't. I'm not allowed outside, because I could die out there. On earth, there were a million places I could go to be by myself. On the moon, there are none. I have no privacy whatsoever. There are security cameras everywhere, half the base is off-limits to me, and even the bathrooms are communal.

So, basically, the only way I could spend any serious time with Zan was late at night, after everyone else had gone to bed.

The night I showed her *Star Wars*, it was well after dinnertime. Mom and Dad had already tucked Violet into bed for the night and were playing chess in our room, while all the other Moonies seemed to be settling down in their residences as well. I wasn't trying to explain anything to Zan by showing her the movie. I had simply referenced it so much, she demanded to see it.

It was hard to talk about life in space without talking

about *Star Wars*. Or *Star Trek*. Or any other space movies. Because space travel always looked so cool in those films, when it wasn't in real life. In the movies, you never saw anyone having trouble walking in low gravity or eating disgusting rehydrated space food or vacuuming their poop out with a space toilet. Instead, gravity was always exactly the same on every planet, the food was delicious, and no one ever even went to the bathroom. Without thinking about it, I'd referenced *Star Wars* over and over again, and finally Zan had said, "Are you ever going to show me this movie?" So I did. I brought her to the rec room and uploaded *Star Wars: A New Hope* onto the SlimScreen.

Zan thought it was hilarious.

She laughed hysterically the whole way through it. And laughter was something that didn't really translate between us. Zan's species actually *had* humor, which was nice, but they didn't express it by laughing; that was a human thing. Instead they made a high-pitched whine that was shrill enough to rattle my eardrums. Plus, there was a strange side effect where Zan would lose control of her projected self and her eyeballs would swell up like beach balls. It was all very disconcerting. Finally, about halfway through, I had to pause the movie and tell her, "It's not a comedy."

She stopped whining, her eyeballs shrinking back down to normal size, and said, "It's not?"

"No," I told her. "It's a science-fiction adventure movie."

"But all the spaceships and the weapons and everything are so ridiculous. Like the laser guns. When they shoot lasers at each other, you can see them moving through space, whereas in real life, light moves so quickly that the shot would be instantaneous. . . ."

"Er . . . yes," I admitted, although this had never occurred to me before. "But . . ."

"And the ships keep jumping to warp speed, which is faster than light speed, which is simply impossible."

"Well, just because you haven't figured out how to do it doesn't mean it *can't* be done."

"Yes, but if it *is* done, it certainly won't be in spacecraft as ludicrous as the ones in this movie. Half of them seem to be using the same type of rudimentary combustion engines that you use on your rockets. They'd be lucky to break the gravity of their planets, let alone travel dozens of light-years in a second."

"I suppose. . . ."

"Plus, all the space creatures are absurd. They're all modeled on humans with two arms and two legs, when there are thousands of other ways a body could be constructed."

"There are?"

"Certainly. Look at your own planet. There are billions

of species of insect and only one species of human. And yet there isn't a single creature in the movie with an insect body structure."

"You mean, you'd think *Star Wars* would be *less* funny if Chewbacca looked like a giant cockroach?"

"Well, it would certainly be more realistic. The chances of Wookiees being so structurally similar to your species is staggeringly improbable. And don't even get me started on the fact that Luke Skystalker and Princess Leo and Ham Bolo look exactly like humans, even though they live in some galaxy far, far away."

"Those aren't their names. . . ."

"Well, you know who I mean. Honestly, the entire film is laughably earth-centric and the physics are preposterous."

I turned the TV off. "Obviously, showing you this was a mistake."

"No!" Zan cried. "It wasn't. I'm really enjoying it. I haven't laughed so hard in a long time." She giggled at the thought, her eyes swelling up again.

"Do *you* look like a giant cockroach?" I asked pointedly.

Zan stopped laughing. Her eyes returned to their normal size. "Why do you ask?"

"Because I don't know anything about you," I told her. "We always talk about me and earth and humanity, but never about *you*. I don't even know what you really look like."

"I don't think you're ready to see me as I really exist. For the time being, it's much better if I appear to you in human form."

"Why?"

"Because it's far easier for you to relate to something that appears similar to you than something that appears alien."

"You don't know that for sure."

"It seems logical to assume as much."

"Now you sound like Mr. Spock."

"Who?"

"Never mind." If Zan had an issue with Wookiees looking too human, she'd probably flip out when she learned about Vulcans.

"I sense frustration in you," Zan said.

"Yes." There was no point in denying it. One of the side effects of Zan communicating directly with my mind was that she could read my emotions as well as I could. Better, sometimes.

"Why?"

"When you first approached me about being your human contact, you said it was extremely important," I reminded Zan. "More important than I could possibly understand. But you haven't told me *why* yet. You haven't told me *any-thing*. Not one thing about you or your family or your planet. While I've told you plenty. I've answered all your questions, and you've had a million of them."

"Dashiell, when we began this relationship, I warned you it wouldn't be easy. . . ."

"You can't tell me what we're doing here? Or why our contact is so important?"

"Certainly you must realize how significant contact is between humans and an alien species for the first time."

"Yes, but there's more to it than that, isn't there? What's so important about it that I couldn't possibly understand?"

"If I told you, you wouldn't understand it."

"See?" I snapped. "Answers like that are why I'm frustrated! Can't you at least *try* to tell me?"

"I don't have authorization for that yet."

"Is the earth in some kind of danger?" I asked.

Zan didn't answer. But something changed in her. I couldn't tell what, exactly; it was almost as though her image had distorted for a fraction of a second. I got the idea that I'd caught her by surprise.

"I'm right, aren't I?" I demanded. "The earth *is* in danger."

"No," Zan told me. "It's not that dire."

"You're lying."

"I'm not," Zan said, but I had the distinct feeling that she was. Or at least hiding something from me.

"What is going on here?" I asked.

Before Zan could respond, voices echoed in the hall outside the rec room. Someone was coming our way.

I suddenly realized that, in my frustration, I'd forgotten to not speak out loud to Zan.

I always tried to keep all our conversations inside my head, but that took a great deal of focus and concentration. When Zan appeared to me, it didn't *feel* like she was only an image being projected into my mind. She seemed as real as any person on the base, and over my twelve years of life, I'd learned that when you speak to someone, you use your mouth, not just your brain. It was a tough habit to break. Often, I thought I *was* keeping quiet, only to realize in mid-sentence that I wasn't.

Zan's eyes flicked toward the door. "We can't discuss this now. I have to go."

"No," I said. "Wait. . . ."

"I'm sorry," Zan told me, then vanished.

A second later, Patton and Lily Sjoberg stormed into the room. Patton and Lily were the biggest bullies at Moon Base Alpha. They were twins, aged sixteen, and at that moment, they were very angry and obviously looking for trouble.

Unfortunately, they'd found me instead.

YOUR FELLOW LUNARNAUTS

Sadly, the most likely cause of pain or injury at MBA is one our engineers can do nothing about: your fellow humans. Statistically, you are much more likely to get hurt by another person than by any equipment malfunction or random disaster. While all lunarnauts were selected in part for their amiability, agreeability, and skill at getting along with others, living with other humans in an enclosed space over an extended period of time has the potential to lead to disagreements, arguments, and even physical violence. Therefore, all lunarnauts are encouraged to work extra hard at resolving interpersonal conflicts—should they arise—as calmly and peacefully as possible. For help with any conflicts that cannot be resolved in this way, lunarnauts are advised to seek the aid of the moon-base commander for mediation. The base psychiatrist is also available for aid in these matters.

It is in everyone's interest to not allow disagreements to escalate to the point of violence, as not only you and your opponent could be injured, but innocent bystanders as well. So please, do your best to be good citizens at MBA and try to get along with everyone. It won't merely be good for your physical health—it will do wonders for your mental health as well!

SELF-DEFENSE WITH PLUMBING

Lunar day 216
Too late to get help

There were a lot of things I didn't like about liv-ing on the moon, but the Sjobergs were the worst by far. And to be more horrible than a space toilet is really saying something. Patton and Lily had come to Moon Base Alpha with their parents, Lars and Sonja, as the first lunar tourists. The whole family was filthy rich and staggeringly mean. They had forked out more than half a billion dollars to visit MBA, and when the whole experience turned out to be far below their expectations, they had taken out their anger on everyone else. They were desperate to go back to earth—and we were all desperate for them to go back as well—but it wasn't that easy. Travel to and from the moon was locked into an inflexible schedule, and the Sjobergs didn't have seats assigned on a rocket for another three months—if everything went smoothly. Which it probably wouldn't. Rockets to the moon got delayed all the time; even someone as rich and powerful as Lars Sjoberg couldn't control that. In the meantime, the Sjobergs were doing their best to make everyone else miserable. Only Cesar Marquez, a Moonie teenager who Lily had a crush on, escaped their wrath. For everyone else, any encounter with them was toxic.

On that night, Patton and Lily seemed to be in a worse mood than usual. Something had really ticked them off.

"Who were you just talking to?" Patton demanded.

"No one," I said.

"Don't lie to us," Lily snarled. "We *heard* you, you little jerk."

The Sjobergs were practically the first purely Caucasian family I'd ever met in my life; back on earth—and at MBA— almost everyone was a blend of ethnicities. I'd heard there were people who actually thought the Sjobergs were quite attractive, and that Lily was particularly exotic and beautiful, with her long blond hair and her fair white complexion. I always found her hideous, though. Maybe because I couldn't help but see the ugliness beneath her skin.

"I meant I wasn't talking to anyone *here*," I corrected quickly.

"I was on a ComLink with my friend Riley back on earth."

"No, you weren't, turdface." Patton moved toward me menacingly. He was a big kid who spent most of his time at MBA in the gym making his muscles even bigger. "You were talking to Roddy, weren't you?"

That would have been Rodrigo Marquez, Cesar's younger brother and the only other boy on the moon my age. Since Lily liked Cesar and Cesar didn't like Roddy, Roddy had become Patton and Lily's favorite target at Moon Base Alpha. Often it was unwarranted, but sometimes Roddy actually did things to deserve it. He could be such an obnoxious know-it-all that there were times when *I* wanted to punch him.

"I haven't seen Roddy tonight," I told them.

"We saw him come this way," Lily said. She stayed by her brother's side as they moved in on me, blocking my escape route.

"That doesn't mean he came in here," I pointed out.

"Where else could he have gone?" Lily demanded.

"His residence," I suggested. "Or the gym. Or the medical bay . . ."

"I'm gonna send *you* to the medical bay if you don't tell me the truth," Patton snarled. "Where's Roddy? What were you two talking about?"

"Nothing!" I exclaimed. "Why are you so upset with Roddy?"

"Just tell us where he is!" Patton lunged across the room, apparently ready to pound the answer out of me.

I was ready for him, though. With Patton, I was always ready for a sneak attack. I ducked under his arm and scrambled for the door.

Patton and Lily both roared with rage and came after me.

I tried to get away from them quickly, but that was hard to do on the moon. The gravity here is only one-sixth of earth's, so you can't run. Instead you just bob along slowly. Each step launches you as high as if you've bounced on a trampoline. Luckily, Patton and Lily had the same issues and couldn't go any faster than I did.

It wasn't like there were many places to run to anyhow. Moon Base Alpha isn't very big. The rec room sits in the center of it, along with the greenhouse and the control rooms, looped by a single circular hallway. On the exterior walls are the gymnasium, mess hall, bathrooms, science pod, air lock, medical bay, and two floors of residences. That's it.

I bounded out of the rec room into the hall facing the residences, hoping to find some adults who could tell Patton and Lily to back off. The hall was two stories tall, with only a metal catwalk to access the upper residences, so I could see every door. Unfortunately, all of them were closed; there wasn't an adult anywhere. Quite possibly, everyone else was already asleep. So I veered toward the science pod. If any

Moonies were up late, they'd be there, working.

Patton and Lily stayed on my heels. We raced through the air-lock staging area, then past the control rooms. Just as I reached the science pod, Patton body-slammed me.

On earth, we would have thudded to the ground. On the moon, we flew. Patton's force sent both of us sailing into the men's bathroom door, which sprang open, and we crashed onto the floor inside. We might have tumbled all the way to the far wall if we hadn't slammed into the first toilet stall, which halted our progress quickly and painfully. Patton ended up on top of me. He pressed his arm against my neck, choking me, fury in his eyes. "Tell me what you and Roddy saw," he growled.

By this point, I was quite sure that telling the truth wasn't going to work out for me. Patton was obviously looking for an excuse to hurt someone, and I wasn't about to give it to him. However, fighting wasn't an option either. Patton was much stronger than me and he already had the upper hand. So I did the only other thing I could think of.

Except for the toilets themselves, the toilet stalls at Moon Base Alpha look exactly like ones you'd see in any public bathroom on earth; the walls don't go all the way to the floor, which meant that my head was disturbingly close to the toilet. Lunar toilets are horrible things. Since we have very little water, they don't flush. Instead they're more like vacuum cleaners for your private parts, designed to suck every last bit of poop and pee away from you. The poop goes into the composter, while our urine heads right into the purifying tank, after which it's recycled into the water supply. (Yet another ordeal of space travel that doesn't occur in *Star Wars*.) The men's toilets all have a suction hose for pee attached, with a wide, clear funnel at one end for you to do your business in. NASA's official name for it was "Splash-proof Urine Receptacle," but we all called it "the Urinator."

The Urinator was dangling only a few inches away from me. I snaked it under the stall wall, slammed it into Patton's face, and turned the suction on.

Patton's head was wide and fleshy enough to make a perfect seal for the funnel, which promptly locked onto his face. Through the clear plastic, I could see his eyes go wide in terror. Air was flowing in the Urinator, so Patton wasn't going to suffocate—but having the receptacle for everyone's pee clamped over his mouth seemed terrifying enough for him. He released his grip on me and tried desperately to yank the Urinator off, but it held fast. He tried to scream for help, but his lips got sucked toward the urine hose and flapped wildly, preventing him from making any noise but guttural squeals.

Unfortunately, I was still pinned beneath him. Patton was sitting on my chest as he writhed around with the Urinator.

Lily burst into the bathroom and gasped in horror at the

sight of her brother. Then she glared at me. "What are you doing to him?"

"It's self-defense!" I argued.

"You get that thing off him right now!" Lily screamed. "Get it off or I will kill you!" She started toward me, her fingernails extended like claws.

"Stop right there!" I warned, smashing the Urinator funnel further into Patton's face. "Or I'll suck his face right off!"

It was a bluff. The Urinator didn't have nearly enough power to remove Patton's face, but I was pretty sure Patton and Lily didn't know that. Patton and Lily didn't know much, period.

Lily froze in her tracks, while Patton gave a blubbery yelp of fear. He waved desperately at Lily, signaling her to back off.

"Okay," she told me, worried. "I'm not going to hurt you. Leave his face where it is."

"I won't suck it off unless you make me." I wriggled out from under Patton and stood, keeping the Urinator pressed firmly against his face the whole time. Patton stayed on his knees, staring at me fearfully with his bugged-out eyes, afraid to move.

"Let's get a few things straight," I said. "I didn't start this. *You* did. I was minding my own business in the rec room when you showed up. I don't know what Roddy did to get you so worked up, but I had nothing to do with it and I haven't even seen him since dinner."

"We thought we heard you talking to him," Lily said weakly.

"Well, I wasn't. And if you two had listened to me instead of attacking me, then Patton wouldn't be French-kissing the Urinator right now. Understand?"

Lily nodded. So did Patton.

I looked Patton in the eye through the plastic funnel. "So do I have your word you won't try to beat me up if I turn this off?"

Patton nodded again.

"I don't mean just right now," I added. "I mean you won't try to beat me up tomorrow, too—and the next day and the next and so on. You're not going to retaliate for this, right?"

Patton hesitated a moment before answering.

I shoved the Urinator into his face a little harder. His lips flapped like willow branches in a hurricane. "Give me your word, Patton."

Patton nodded once more, desperation in his googly eyes.

"Okay," I said, then turned off the Urinator and popped the funnel off Patton's face.

I was ready to run. I figured there was a decent chance Patton would immediately go back on his word and try to cream me. Instead he was so disgusted from having his face in the Urinator, he ran screaming for the shower. To conserve water, we were only supposed to shower once a week, if that, but Patton completely ignored the rules. He also didn't bother to take his clothes off. He just ran in, cranked on the water (which was really only a trickle, given how precious a resource it was), and scoured his face with it. Lily forgot about me too for the moment. She hovered around the shower, asking Patton, "Are you all right? You didn't swallow any pee, did you?"

While they were distracted, I quickly headed for home. I was quite sure the Sjoberg twins weren't done with me, but for the time being, I'd be safe in my family's residence.

And besides, given my conversation with Zan about the fate of the earth, I had bigger things to worry about than the Sjobergs.

Excerpt from *The Official Residents' Guide to Moon Base Alpha*, "Appendix A: Potential Health and Safety Hazards," © 2040 by National Aeronautics and Space Administration

TOILETS

The toilets at Moon Base Alpha are not like the ones you are used to on earth. To counteract the lack of water and minimal gravity, the space toilets use suction instead. Please exercise extreme caution around the suction hoses and vacuum bowl, as they can cause harm to any body parts caught in them accidentally. In addition, do not dispose of any garbage down the toilets other than human waste, as this could cause blockages that could then lead to burst pipes, ruptured tubes, or even explosions of fecal matter—which are not only dangerous, but unsanitary as well.

THE SPACE TOILET INCIDENT
INVESTIGATION

Lunar day 216

Well after bedtime

Given where our conversation had left off, I was desperate to get back in touch with Zan and find out what danger lay in store for the earth. But I had no way to contact her. Zan only appeared to me when she wanted to and that was that. There was nothing I could do but wait for her to show up again.

In the meantime, the Sjobergs reported me to the moonbase commander.

That was Nina Stack, who was as tough and straitlaced as any person I'd ever met. Nina had come to NASA from the military and she still acted like she was in it. Behind her back, all the kids called her "Nina the Machina," because she had the same range of emotions as a kitchen appliance: none.

She knocked on the door of our residence while my parents and I were getting ready for bed. Violet was already snoring in her sleep pod. We had set our wall-size SlimScreen to project a nighttime view of Hapuna Beach in Hawaii. We were from near there, on the Big Island, and it always made us feel like we were back home, rather than stuck in a tiny outpost on a barren rock floating in space.

Nina didn't even say hello when Mom opened the door. That type of normal human interaction was alien to her. Instead she said, "I need to speak to Dashiell in my quarters."

I had already informed my parents of everything that had happened that night. Everything that didn't involve Zan, at least. "Dash should not get in trouble for this," Mom told Nina. "He was protecting himself from Patton Sjoberg."

"I'm not here to punish Dashiell," Nina said flatly. While everyone else at MBA dressed casually in shorts and T-shirts, Nina always wore her official NASA flight suit. Even this late at night, it looked as though it had just been ironed. "However, I am required by NASA to get his statement as to what occurred in the space toilet incident."

Mom opened the door wide and waved Nina inside. "Fine. Then you can do it right here."

Nina remained on the catwalk outside our residence.

"Rose, my orders are to get Dashiell's statement, not yours or your husband's. To prevent you from interfering, this really ought to be done in my quarters."

Mom started to protest, but I cut her off. "It's okay. I'll go." I turned off my e-book and headed for the door.

"This can't wait until morning?" Dad asked. "It's bedtime for all of us."

"We have an extremely busy day tomorrow, so I'd prefer to get this done now," Nina said. Without so much as a good-bye—or an apology for disturbing everyone so late— she turned away and led me down the catwalk to her residence.

This didn't take long, as Nina lived right next door to us. All the residence doors at MBA have electronic sensor locks linked to our smartwatches. Nina waved her watch in front of the sensor pad and the dead bolt automatically slid open.

It was only the second time I had ever been in Nina's quarters. The previous time had been a month before. Nothing had changed. Although Nina's residence was larger than my entire family's (or anyone else's quarters, save for the Sjobergs' "tourist suite"), she had almost nothing in it. Furniture was too big and bulky to haul much of it to the moon, so except for the standard bureau, SlimScreen table, and inflatable cubes that served as chairs, Nina's only extra item was a spindly self-assembled desk. We had all been allowed to bring a few personal items to MBA, but Nina hadn't bothered with any of those. Her SlimScreen wasn't on, leaving only a blank gray wall. Even the view out Nina's window was exactly the same as it had been before. Since there was no wind, rain, or any other type of weather on the moon, every speck of dirt was probably exactly where it had been not only a month earlier, but for the last hundred thousand years as well.

Nina sat on an InflatiCube on one side of her desk, then pointed me to the one on the other side. "Sit," she said. Like I was a dog.

I sat anyhow, trying not to make waves. I wanted this to be over with as quickly as possible. The InflatiCube, being cheap plastic, made a farting noise as I put my weight on it. This happened a lot with those. Most people at MBA found this funny—Violet in particular—though Nina never found anything funny. I had never seen her laugh once in the four months we'd been on the moon.

"I'm revoking your communication privileges with earth," she told me. "For the next two weeks, you will not be able to use the ComLinks for any purpose other than school."

"What?" I asked. "I thought you said I wasn't going to be punished!"

"Use of the ComLinks is a privilege, not a right," Nina

said robotically. "Therefore, temporary suspension of your privileges is not technically a punishment. . . ."

"It's still not cool! I thought you said you were going to take my statement on the space toilet incident!"

"There's no need for that. I have reviewed the security footage from the men's bathroom and observed what happened."

"I did that in self-defense!" I argued. "Patton was trying to strangle me!"

"The space toilet is not intended for use in self-defense," Nina told me. "It is *only* designed for the hygienic disposal of human urine and feces. Should you have broken it, the fabrication, shipping, and installation of a replacement would have cost NASA over half a billion dollars."

"Well then, the Sjobergs should pay for it. A half a billion dollars is petty cash to them."

"This isn't merely about the cost, Dashiell. There are only three toilets for all the men on this base. A reduction of those by a third could have severe consequences, especially given the unfortunate effects of some of our space food on everyone's digestive tracts."

She was probably talking about the chicken parmesan, which often sent us Moonies to the bathroom for extended periods of time. Sure, everyone could have avoided it, but it had already been shipped to MBA, and on the moon our options for dining out were limited. The nearest pizza delivery was 238,900 miles away.

"Are Patton and Lily losing their ComLink privileges too?" I asked. "Seeing as they were trying to beat me up?"

Nina broke eye contact with me for a second. "For the Sjobergs, the ComLinks aren't a privilege. They paid for them, so usage is guaranteed."

"Hold on," I said. "They attacked *me*, but they get off free and clear, while I get punished for defending myself?"

"With the space toilet," Nina reminded me. "You could have caused serious harm to Patton with that."

"He was trying to cause serious harm to *me*! For no reason! What was I supposed to do, let him beat me up?"

Nina completely avoided answering the question. Instead she said, "I'm sure you're aware that our relations with the Sjobergs have been strained over the past few weeks. NASA is adamant that we not do anything to make the situation worse."

"So that gives them the right to beat us up?"

Nina sighed, as though I was being foolish. "Our government does not provide adequate funding for the moon base program. We need the income from space tourism to make up the difference. And once Moon Base Beta is built, it will derive even more of its operating costs from tourism. The Sjobergs could ruin all of that. If they start spreading lies about how bad things are up here, the tourists won't come and the entire lunar colonization program will have to be scuttled."

I frowned, annoyed by Nina's argument. If the Sjobergs started talking about how bad life was at MBA, they wouldn't have really been spreading lies at all; they would have been spreading the truth. All the Moonies knew that. The only thing that stopped any of us from letting people back on earth know that life there stank was that we *couldn't* do it. NASA's public relations department censored all our communications. Plus, we'd had to sign these complicated nondisclosure agreements preventing us from bad-mouthing the place when we got back to earth. If we did, we could be sued. But as tourists, the Sjobergs hadn't signed any agreements like that; NASA had feared that would scare them off. When the Sjobergs got home, they could say whatever they wanted, so NASA was desperately trying to appease them in the meantime. Shoving the Urinator into Patton's face didn't really jibe with that plan.

As I considered this, I had a sudden flash of insight. "The Sjobergs are behind this, aren't they?" I asked. "*They're* the ones making you punish me, not NASA."

For the second time, Nina dodged my question. "What you did warrants punishment, Dashiell. You could have really hurt Patton with that urine hose."

I wasn't about to let Nina get away without answering me. "That's it, isn't it? They want me punished, even though their kids are jerks. And because they're so rich, you have to do it."

Nina started to say something—probably a denial—but then changed her mind and told me, "Yes. And to be honest, they wanted a lot worse than merely cutting off your communication privileges for two weeks. If they'd had their way, you'd have been restricted to your room for the next three months."

"This is so unfair," I grumbled. The ComLink was the only thing that kept me sane at MBA. It was how I talked to my friends back on earth and uploaded all my books and movies. "I was just sitting there, minding my own business, and they came after me. Roddy was the one who got them all worked up in the first place."

Nina arched her eyebrows slightly, which was as close as she ever came to expressing surprise. "Roddy was involved in this?"

"The Sjobergs didn't tell you that?"

"Lily said they came into the rec room to play a game and you started mouthing off to them."

"That's a big old lie. They came in looking for Roddy. He'd done something to get them angry and they thought he and I were in on it together."

"What had he done?"

"I don't know. I tried to find out, but Patton was more interested in trying to kill me."

Nina stroked her chin, thinking things over.

I said, "I'll bet those two were up to no good and Roddy saw them. That's why they didn't tell you about him. Because they knew you'd go talk to him and find out what really happened."

Nina considered this, then sighed again. "I suppose I should. I'll see if . . ." A soft ping from her watch interrupted her, indicating a message had come in. She glanced down at it—and something about her changed. Nina was generally as focused as a laser, but she suddenly seemed distracted and flustered. She completely forgot what we'd been talking about, stood, and said, "We're done here. You can return to your quarters."

Normally, I would have jumped at the chance to get out of Nina's room, but I stayed put on my InflatiCube. "Wait. Are you going to talk to Roddy?"

"What?" Nina asked, like her mind was already somewhere else.

"Are you going to ask Roddy what really happened?"

"Oh, yes. Of course. A full inquiry into the matter will be made. Run along now." Nina made a shooing motion with her hands, then started to look through her desk drawers.

I stood and headed for the door. "And if Roddy tells you the Sjobergs were doing something wrong, you'll punish them for it?"

"Definitely," Nina said.

"Maybe you could roll them in peanut butter and then dip them in chocolate," I suggested, just to see if Nina was paying attention.

"Sure," Nina said distractedly.

"And then shove a flaming octopus up their noses."

"Of course." Nina suddenly looked up, having realized I'd been teasing her. She frowned at me. "I said we're done, Dashiell."

"Okay. Have a nice night."

Nina returned her attention to her desk as I slipped out the door.

That was the last time anyone saw her before she disappeared.

Excerpt from *The Official Residents' Guide to Moon Base Alpha*,
"Appendix A: Potential Health and Safety Hazards,"
© 2040 by National Aeronautics and Space Administration

SHARP OBJECTS

For any object that you would normally exercise caution with on earth, you need to exercise *extra* caution on the moon. Nowhere is this more serious than with sharp objects.

Consider a knife, for example. In the moon's lower gravity, even doing something as simple as slicing a tomato can be more dangerous than you realize; if you exert the exact same force on the knife as you would back on earth, this force will be *six times greater* on the moon. Which means the knife will move much faster and harder than you might expect, with the power to do bodily harm.

That's a case where someone is still being cautious. Now imagine a scenario where a lunarnaut is being cavalier with a sharp object: running with scissors. Should that person trip and lose their grip, those scissors will fly much farther than they would on earth, with the potential to hurt more people and do far more damage.

Therefore, all lunarnauts are advised to be *extremely* careful with any sharp objects and to handle them with great vigilance. Furthermore, be aware that, at MBA, there are many other sharp objects besides the standard knives, scissors, and scalpels.* There is a great deal of machinery that may have honed edges, and robots with pointy metal joints. Even the SlimScreens can have sharp edges. So take care and keep a *sharp* eye out for potential danger!

---

* All scalpels ought to be kept in the medical bay at all times.

MALICIOUS BLUEBERRIES

Lunar day 217

Breakfast time

"Blecch," Violet said, spitting a hunk of chewed food onto her plate. "I hate waffles."

"What are you talking about?" I asked her. "You liked waffles yesterday."

My whole family was in the mess hall for breakfast. Mom, Dad, and I were dressed in our usual moon base clothing: shorts and T-shirts. Violet was still wearing her pink unicorn pajamas.

"No," Violet insisted sternly. "I never liked waffles."

"You sang a whole song about how much you liked them," I pointed out.

"I like *bacon*," Violet replied. As if that was an argument.

In truth, I couldn't blame her for hating the waffles. Nobody liked the waffles at Moon Base Alpha. Or most of the other food, for that matter. Everything we ate at MBA had once been actual edible things, but then they'd all been precooked, irradiated, thermostabilized, dehydrated, and compacted into little cubes of disgustingness. And if that weren't bad enough, we had to rehydrate it all with water reclaimed from our own urine.

For this reason, most Moonies didn't spend much time in the mess hall. They wolfed their food down as fast as possible, the idea being that the less time it was in your mouth, the less time you had to taste it.

Violet hadn't quite grasped this concept, though. Or the fact that there were certain foods that would never show up at MBA, no matter how much she wanted them.

"There is no bacon," Dad told her. "They don't have it on the moon."

"But I waaaant it," Violet pleaded.

"How about blueberry muffins instead?" Mom asked.

"Okay!" Violet instantly returned to her usual perky self, having forgotten all about bacon, and began to sing a song about how much she liked blueberry muffins. Violet was normally so cheerful, it was like living with an animated cartoon character, right down to breaking into song at random moments.

"Good," Mom said. "Let's go get some."

The two of them headed across the mess to dump Violet's waffles and get some muffins, which weren't really muffins at all, but more like muffin-flavored substance cubes.

At the other tables in the mess were the Brahmaputra-Marquez family—except for Roddy—the Goldstein-Iwanyi family, and Kira Howard, the only girl at MBA my age, who was eating with her father. As usual, Kira's father, Maxwell, wasn't paying much attention to her. He was staring at his fork, lost in thought. As one of the main engineers for Moon Base Beta, he was constantly coming up with things to improve; at the moment, he was probably thinking of a better eating utensil. Kira's mother had passed away several years earlier; with her father's mind constantly somewhere else, it was sometimes like she didn't have any parents at all.

Kira was tapping at a SlimScreen tablet while she ate, probably coding. Kira was talented with computers, and she filled the long gaps of free time at MBA with hers. She'd developed several programs to improve life at MBA. Some were beneficial to everyone—like an oxygen-monitoring system for the air locks—although most were just for fun. My favorite allowed us to simulate a transmission failure during our school classes, which we could use to cut off our teachers back on earth if they ever tried to spring a pop quiz on us.

The Sjobergs, the only other family on the moon, were

nowhere to be seen. The other Moonies didn't have kids and were probably eating at their workstations. This was usually the case, which was why no one had noticed that Nina was missing yet. Everyone probably figured she was somewhere else at MBA, taking care of something important.

Kira looked up from her tablet and waved to me.

"You can go sit with her if you want," Dad told me. "I won't be offended."

"I'm fine here," I said. "I'll spend the whole day with her in school."

Dad poured Tabasco sauce onto his reconstituted eggs. Like many Moonies, Dad put Tabasco sauce on almost everything. Even stuff it shouldn't have been on. Like pancakes. It was one of the only ways to give the rehydrated food flavor. "I really like Kira," Dad told me. "I'm glad she's up here with us."

I shrugged. "Yeah. Me too, I guess."

"You guess?" Dad repeated. "You've seemed a whole lot happier since she got here, now that you have someone else to hang out with besides Roddy."

Dad was right. Kira was a lot more fun than Roddy, and I did really like her as a friend. But her presence at MBA was also a little awkward for me. All us Moonies have lots of fans back on earth—they usually call themselves "Moonatics"— and shortly after Kira arrived, it seemed as though every one of them had decided that we ought to be a couple. This wasn't because any of those Moonatics really knew us; it was because we were a boy and a girl, we were the same age, and there weren't any other options. It was a Noah's ark kind of thing. There were thousands of gossip sites that claimed we were going to become a couple any day—while thousands of others claimed we were already dating. (I think I was chosen over Roddy because he was an oddball and the public didn't like him as much as me.) While I liked Kira as a friend, the idea of dating her seemed kind of weird; we were only twelve, after all. And yet, sometimes, it seemed that even our fellow Moonies—including my parents—felt we should be going out.

"I wonder where Roddy is," I said, trying to change the subject.

"Bet you a million dollars he's playing virtual-reality games," Dad replied. "If you want to find out what he saw last night, you're going to have to jack in."

"Great," I grumbled, then forced down a forkful of space eggs and flushed my mouth with a swig of orange-flavored water.

Beyond Dad, I could see into the greenhouse, which was a large atrium in the center of MBA across from the mess hall. The biggest window in all of the base was in the roof, allowing sunlight to spill down through it, illuminating the plants inside. Dr. Shari Goldstein, the lunar-agriculture specialist, was already at work. Despite her name, Dr. Goldstein was actually mostly of Chinese descent; everyone in her family had been Asian except her paternal great-grandfather. Normally, she was one of the more cheerful people at MBA, though she sometimes got too invested in her plants, as though they were pets. That morning, she seemed extremely distraught over a sick-looking squash plant. Its leaves had turned brown and she was now cradling it in her arms and crying.

Thankfully, most of the other plants in the greenhouse were doing far better than the squash. They hadn't grown nearly as well as NASA had hoped, but Dr. Goldstein had been having some success lately. The rumor was that she'd upped the amount of our own recycled poop she was using in the fertilizer. It was disgusting but effective. Around Dr. Goldstein, I could see the bright red fruits of a few dozen precious strawberries, as well as some tomatoes ripening on the vine. No one had been allowed to eat any of them yet; they were being saved so that everyone on the base could share them at the peak of flavor. In the meantime, it was torturous to look at them while trying to swallow rehydrated space eggs. I was dying for a taste of fresh strawberry. And while I hadn't been a big fan of tomatoes back on earth, now merely looking at them made my mouth water like Niagara Falls.

"How many more days do you think it'll be until the berries are ready?" I asked.

Dad glanced back over his shoulder at them. "They look awfully ripe. I'm sure it won't be much longer."

"They looked good to me two days ago."

Dad laughed. "Shari knows what she's doing. We wouldn't want to wait all this time and then eat them before they were ready."

"I wouldn't care. An unripe berry would be a billion times better than this." I shoved my eggs away, unable to stomach another bite.

"Shari's making a lot of progress," Dad told me. "Hopefully, pretty soon we'll be eating fresh fruit a lot more often. And the greenhouse at Moon Base Beta is going to be thirty times the size of this one. Once that's built, there'll be fresh food all the time."

"That'll be like ten years from now."

"It's scheduled to be done much sooner than that."

"If there aren't any construction delays. Which there will be. I'll bet we'll be back on earth before they even *start* building MBB."

Dad didn't argue the point, which probably meant he thought the same thing. Instead he asked, "When'd you get so cynical?"

"Since I moved to this fabulous location." I gestured

with false excitement to the rest of MBA. "I promise, when we get back home, I will never complain about eating my vegetables again."

"I'm going to hold you to that," Dad said.

My watch buzzed, indicating a text had come in. I glanced at it, knowing it wouldn't be from any of my friends back in Hawaii. There was no real day or night on the moon—the sun was overhead hundreds of hours at a time—so MBA kept to a twenty-four-hour schedule synced to Central Standard Time and Mission Control in Houston. Hawaii was five hours behind, meaning it was still nighttime there.

The text was from Dr. Levinson, my math teacher back on earth, alerting me that our class on the ComLink that day was going to be delayed fifteen minutes. All teachers at MBA taught our classes remotely from earth, and most weren't merely teachers; they were NASA scientists who spent a few hours a week educating us for extra pay.

"That's strange," Dad observed. "I thought Nina was shutting down your ComLink access."

I stared at him, realizing he was right. All texts came via ComLink. "She said I'd be able to use it for school, though."

"I thought she only meant for class," Dad pointed out. "Any texts would probably still be blocked."

"Let's see." I opened the message center on my watch. I hadn't bothered checking it that morning because it wasn't supposed to be working. Instead, it was. I had sixty-five texts in my folder. The first was from Riley Bock, who'd probably sent it long after I'd gone to sleep. "Yeah, there's messages."

"What's going on?" Mom asked, sitting back down with Violet, who was happily devouring blueberry muffin cubes and singing about blueberries with her mouth full.

"Nina never shut down Dash's ComLink," Dad said.

"Oh." Mom seemed pleasantly surprised. "Maybe she had a change of heart about it."

"I didn't know Nina *had* a heart," Dad said, keeping his voice low so no one else would hear.

"I love blueberries!" Violet sang. "They're delicious and nutritious and malicious!"

"'Malicious' means 'evil,'" I told her.

"There could be evil blueberries," Violet shot back. "Blueberries who try to take over the world so that no one eats them anymore. Luckily, I can defeat them!" She crammed a blueberry cube into her mouth and made a show of crushing it with her teeth.

I turned back to my parents. Our food was disgusting enough without having to see Violet chewing it with her mouth open. "You really think Nina changed her mind? Because she seemed awfully determined to punish me."

"Maybe she was only making a show of punishing you,"

Mom suggested. "So the Sjobergs would *think* she was doing it and be satisfied."

"I don't know," I said skeptically. "That sounds awfully human for Nina."

"Don't question it," Dad advised me. "Just be happy you're still on the Link."

"Know who else likes blueberries?" Violet announced suddenly. "DeeDah!"

"Who's DeeDah?" Mom asked, humoring her.

"She's my new friend!" Violet grinned. Her teeth were stained purple with blueberry.

"Oh?" Dad asked. "Where's she from?"

"Here," Violet replied. "She lives in the bathroom."

Dad and Mom looked at each other and tried not to laugh. They always found Violet's stories amusing. "Is DeeDah a little girl like you?" Mom asked.

"Oh no," Violet said seriously. "She's a walrus."

Mom and Dad couldn't keep their straight faces any longer and cracked up. "Oh, Violet," Mom giggled, tousling my sister's hair. "You're such a goofball."

I forced down the last of my breakfast and stood. "I'm going to see if I can find Roddy and talk to him before school starts."

"All right." Mom blew me a kiss. "You know where to find us."

I took my plates to the cleaning station, then headed out of the mess hall. I could have just stopped by the Brahmaputra-Marquez family table to ask where Roddy was, but then I would have had to talk to them. Dr. Brahmaputra-Marquez and Inez were nice, but Cesar was a jerk and Dr. Marquez, our base psychiatrist, was always trying to psychoanalyze everyone else even though he was the looniest person at MBA. He had hundreds of weird tics; at the moment, he was sticking his pinky finger into his nostril so deep it looked like he might poke himself in the brain. One of the biggest problems with living on a moon base is that you're stuck with your fellow Moonies no matter what. So I took any chance I could to avoid the ones I didn't care for.

"Where are you going?" Kira asked as I walked past.

"To talk to Roddy."

Kira jokingly faked a shudder of disgust. "Why would you do that?"

"He had something to do with why Patton tried to beat me up last night."

"Oh. I heard about that. Nice move with the Urinator."

"Thanks."

"See you in class."

"You too," I said.

As I left the mess hall, I gave Dr. Goldstein a friendly wave through the greenhouse window, hoping it might lift her spirits, but she was too distraught over her sick squash to even notice me. My route to the rec room then took me past the science pod. Sure enough, most of the adults at MBA were already at their workstations: Dr. Janke in astrobiology, Dr. Kowalski in chemistry, Dr. Balnikov in astrophysics, Dr. Kim and Dr. Alvarez in geology. Dr. Daphne Merritt, the base roboticist, was also in her office, right by the air lock, examining something on her computer.

As Dad had guessed, Roddy was already in the rec room, playing virtual-reality games. This wasn't an amazing deduction on Dad's part. Roddy was almost always playing virtual-reality games; sometimes he logged as much as fourteen hours a day. Now he was obviously trying to squeeze in some time before school. A set of hologoggles was strapped over his eyes, and his hands were sheathed in sensogloves. He was whirling around madly, pausing now and then to pounce forward with a stabbing motion. I assumed this meant he was having an imaginary battle, though to me it looked like he was dancing ballet with a bad case of stomach cramps. One of the big problems with veeyar games is that no matter how cool you looked *inside* the game, you always looked like an idiot to anyone watching you play it from the outside.

"Roddy!" I shouted, so he could hear me over the game's audio. "It's Dash! Can you talk?"

"Sure!" Roddy made a pirouette and stabbed an invisible

enemy beside me. "Jack in! I could use some backup."

"All right." I didn't really want to jack in, but I had little choice. I needed to find out what Roddy knew. So I slipped on some sensogloves, strapped on some hologoggles, and fired them up. There was a flash of light, and then I was plunged into a world even more bizarre than I'd imagined.

Excerpt from *The Official Residents' Guide to Moon Base Alpha*,
"Appendix A: Potential Health and Safety Hazards,"
© 2040 by National Aeronautics and Space Administration

VIRTUAL-REALITY DEVICES

Moon Base Alpha has been equipped with the latest virtual-reality entertainment systems to provide endless hours of enjoyment for you and your fellow lunarnauts. However, please remember that, when you use the veeyar system, you are doing it in a public space, rather than in the comfort and safety of your own home. People wearing hologoggles often fail to be aware of the *real* world around them, so make sure that other people and objects are not close by before you jack in. Many veeyar games require the players to make sudden dramatic, potentially dangerous motions such as kicks, punches, and karate chops. Try to only deliver these to your virtual opponents and not your fellow lunarnauts.

In addition, if you encounter anyone using the veeyar system, remember that they probably are unaware of your presence, and keep your distance until you can make sure they know you are close by. Otherwise, you might receive an attack meant for a virtual enemy, rather than yourself.

STEALING JULIET

I had expected to find myself on a bizarre virtual planet, fighting some sort of terrifying aliens. The last time I'd jacked into a game with Roddy, I'd been transported to a moon made of broken glass, where I'd battled beings who looked like giant, angry blobs of snot. But this time, I actually found myself on earth. We were in a charming little Italian village, and our enemies appeared to be completely normal humans. Angry and deadly humans, but humans nonetheless. The only odd thing about them was their clothing, which was straight out of the Renaissance: puffy white shirts, leather pants, and floppy feathered hats.

Their weapons were simple swords, rather than ray guns or photon blasters. It was so disorienting, it took me a few seconds to get my bearings.

This was a few seconds too long for Roddy. "Don't just sit there!" he yelled. "Help me kill these guys before they kill us!"

I spun around to find Roddy's avatar beside me. While real Roddy was short, flabby, and pear-shaped, virtual Roddy appeared to have stepped out of a comic book. He was nearly seven feet tall and every inch of him bulged with muscles. He was also dressed in a puffy shirt and a floppy hat. Normally, Roddy's avatar wore high-tech body armor, with multiple guns strapped to his chest. Now he looked like a member of a juggling troupe. His only weapon was a sword with an extremely thin blade.

I had never bothered to modify my avatar, so it looked exactly like me—though the game automatically outfitted me. I found myself in medieval clothes and armed with a sword as well. I raised it as one of the enemy attacked, deflecting his blade. Even though the contact was completely imaginary, it felt unsettlingly real. My sensogloves gave me the feeling of our swords clanging together, while speakers embedded in the hologoggles made the sound ring in my ears.

"Why do these guys want to kill us?" I shouted, fending off another attack.

"Because I kissed their cousin!" Roddy shouted back. While I was fighting only one guy, he was taking on three at the same time.

"That's it?" I ducked to the side of a fruit cart as my opponent lunged at me. He missed me and cleaved a watermelon in half.

"Yeah," Roddy replied. "They're Capulets, we're Montagues, and our families hate each other."

"Hold on," I said. "This is *Romeo and Juliet*?"

"Duh." Roddy calmly speared one of his opponents through the chest. "You've never played it before?"

"I didn't even know there was a veeyar version of it."

Roddy looked at me as though I'd just said I'd never drunk water. "How could you not know that? William Shakespeare was one of the world's greatest game creators."

"Shakespeare didn't create games," I told him. "He was a playwright."

Roddy laughed disdainfully, like I was an idiot. "Please. I know what I'm talking about. He created a ton of games: Macbeth's Battle for Scotland, Revenge of Hamlet, Shrew-Tamer . . . I've played them all."

I would have argued the issue, but it would have been pointless. Once Roddy thought he knew something, there was no talking him out of it. Besides, I needed to save my breath. I didn't have a lot of practice sword-fighting and my opponent was awfully determined to lop my virtual head off. I was deflecting his attacks as well as I could, but they kept coming. I quickly found myself backed against a wall with nowhere to run.

"Die, Montague scum!" the enemy screamed, raising his sword above his head.

At which point, Roddy came to my rescue, slicing him in half. From head to toe. Both halves thudded to the cobblestones in front of me. Thankfully, no blood or internal organs spilled out; Roddy must have had the game's violence settings set to Teen.

He'd taken care of his opponents in a similar way. The three of them were now in a dozen large pieces scattered about the plaza.

The dead bodies faded away and were replaced by the words EXCEPTIONAL SWORDPLAY! LEVEL ONE HATH BEEN COMPLETED.

"C'mon," Roddy said, leading me down a narrow alley. "The Capulets are a big family. More of them will be coming for us soon. We have to get to Juliet."

"So you can marry her?" I asked, trailing after him.

"Marry her?" Roddy's avatar stuck out his tongue in disgust, which meant that real Roddy had done the same thing. "Dude, she's only, like, thirteen."

"I know, but in the play . . ."

"It's a *game*, dimbulb. The whole point is just to kiss the girl. She's crazy beautiful. And then her cousins try to kill you and your family. But if you defeat them all, you get to kiss her again. For, like, thirty whole seconds."

"You can kiss a virtual girl?"

Virtual Roddy shot me another you're-an-idiot look. "Yeah. It's cosmic. And good practice for when Kira and I start making out in real life."

I shuddered just thinking about this. Roddy truly believed that he was a great catch and the only reason Kira hadn't succumbed to his charms yet was that her father didn't want her dating anyone at the moon base. In truth, the reason was that Kira thought Roddy was a weirdo and a creep. Learning that he'd been making out with virtual Shakespeare characters wasn't going to improve her opinion of him.

We appeared to have settled into an exploration mode in the game, slinking about Verona in search of Juliet while trying to elude angry Capulets. Even though it was completely fake and ridiculous, being on virtual earth felt fantastic. It was easy to imagine I was wandering through one of the thousands of real Italian country towns, breathing fresh air and feeling the sun on my face. Yes, it was only a matter of time before sword-wielding hooligans tried to kill us, but for the moment, it was a welcome break from the dull, sterile surroundings of Moon Base Alpha.

In the lull between attacks, I asked, "Did you do anything to get Patton and Lily angry at you last night?"

Virtual Roddy shot a wary glance at me. "Sort of."

We came upon a large, open-air market and wove through the maze of stalls and merchants. All around us, imaginary people were selling imaginary cheese, fruit, and goats. "What'd you do?" I asked.

"I was spying on them."

"Why?"

"Because they were obviously up to no good. I saw them in the gym after dinner, and they looked like they were trying to be all sneaky. . . ."

"Wait a minute. *You* were in the gym?" We were all supposed to work out in the gym for two hours a day to counter the effects of low gravity on our bodies, but Roddy hadn't done this in months.

"No," he corrected. "*They* were in the gym. I was just passing by. But I could tell they were up to something, so I decided to spy on them."

I wondered if this was true. I knew that, in addition to being attracted to Kira, Roddy also had a crush on Lily Sjoberg. In fact, Roddy had a crush on pretty much every woman at MBA who wasn't related to him; he was a year older than me and his body was already surging with hormones. Lily was the girl who grabbed his attention most of all, though. Every time he saw her, his train of thought would immediately derail and he'd stare at her, slack-jawed with puppy love. Chances were, Roddy hadn't been randomly passing by the gym; he'd probably been lurking around, watching Lily use the exercise equipment. I decided not to call him on this, though. "And? Did you see them do something?"

"I'll say. After a while, they snuck out of the gym and went into the base control room."

A virtual fishmonger waved several handfuls of dead eels in my face, trying to sell me the slimy things for breakfast. I ducked around him. "What'd they do in there?"

"I don't know. I couldn't see."

"Why not?"

"Because they were *inside* the office and I was *outside* it. Duh. I don't have X-ray vision."

"You don't have any idea what they did?"

"Nope. But I'll bet it was bad."

"Why?"

"Because when they realized I was spying on them, they came after me."

I slipped between two oxcarts as they rumbled through the main square. "How'd they realize you were spying on them?"

"I don't know. I was being as quiet as a ninja. They just

sensed my presence somehow. Maybe they're psychic."

I was sure that wasn't the case. Roddy wasn't exactly a master of stealth. He had probably sneezed or knocked something over and given himself away.

Roddy's avatar stopped in front of me so suddenly that I almost slammed into his broad backside. He was looking up above the market plaza. I followed his gaze to an enormous mansion, obviously the home of somebody wealthy and powerful. A teenage girl stood on a second-floor balcony, staring off into the distance.

"There she is!" Roddy sighed. "Juliet!"

Since the girl had been designed by a team of programmers who were most likely male, she looked less like a teenager in medieval Verona than a modern-day swimsuit model. She was actually wearing a bikini, even though they wouldn't be invented for another five hundred years.

"Oh, Romeo, Romeo," she trilled. "Wherefore art thou, Romeo?"

"I'm right down here!" Roddy yelled, unaware this was the beginning of her famous speech.

Juliet didn't notice him. She continued speaking to herself, as in the play. "Deny thy father, and refuse thy name; or, if thou wilt not, be but sworn my love, and I'll no longer be a Capulet."

Roddy groaned. "Something must be wrong with the

language settings on this game. She's not speaking English."

"That *is* English," I pointed out. "But it's from a long time ago. She wants you to give up your family to marry her."

Roddy looked at me curiously. "I thought you'd never played this game."

"It's based on a play!" I repeated. "Like, the most famous play ever."

"'Tis but thy name that is my enemy," Juliet continued. "Thou art thyself, though not a Montague. . . ."

"Ugh," Roddy muttered. "I have no idea what she's talking about. C'mon. Let's see if we can find the door to that mansion." He started shoving his way through the crowded marketplace again.

I followed him. "What happened after the Sjobergs saw you outside the office?"

"I took off and hid in the greenhouse. They came looking for me but, luckily, they didn't find me."

"No," I said. "They found *me*. And they thought you and I were working together."

"I know." Roddy laughed. It was a weird, high-pitched laugh that sounded bizarre coming from his muscle-bound avatar. "I heard the whole thing."

"And you didn't do anything?"

"Like what?"

"Get an adult and tell them what was going on."

"If I'd done that, they might have seen me."

"So you just sat there and let them threaten *me* instead? Even though I was innocent? I almost got my face pounded in because of you."

"But you didn't. Instead you nearly sucked Patton's tonsils out with the Urinator! That was awesome!" Roddy laughed again.

"It's not funny!" I told him.

"Incoming!" Roddy shouted. He suddenly wasn't laughing anymore.

An entire horde of angry Italians was charging across the plaza at us. Unlike the relatively normal men who had attacked us before, these guys were all as enormous and muscular as Roddy's avatar. Instead of mere swords, they carried scimitars as big as I was.

Even though the entire assault wasn't really happening, it was still scary. I felt real sweat bead on my forehead and prepared to be filleted.

"Time to upgrade my weaponry," Roddy announced. He opened a leather bag clipped to his belt, revealing several pieces of gold. They vanished as the game accepted the payment, and a suit of futuristic armor instantly appeared on Roddy's body. In addition, his thin sword suddenly became some sort of bizarre space-age gun.

"What is that?" I asked.

"Photon blaster," Roddy replied, then fired several bolts of green light from it. A dozen Capulets were instantly vaporized, leaving nothing behind but smoking piles of ash.

I didn't have any gold, nor did I have any idea how to cash it in and obtain a photon blaster. I could only shake my sword threateningly and hope Roddy wiped out all of our enemies before they reached me.

"What are you doing?" Roddy screamed at me. "I need help here! Don't you know how to upgrade?"

"There's no upgrading in Shakespeare!" I shouted back. "There were no photon blasters in *Romeo and Juliet*!"

"Dash! Troll on your right!" Roddy yelled.

"Troll?" I repeated, then spun around to find that there was, in fact, a troll bearing down on me. I was quite sure there weren't any trolls in *Romeo and Juliet*, but obviously the game's designers didn't really care about staying true to the story. This one appeared to have wandered in from *The Hobbit*; it was the size of a garbage truck, it was vomit green, and unfortunately, it was extremely angry. It galumphed across the plaza, wielding a club that looked like an uprooted tree with spikes jutting out of it.

Roddy fired a few photon blasts, but they glanced off the troll harmlessly. It roared loud enough to rattle my brain, then leaped high in the air, club raised, ready to flatten us.

"We're gonna die!" Roddy cried, and curled into the fetal position.

Something tapped my shoulder.

The troll suddenly froze in midair.

All around us, the Capulet assault team froze as well.

Someone had paused the game.

Whoever had been tapping my shoulder was now shaking me.

I pried the hologoggles off and blinked in the fluorescent lights of the common room. To my right, real Roddy was curled in the fetal position, just like his avatar. He was slowly coming to the realization that the game had been paused as well.

My father was standing next to me. Despite the fact that it had only been fifteen minutes since I'd last seen him, he'd changed dramatically. He was now extremely nervous and worried, so much that it seemed as though he'd aged five years.

"Sorry to interrupt your game," he said, "but it's important. Do you have any idea what Nina did after you saw her last night?"

"No," I said, feeling a little bewildered. It was always hard to adjust back to reality after a veeyar session. Even though my near death-by-troll had been fake, it still felt disturbingly real. "Why?"

"We can't find her," Dad told me. "We've looked every-where."

I stared at him blankly, trying to make sense of this. "You mean, she's not at Moon Base Alpha?"

"No. She's completely vanished."

"How is that possible?" I asked.

Dad shrugged helplessly. "To be honest," he admitted sadly, "no one has the slightest idea."

Excerpt from *The Official Residents' Guide to Moon Base Alpha*,
"Appendix A: Potential Health and Safety Hazards,"
© 2040 by National Aeronautics and Space Administration

THE LUNAR SURFACE

While MBA is an extremely safe habitat, the lunar world outside the air locks is not. In fact, the lunar surface is exceptionally hostile to human life. Temperatures can fluctuate from -387 degrees Fahrenheit (-233 degrees Celsius) at night to 253 degrees Fahrenheit (123 degrees Celsius) in direct sunlight. In addition, there is no oxygen. For these reasons, visits to the lunar surface should be limited only to cases of extreme necessity, and no children under the age of eighteen are allowed on the surface except for 1) transits to and from the rockets on arrival and departure, and 2) emergencies in which the base must be evacuated. Should you need to exit the base for any reason, *never go outside without a partner*. In addition, take extreme caution when putting on your space suits, as any mistake or oversight could cause you severe injury—if not cost you your life.

FRUITLESS SEARCHING

Lunar day 217

Midmorning

On a normal day at MBA, most of the adults worked from breakfast to dinner, and sometimes after that as well. There wasn't much else for them to do. Weekends didn't really exist in space. The scientists would have been at their stations in the science pod, while Nina and Daphne Merritt would have been in their offices. Dr. Marquez conducted his surveys of our mental states—or at least tried to—in the medical bay. Since our doctor was dead and our maintenance man was on trial, we were short both positions. Reinforcements were scheduled to arrive on the next rocket in a month. In the meantime, Chang "Hi-Tech" Kowalski, our chief geochemist and resident genius, was doing everything he could to keep us healthy and the base functioning. The only adults who didn't work were the Sjobergs, who usually hung out in their suite, doing their best to avoid everyone else. It had been three days since anyone had seen them. We had no idea what they were doing, but we didn't really care; we were happy to not have to deal with them.

During the time that I'd been battling Capulets with Roddy, however, things had changed. Instead of working, everyone was now frantically combing Moon Base Alpha for Nina. The place was a hive of activity. Since MBA was only the size of a soccer field, there weren't many places Nina could have been, but they were being searched over and over again anyhow. It was ridiculous, but then, so was the idea that Nina wasn't in the base anymore.

"You've checked her quarters?" I asked, as Dad and I walked out of the rec room.

"A dozen times and counting." Dad pointed up to Nina's residence. The door was open and Moonies were shuttling in and out.

"Her door wasn't locked?" Roddy asked, tailing behind us.

"Er . . . it *was*," Dad said. "But Chang kicked it in."

Now that he mentioned this, I could see that the doorjamb was splintered where the lock had torn out of it.

"We were worried," Dad explained. "She wasn't anywhere else on the base or answering her phone. We thought maybe she'd had a stroke or something and collapsed in her room."

We entered the staging area and nearly slammed into Daphne Merritt and Jennifer Kim.

Besides Violet, Daphne was the most chipper and effusive person at MBA. Even now, in the midst of crisis, she was upbeat and smiling. Dr. Kim, a seismic geologist, was almost the opposite: reserved and extremely quiet. She actually spoke a normal amount, but always did so in a very meek way, as though she were slightly embarrassed about what she had to say.

"We checked the women's room," Daphne reported to Dad.

"And?" Dad asked.

"She's not in there," Dr. Kim said apologetically, as if this were somehow her fault.

"You're sure?" Roddy pressed.

"We both have PhDs," Daphne teased. "We know how to check a bathroom. We're going to give the gym another look." With that, she led Dr. Kim around the corner.

Dad sighed, looking even more worried than before. "This just doesn't make sense," he said, more to himself than to me.

"If Nina isn't here, could she have left the base?" I asked.

"She didn't," Dad told me. "Her space suit is still here." He pointed to the space suit storage area. The door to Nina's locker hung open, revealing her suit, helmet, boots, and gloves, right where they should have been. Given that there was no oxygen on the surface of the moon, she wouldn't have gotten very far outside without them—only a few feet at most.

"Maybe she went out anyhow," Roddy said. "You know, like she got space madness and lost her mind and left in her regular clothes and croaked."

"I don't think that happened," Dad said, but then told me, "Although your mother and Chang went out to make sure."

I glanced toward the air lock. Through the windows, I could see my mother and Chang in their space suits, returning to base. I couldn't tell who was who, because they had the reflective visors down in their helmets to protect them against the sun's heat. I asked, "If Nina went out the air lock, there'd be a record of it, wouldn't there? There's some sort of electronic log, right?"

"Right," Dad agreed. "And there wasn't any record of the air lock opening last night. But Chang thought maybe Nina had the ability to override it."

"Why?" I asked.

Roddy laughed knowingly. "Don't be such a dork, Dash.

NASA has a buttload of secrets, and Nina's their main gate-keeper."

Dad narrowed his eyes at Roddy. He looked like he wanted to smack the smile right off Roddy's face for insulting me.

I saw Mom and Chang enter the air lock's pressurization chamber and shut the outer door behind them. There was a loud whoosh as the air inside the chamber repressurized from the moon's atmosphere to MBA's. Mom and Chang popped their helmets off, but didn't open the inner air-lock door right away. Before coming into the base, they needed to remove the moon dust from their suits. Moon dust is very different from earth dust. Earth dust is mostly decaying matter. Moon dust is mostly very tiny shards of glass created in the heat of meteorite impacts—and it sticks to everything. If any got inside the base, it would be extremely difficult to get back out again. Cleaning it off the suits involved two hoses: one that fired air at high pressure to knock the dust off, and a high-powered vacuum to suck it up.

It was obvious that Mom and Chang hadn't found Nina: They weren't carrying a dead body and they looked concerned, rather than saddened. But the rest of us gathered around the air lock anyhow.

There was an intercom built into the door that we could

talk through. Mom flipped it on and reported, "There's no sign of her out there."

"Any luck in here?" Chang asked. Normally, he sported a spiky Mohawk, but it had been squashed flat by his space helmet, making it look like a small mammal that had died on his head.

"None," Dad replied.

Dr. Brahmaputra-Marquez came through the staging area. Somehow, she'd ended up chaperoning all three of the youngest children at MBA. Violet, Inez, and Kamoze were skipping along after her, apparently thinking of Nina's disappearance as a game. "Nina!" they called, as though she were merely hiding. "We give up! Come out, come out, wherever you are!"

Everyone else at MBA, having run out of places to look for Nina, was pouring into the staging area expectantly. Dr. Janke and Dr. Alvarez emerged from Nina's quarters onto the catwalk. Kira and her father exited the medical bay. Dr. Marquez and Dr. Iwanyi rounded the corner from the mess hall, while Dr. Balnikov and Dr. Goldstein came from the science pod.

The Sjobergs were still nowhere to be seen. Either they didn't care about where Nina was or they hadn't been notified she was missing.

"Isn't there some way to track Nina's location?" I asked my father. "Like with a GPS chip or something?"

"In theory," Dad told me. "There's a chip in her space suit for exactly this sort of scenario—but it doesn't do any good if the space suit is *here*. And her smartwatch is traceable as well. Only she's not wearing it."

"Where is it?" Roddy asked.

"Up in her quarters," Dad replied. "She left it on her desk."

"That's weird," I said. "I mean, she usually wore it, didn't she?" As far as I knew, most people wore theirs all the time, except maybe at night or when showering.

"I never take *my* watch off," Roddy volunteered.

"That doesn't mean Nina never did," Kira told him.

"But it'd be weird for her to go somewhere without it, wouldn't it?" Roddy pointed out.

"Maybe," Kira said. "I don't really know Nina all that well."

"Does *anyone*?" Dr. Goldstein asked.

Everyone within earshot looked at one another awkwardly, aware of the truth. No one at MBA was friends with Nina.

Mom and Chang emerged from the air lock, having finally cleaned the moon dust off their suits. Or at least, they'd done the best they could.

Dr. Balnikov approached Chang as he lugged his space suit to the storage area. Balnikov was a Russian astrophysicist, a big, hulking man who was surprisingly gentle. "I think we should dig up the blueprints for this base," he suggested. "Maybe there are ducts or crawl spaces Nina could be inside."

"Why would Nina be inside a duct or a crawl space?" Dr. Alvarez asked. He was a water-extraction specialist who'd seemed very straitlaced at first—and then turned out to have a love of practical jokes. In his allotment of personal stuff from earth, he'd brought a dozen whoopee cushions. (They'd turned out to be pointless, though, as the squeaky Inflati-Cubes acted like whoopee cushions anyhow.)

"I don't know," Dr. Balnikov admitted. "But she's obviously not anywhere else inside MBA."

"I don't think the ducts are big enough to let a human inside," Chang told them. "And I doubt there are any crawl spaces in this structure. It'd be a big waste of space."

"It still couldn't hurt to check, though," Dr. Iwanyi said. He was an astronomer from Tanzania who had been raised as a Masai warrior. After Nina, he was probably the biggest stickler for the rules on the base. "We have searched all the rooms here many times over. Where else could Nina be?"

Chang considered this, then shrugged. "Good point. Let's see if we can find some blueprints." He placed his space suit in his storage locker.

"What about the Sjobergs' room?" Roddy asked loudly. "Has anyone checked in there yet?"

Kira shot him a disdainful look. "What are you saying? That the Sjobergs have kidnapped Nina or something?"

"Maybe," Roddy said. "The Sjobergs are jerks. They could be holding her hostage until we give them a spaceship back to earth or something."

"That's ridiculous," Kira argued. "If the Sjobergs were holding Nina hostage, wouldn't they let us know? That's the whole point of hostages, isn't it? You don't keep them a secret."

"Maybe they're still working on the note," Roddy suggested.

Kira looked at me and rolled her eyes.

All around us, the staging area was now a babble of conversation. Everyone was comparing notes about where they'd searched for Nina. Dr. Marquez was admitting that he was completely stymied, which wasn't that surprising, as he was often completely stymied, even by things he was supposed to be an expert on, like psychiatry. Dr. Goldstein, who had finally recovered from the loss of her squash plant, looked like she was about to burst into tears again. Meanwhile, Violet and the other little kids were still chanting for Nina to come out from hiding.

Dad pulled me aside from all the chaos. "Dash, the whole reason I came to get you was that, from what we can tell, you were the last person Nina talked to before she disappeared."

"I was?"

"No one else saw her last night—or this morning."

"You're sure about that?"

"No," Dad conceded. "I'm not sure of anything. But if anyone else *did* see Nina before she vanished, they haven't admitted it. Did she say or do anything strange last night?"

"Nina is always strange."

Dad gave me a disapproving look, as though I'd spoken badly about someone who'd just died. "You know what I mean."

"Sorry." I thought back to my time in Nina's room and realized something strange *had* happened there. "Nina got a text while she was chewing me out. I think it upset her somehow."

"Why do you say that?"

"She reacted kind of funny after she got it."

"How so?"

"Really distracted, I guess. Then she got rid of me as fast as she could—and I think she forgot all about me after that. I'll bet *that's* why she didn't cut off my ComLink privileges. She was too focused on this other thing."

"Or maybe something happened to her before she had a chance to cut off your ComLink," Dad said thoughtfully. He signaled me to come with him, then led me through the crowd in the staging area.

Violet dropped in beside us. "Nina is *really* good at hide-and-seek," she announced. "All these people can't find her!"

I started to tell Violet that Nina was missing, not hiding, but Dad cut me off before I could get a word out.

"She *is* very good," he agreed. "But don't worry. We'll find her."

"She should just come out already," Violet said. "This game is getting boring."

"Why don't you and Inez and Kamoze go play something else, then?" Dad suggested. "You can use the SlimScreen in the rec room if you want."

"Ooh!" Violet gasped. "Can we play Candy Attack?"

"Sure," Dad said.

"Candy Attack!" Violet whooped. Inez and Kamoze joined in, and the three of them scurried toward the rec room.

Dad and I reached the space suit storage area. Mom was now there, putting her suit in her locker. Everyone had their own space suit at MBA, even the kids. They were all made specially for us.

Dad snaked an arm around Mom's waist. "How was it out there?"

"Hot," Mom groaned.

There had been a time, right after we'd arrived at MBA, when moonwalks had been fascinating and exciting to my parents, as well as all to the other adults. After all, very few humans had ever been lucky enough to take so much as a step on the moon. Now, four months later, the thrill was gone. Everyone considered going onto the lunar surface a chore rather than an adventure.

Dad turned to Chang, who was checking his suit for any damage it might have suffered on the surface. Chang was wearing a sleeveless T-shirt, allowing a great view of his tattoos. His arms and legs were covered with his favorite scientists, reimagined as action heroes. Albert Einstein was on his right bicep, wearing a cape and spandex and flying at light speed, while the great physicist Werner Heisenberg was on his left bicep, punching Adolf Hitler in the face.

"Is Nina's watch still in her room?" Dad asked.

"It ought to be," Chang replied. "Everyone was ordered not to disturb any of her stuff."

"Do you have any idea what kind of security protection she might have on it?"

"Are you proposing something illegal here?" Chang asked, although he had a slight smile, as though he actually liked the idea.

"Dash says Nina got a text when they were together last night," Dad told him. "She reacted oddly to it. Got very distracted. And then no one ever saw her again. I'm guessing there's a good chance it's related to all this."

Dr. Iwanyi interrupted, having overheard them. "We can't do anything with Nina's watch," he insisted. "Technically, it's NASA property. And NASA protocol is that we can't violate anyone's privacy without authorization."

"Whose authorization?" Mom asked.

"The moon-base commander's," Dr. Iwanyi replied.

"Nina's the moon-base commander," Dad pointed out. "And she's missing."

"Then we'd have to ask the second in command," Dr. Iwanyi said.

"Our S-I-C was Dr. Holtz," Dad said. "And seeing as he's dead, we probably can't ask him to authorize anything."

"NASA didn't officially name a new S-I-C?" Mom asked.

"They named a temporary one," Chang said.

"Really?" Dr. Iwanyi asked. "Who?"

"Me," Chang replied.

Everyone within earshot stopped talking, surprised.

"You?" Dad asked. "You're the S-I-C? Since when?"

"Four weeks ago," Chang answered. "Right after Dr. Holtz died."

"Why didn't anyone tell us?" Dr. Marquez demanded.

"Nina didn't think we should make a big deal about it," Chang explained. "She figured people might be upset that I was picked and not them. It never occurred to us that NASA would take so long to make an official choice for S-I-C."

"Well," Dad said, "sounds like it's your decision, then. I have no idea if this text Nina got is really important or not, but so far, it's the only lead we have."

"Then let's get the watch." Chang shut his locker and headed for Nina's room. As he shoved through the throng of Moonies gathered by the air lock, he announced, "Meanwhile, the rest of you should get back to your regular work."

There was a general murmur of annoyance from the crowd.

"But Nina's still missing," Dr. Goldstein pointed out.

"I'm well aware of that," Chang told her. "However, there's also plenty of work that has to be done here. If I had something constructive to assign you right now, I'd do it . . . but I don't. And tripping all over each other while we search the base for the umpteenth time isn't going to help Nina."

"What about finding the blueprints for the base?" Dr. Balnikov asked.

"The base computer can do that faster than any of us can," Chang replied.

"And doesn't someone need to inform NASA of what's going on here?" Dr. Iwanyi asked.

"As the temporary second in command, that's my job," Chang said. "I'll do it right after I find Nina's watch."

"I could notify NASA if you needed me to," Dr. Brahmaputra-Marquez offered.

"I can handle it," Chang told her. "The best way you can all help me right now is to get your own work done. You all know that if someone else was missing out there and Nina was still in charge, that's exactly what she'd ask of you."

There was a general muttering of agreement with this.

"Good," Chang said. "So all of you, back to work. And kids, school is back in session."

"Awwww," Roddy whined.

"That's an order!" Chang barked.

The staging area quickly cleared as everyone headed to their stations.

"I'll let you all know if I find anything," Chang told us, seeming to already feel bad about raising his voice. "Frankly, this whole thing's probably a wild-goose chase anyhow. Nina's the most competent person at this base. I wouldn't be surprised if she shows up soon on her own."

"Fat chance," Roddy muttered as we headed to the rec room for class.

I didn't bother arguing with him, because I didn't believe Chang either. In fact, I didn't even think Chang believed what he was saying. He was only trying to bolster everyone's spirits.

I glanced back out the air-lock window at the surface of the moon.

It looked calm, but it was an incredibly hostile place.

The lunar surface was 14.6 million square miles, bigger than North America and Europe combined—and in that entire vast expanse, Moon Base Alpha was the only safe place for humans.

So if Nina wasn't there, where was she?

Excerpt from *The Official Residents' Guide to Moon Base Alpha*,
"Appendix A: Potential Health and Safety Hazards,"
© 2040 by National Aeronautics and Space Administration

POOR PREPARATION

We all make mistakes. Unfortunately, sometimes those mistakes can lead to injury . . . or worse. Therefore, all lunarnauts are advised to try to make as few mistakes as possible. If you are going to be doing anything risky—such as taking a moonwalk or cleaning the evaporator units—take the time to plan ahead. Think through every step of what you are going to do, analyze all potential risks, and have multiple backup plans in case of emergency.

However, it also makes sense to use this type of caution in all aspects of your life at MBA. After all, even a space toilet can cause injury if one doesn't exercise the proper caution around it. To stay safe, follow the motto of the Boy Scouts and be prepared!

DIRE WARNING

Lunar day 217
Midmorning

Zan showed up in the middle of math class.

School at MBA took place in the rec room, but since there were nine kids in several different grades, the logistics were complicated. We were usually lumped into three groups: the high school kids (Cesar and the Sjobergs), the middle schoolers (me, Kira, and Roddy), and the elementary schoolers (Violet, Inez, and Kamoze). All our classes were taught over ComLinks from earth. The high schoolers and middle schoolers normally jacked in to individual tablets with headphones for our classes, while the elementary schoolers gathered around the large SlimScreen together.

This was because the little kids couldn't manage their own equipment or even keep their headphones on for more than five minutes. It wasn't a great system, because the little kids usually made a lot of noise, which could be distracting—and they easily got distracted themselves. The high school kids were supposed to wrangle them, but they never did. In fact, the Sjobergs barely ever showed up at all, which explained why both of them were about as smart as stalks of celery. (They were absent that day as well.) So it usually fell to Kira and me to deal with the little ones.

That morning, the elementary schoolers were being more distracting than usual. They were learning about dinosaurs, and all three were eagerly trying to prove that they could make the loudest velociraptor noises.

Of course, I was distracted by the Nina situation as well. Questions kept tumbling through my mind as I tried to work: Where could Nina be? There was no evidence that she'd left the base, but she certainly didn't seem to be anywhere inside it either. Only, how could she have left without a space suit? And what could have possibly motivated her to leave?

Meanwhile, there were still the Sjobergs to think about. What had they been doing in the offices when Roddy saw them? Why had the family been so quiet that morning? Were they connected to Nina's disappearance? And if so, why?

My last conversation with Zan was also disturbing me. I desperately wanted to know what kind of danger the earth was in. So I was excited to see her—even though she nearly scared the pants off me when she showed up. One second, I was doing word problems. The next, she was sitting beside me.

One of the most unnerving things about having an alien beam herself into my brain was how abruptly she could appear. Zan usually tried to make this easier on me by projecting an image of herself walking into the room like a normal person, but sometimes she forgot—or simply couldn't make it work. At those times, her sudden presence could be startling, kind of like when you were crossing what you thought was an empty street and then realized there was a truck bearing down on you.

I did my best not to overreact. I managed to only jump in my seat a bit.

Roddy looked my way, but I acted like I was stretching. Roddy bought it and returned his attention to his work. Or rather, pretending to work. He was secretly reading a graphic novel instead of doing his math problems. Since our math teacher, Dr. Levinson, was back on earth, it was hard for him to keep tabs on all of us.

I did my best to pretend I was doing my math as well while speaking to Zan inside my head. "Where have you been?" I asked. "I really need to talk to you."

"I am sorry I couldn't get back to you sooner. Some things came up."

What could possibly have been more important than the future of earth? I thought. If I'd been talking to a human, I would have kept it to myself, not wanting to antagonize her, but since Zan could read my thoughts, it was as though I'd said it anyhow. Yet another unnerving thing about communicating directly from your brain.

"It would be very hard for you to understand," Zan said, which was her standard answer to almost any question I asked about her planet.

"Can you tell me about the danger earth is in, then?"

"Earth is not in danger."

"But you said it was. . . ."

"No. I said it was important for us to be in contact with one another. You made an assumption that earth was in danger. I am sorry if there was any miscommunication on my part. As you know, I sometimes have trouble with your language. It is quite difficult to master."

I stared at Zan. Once again I had the sense she wasn't being completely honest. As I gazed into her crystal-blue eyes, though, I began to feel okay about that. And then I found myself wondering if Zan was calming me herself, somehow manipulating my brain. I had the very faint sensation of something working on my mind that wasn't me.

"Dashiell, why aren't you doing your work?"

I looked up, startled, to find Dr. Levinson staring at me on the SlimScreen. When he wasn't teaching us math, Dr. Levinson was a rocket scientist at the Jet Propulsion Laboratory in Pasadena, California.

"Sorry," I said. "I'm finding it hard to concentrate today. With Nina being missing and all."

Chang had told his superiors at NASA about Nina's disappearance. They were doing their best to keep the story secret, even from other divisions, so that the public didn't find out, but Chang had insisted upon letting our teachers know. He thought all us kids—especially the little ones—might need some additional emotional support dealing with the crisis.

Dr. Levinson tried to give me some right then. "I understand," he said supportively. "An event like this can be quite unsettling."

Roddy perked up at this. "I'm having trouble concentrating too! Maybe we should cancel class for today."

"Rodrigo," Dr. Levinson said sternly. "Please tell me you're not trying to use a crisis situation for something as petty as getting out of math class."

"No, I would never do that!" Roddy replied, even though that was exactly what he'd been doing.

Of course, that was exactly what I was doing too. But I

was better at selling it than Roddy. "I just thought of something Nina said to me last night that might be important," I told Dr. Levinson. "Can I go tell Chang and my father?"

"All right," Dr. Levinson said. "But come right back."

"I will. Thank you." I got up and headed for the door.

Zan followed me. Or at least she projected an image of herself following me into my brain. "What's going on with Nina?" she asked curiously.

"She's not in the moon base anymore," I said in my mind.

Zan gave me a doubtful look. "That's not possible."

"That's what everyone keeps saying. But she's still gone."

I passed Violet and her class on the way out. The kids had grown tired of dinosaur noises and were now making other animal noises instead. Violet was proudly demonstrating how loudly she could imitate an elephant. Her teacher, Miss Driscoll, was on the big SlimScreen, desperately trying to get them all to calm down and pay attention. It was only fifteen minutes into her lesson, and she already looked like she needed a nap.

I headed for my family's residence, figuring no one would be there. On the way, I quickly explained what had happened to Nina, doing my best to keep the words inside my head. Zan listened intently the whole time.

When we got to my residence, I unlocked the door and led Zan inside. It didn't take long to make sure no one was there. I could see the entire room from the doorway, though I still checked the sleep pods, just to be safe.

Zan sat on an InflatiCube. It didn't make an embarrassing noise beneath her, because she wasn't really there. I was too amped up to sit. Instead I paced.

Zan said, "Your species has an extremely limited temperature range in which it can survive. Plus, you need oxygen. Moon Base Alpha is the only place on the lunar surface that meets those needs, correct?"

"Yes." In the privacy of my family's residence, I felt comfortable enough to speak my words, rather than only thinking them. It was a huge relief.

"Then Nina must still be here," Zan concluded.

"She's not. We've looked everywhere."

"There must be someplace you've missed."

"There isn't. MBA isn't that big and we've been here four months. Trust me, we know this place inside and out."

"Logic says that must not be true."

I started to argue about this, then thought of something. "Hey. *You* could help us find Nina!"

Zan looked at me curiously. "How so?"

"You could project yourself into her mind the same way you do with me and then just ask her where she is."

Zan frowned. "I'm afraid it's not that simple."

"What do you mean? You do it with me all the time."

"Yes, but I can't do it with *anyone*. First, as you know, my appearing to you is a significant event. My species has known about yours for nearly a hundred of your years and you are only the second person with whom we have made contact. We do not take this selection lightly."

"I get that, but Nina's life might be in danger. . . ."

"Millions of humans' lives are in danger every day. I can't help them all."

"This is different."

"No, it's not. I am not authorized to alter the fate of any human being. It would be wrong to do so."

"You altered the fate of Dr. Holtz," I pointed out.

Zan recoiled from me, like I'd offended her. "Garth Grisan was the one who killed Ronald, not me," she snapped.

"I know," I said. "But he still did it *because* of you."

Zan calmed down and sighed sadly. "I suppose you're right. If I had never made contact with Ronald, he would still be alive. Which is exactly why we are now keeping our contact a secret. But even if I *wanted* to contact Nina, there is a good chance it wouldn't work. I can't appear to just anyone. Only those with minds open to it."

I stopped pacing, intrigued. "What do you mean?"

"It's hard to explain. As you know, every human is different. For example, some are far more open to new ideas and experiences than others. In a way, I can sense those who are the most agreeable to contact. With you and Dr. Holtz, I immediately knew it would work. With others, I am not sure. And with most, I know it won't. It's as though there is a shell around their minds."

If there was anyone I could imagine with a shell around her mind, it was Nina. "So, you couldn't even *try*?"

"It takes a great deal of effort for me to even appear to you. I would hate to expend so much energy for no reason."

I suddenly had another idea. "If you can sense our minds, then can you at least *sense* Nina's right now? You wouldn't have to appear to her. But you could still figure out where she is, right?"

Zan didn't answer me for a bit. She seemed to be considering her options. "I don't know."

"Well, could you give it a shot? Please? I think she's in danger."

Zan sighed. "If it means that much to you."

"It does."

"It won't be easy. And I can't promise anything."

"Whatever you could do would be great. Anything at all."

Zan stood, her eyes locked on mine. And then I felt her leave my mind. For a few moments, her body was still there, but her eyes were vacant, as though her own mind was somewhere else. Then the image of her flickered and disappeared.

I started pacing again, unsure what to do. I hadn't

expected Zan to completely vanish, and now I wasn't sure when she'd be back.

The SlimScreen in the room chimed, indicating a message over the public address system. "Attention, all MBA residents," the base computer announced. "The unmanned rocket is en route to deliver Supply Capsule Twelve. Capsule Drop will commence at the Moon Base Beta drop zone in one hour."

So much had been going on, I had forgotten a drop was scheduled for that day. Although the delivery of a supply capsule wasn't nearly as momentous as the arrival of a new crew of Moonies, it was still a break from our usual routine. And any break from our dull routine in space was like a holiday back on earth.

NASA was gearing up for construction of Moon Base Beta, which would be significantly larger and far more impressive than Moon Base Alpha (or so they claimed). MBA would serve as the base for some of the construction personnel, but because the MBB site was a mile away, an operations pod had already been erected there so people wouldn't have to commute. Meanwhile, capsules filled with construction equipment and supplies were arriving every week. Each of these was quite large, holding as much stuff as a moving van.

The delivery rocket wasn't even going to land on the moon. That would have been a waste of fuel. Instead, Supply

Capsule 12 was going to be dropped from a few miles up while the rocket returned to earth. The capsule would then guide itself down to the site, using retro rockets to slow its descent. Since there were no humans in the capsule, the rocket delivering it was a drone. The entire flight was automated.

I paced around my room for another minute, then decided I couldn't wait for Zan any longer. I had to get back to school. Dr. Levinson would be wondering where I was.

As I was heading for the door, Zan suddenly reappeared in front of me. Her image wasn't perfect, though. I could see through her. I got the sense that whatever she had done to find Nina had taken a lot out of her.

"Did you find her?" I asked.

"Sort of."

"Where is she?"

Zan frowned. "It doesn't work like that. I only know where you are because you let me into your mind. I can only see things because *you're* seeing them. I couldn't get into Nina's mind. I could only sense she was there. And that there was darkness around her."

"You mean, she's somewhere that's dark?"

"Maybe. Or maybe it only felt dark because of how *she* felt."

"So she's still alive?"

"Yes, but you were right. She's in great danger. Her vital signs were extremely weak. I don't think she has much time left."

"Do you know how much?"

Zan shook her head sadly. "I can't be sure, but . . . I suspect that if you don't find Nina in the next few hours, she will die."

ROBOTS

Just as on earth, many of the everyday tasks at MBA are performed by robots, rather than humans—particularly outside the base. In fact, given the highly technical nature of MBA, perhaps you will find more robots than you are used to. While the robots are extremely helpful, keep in mind that they are also potentially dangerous, with many moving parts and sharp edges. And though some of the smaller robots might look harmless, they are not toys! They serve extremely important functions. To avoid injury, all lunarnauts are advised to avoid touching or handling the robots in any way—with the exception of the moon-base roboticist.

DEAD ENDS

Lunar day 217

T minus 55 minutes to Capsule Drop

Instead of going back to school, I went to look for my parents. If Zan was right, every minute counted for Nina.

I found them with Chang in the control room, examining an image of the blueprints for MBA on the SlimScreen. Daphne Merritt was there too, though she appeared to have something on her mind other than Nina.

"I don't know what could have happened to them," she was saying. She sounded unusually stressed out. "I've never had anything like this occur before."

"What's wrong?" I asked.

Most adults probably would have told me it was none of

my business, but Daphne did her best to flash a smile and said, "My robotics logs from the last week have vanished."

Mom looked at me and said, "Aren't you supposed to be in math right now?"

"Dr. Levinson gave me permission to leave," I said.

"For what?" Mom asked.

I hesitated a moment before answering. I couldn't tell my parents the truth about why I was there—the alien that only I could see had sensed that Nina was running out of time to live—and I'd been in such a hurry, I hadn't concocted a suitable lie yet. So I went with bending the truth. "I was worried about Nina. I think she's in serious trouble."

For a moment, it looked as though Mom was going to say I still ought to be in school, but then she softened. "You're probably right."

"We're doing everything we can to find her," Dad said. He sounded frustrated with himself, and Chang looked frustrated too. Everyone in the room was extremely intelligent. They weren't used to not understanding things.

"Have you found anything out?" I asked. "Did you get the text off her watch?"

"I don't know that we should be discussing this with you right now," Chang said.

"What could it hurt?" Dad asked. "Dash was the one who figured out who killed Dr. Holtz."

"Or that he'd even been killed at all," Daphne added.

"And he's the one who told us about the text Nina got in the first place," Mom pressed. "We might as well have another mind on this. . . ."

"All right, I give!" Chang raised his hands in surrender, then turned to me. "The text wasn't quite as helpful as we'd hoped. It was only someone sending her some music."

"Music?" I repeated.

Chang tapped on the computer keypad and brought a list of text messages up on the SlimScreen. "NASA gave me authorization to hack into Nina's personal account. According to your parents, you came back from her room at eleven forty-five last night. This was delivered to her at eleven forty-one."

He highlighted a text from someone named Charlie. All it said was, "Heard these and thought of you."

There were two songs attached. One was "Fifty Miles of Elbow Room" by Coronal Mass Ejection, which was Violet's favorite band. The other was "Gimme Shelter" by an old group called the Rolling Stones. I knew about them because they'd been one of my great-grandfather's favorites.

"Are you sure this is right?" I asked.

"It's the only message she received during the time you were with her," Chang replied.

"Maybe she got another and erased it," I suggested.

"It wouldn't matter," Chang said. "Every communication to and from this base is logged by NASA. Even if Nina erased the message, there'd still be a record of it having come in. But there isn't. This is all she received within a twenty-minute window."

"That doesn't make sense," I said. "If you'd seen her then . . . well, she didn't *look* like she'd only received some music. . . ."

"We know something's important about this," Dad told me. "Nina received other texts *after* this one came in, some of which were very important base business—but she didn't open any of them." He pointed to the list of messages on the SlimScreen. After the one from Charlie, they were all marked as unread. The first had come in at 11:47. "That's not like Nina. It's as though she disappeared right after Charlie's music showed up."

"And then," Chang added, "this 'Charlie' isn't a real person. It's an alias someone set up."

"Have you figured out who?" I asked.

"No," Chang sighed. "Charlie did a darn good job of protecting himself through encryption. We've tipped NASA off, though, and they have people working on it."

I said, "So, was whoever did this some kind of computer genius?"

"Probably not," Chang replied. "It's not all that hard to

create a decent alias. I could do it when I was six."

"But you *are* a genius," I pointed out.

Chang laughed. "I'm not any smarter than anyone else on this base," he said. "Including you."

I was quite sure he was only being humble. Chang's IQ scores were rumored to be higher than Albert Einstein's. In addition to knowing everything about physics, chemistry, biology, and astronomy, he could also fix anything that broke at MBA and was a world-class pianist.

"Was Charlie's message really about music?" I asked. "Or do you think it was really about something else?"

"Well, this Charlie actually sent the songs," Mom said. "We listened to them. They weren't encrypted files or anything."

"And no additional files were piggybacked on them," Dad added. "So we figure the music meant something to Nina somehow. A message of some sort. Only we have no idea what it could be."

Mom asked me, "Can you be more specific about Nina's reaction to this text? How was she distracted exactly? Was she scared?"

I thought back to my encounter with Nina the night before. "I don't think so. It was more like she realized she had to do something."

"Was she excited?" Daphne asked.

"No." It was hard to even imagine Nina expressing

excitement. Or think of anything she would even be excited about. "She just wanted to get rid of me."

The adults all looked from one to another, like this might have meant something.

"Have you checked the video feeds from last night?" I asked. There were thousands of cameras around MBA, inside and out. Even in the bathrooms. The only place we weren't recorded was in the privacy of our residences.

"That was the first thing we did," Chang told me. "Only there was a glitch. The entire system went down for an hour last night."

"Every single camera?" I asked.

"Yes," Chang replied. "Starting a few minutes before midnight and lasting until shortly after one a.m."

"That's weird, isn't it?" I asked.

"Definitely," Chang agreed. "I've never really dealt with the cameras before, so I don't know if them all cutting out like this is common, but the fact that it happened on the same night that Nina disappeared is certainly suspicious. We're assuming both events are connected."

"Is there any way to recover the lost footage?" I asked.

Chang sighed. "Maybe. Unfortunately, the two people who knew the most about this system aren't here. Garth Grisan is back on earth and Nina is missing."

"Just our luck," Dad muttered.

"Do you think that all this could be connected to the robots, too?" Daphne asked. "I mean, I haven't had any trouble with the logs like this the whole time we've been up here. And now, the same night Nina disappears and the cameras go down, they get wiped out too? That can't be a coincidence, can it?"

"There's ten million things that can go wrong at this base," Chang said. "To have three happen at once is easily within the realm of probability. But my gut says they're probably linked."

"What's in the robot logs?" I asked.

"Detailed reports of everything the robots have done each day," Daphne explained. "For some, like the maintenance bots, it's nothing much, only a record of where they went and what they did. But for the drones and the surveillance bots, it's all the data they've collected."

"Patton and Lily were fooling around in the offices last night," I reported. "Roddy saw them—and they got really upset when they realized he was spying on them. That's why Patton tried to beat me up. He thought I was spying with Roddy."

Daphne frowned at the thought of this. "He tried to beat you up for that? I'm glad you stuffed that jerk's face in the toilet."

Chang looked at me accusingly. "Patton and Lily were in here? Why didn't you say anything about this before?"

"I only found out from Roddy this morning," I said.

"And then I heard about Nina being gone and kind of forgot all about it."

Chang still looked annoyed about this, but Mom put a hand on his shoulder to calm him. "That's perfectly understandable," she told me.

Dad said, "So maybe Patton and Lily are the ones who wiped out the logs. And whatever they did might have knocked out the cameras, too." He looked to Daphne. "Did you find any evidence of tampering on the computers?"

"No," Daphne admitted. "But someone who knew what they were doing might have been able to hide that."

"We're talking about the Sjoberg twins here," Dad said. "I'm surprised those two can even breathe, let alone hide evidence of hacking a computer."

"Maybe their dad helped them somehow," I suggested. "He's not that dumb, right?"

"You don't earn a trillion dollars without *some* smarts," Daphne agreed.

Mom asked, "What if the Sjobergs were connected to Nina's disappearance? Like, Nina caught them doing something they weren't supposed to and they retaliated." When everyone stared at her, she added, "I know it sounds crazy. But I can't think of anything more rational."

"The Sjobergs *have* been acting very suspicious lately," Daphne said supportively. "Lars and Sonja haven't come out of their room in days. It's like they're plotting something. And we know they were angry at Nina for making them stay at MBA when they wanted to go home."

"Nina didn't *make* them stay here," Dad countered. "There was no room on the rocket to send them back. All Nina did was deliver the bad news."

"She probably could have handled it better," Daphne said. "She was awfully blunt with them. I know they don't like her very much."

"They don't like *any* of us," Chang pointed out. "And they're certainly not holding Nina in their room. I searched it myself with Balnikov. Twice. She's not there."

"Maybe they're holding her somewhere else," Mom said.

Chang blew out a sharp breath, sounding exasperated. "Where?" He brought the MBA blueprints back up on the SlimScreen. "We've been poring over these for an hour. There's no crawl space or anything like that in this building large enough to hold a person Nina's size."

"Maybe the blueprints are wrong," Daphne suggested. "Maybe there's a hidden space somewhere."

"And the Sjobergs know about it while we don't?" Chang snapped.

"Don't be so testy," Daphne scolded. "I'm only trying to help."

Chang rubbed his temples, trying to calm himself down.

"I'm not angry at you. I'm frustrated. I can't make any sense of Nina's disappearance. It's completely impossible!"

"Obviously not," Mom pointed out calmly. "Nina must be somewhere. She didn't evaporate. So maybe Daphne's right. Maybe there is a secret hatch or something in the base."

"Why would there be a secret hatch?" Chang asked, still sounding testy.

"I don't know," Mom admitted. "For military purposes, maybe. After all, NASA let the military send Garth Grisan up here without telling us about it. Maybe there are other things they didn't tell us as well."

Everyone considered that for a bit. It was hard to believe there could be any hidden spaces at MBA, though. The base was kind of like a boat; it had been built to utilize every last inch of space. When room was limited, you couldn't afford to waste one bit of it.

I suddenly found myself wondering if my mother was wrong. What if Nina *had* evaporated—or something like that? A month before, I would have thought this was ludicrous, but now I was friends with an alien who vanished into thin air all the time. Could Nina have been an alien too? I knew she wasn't a mental projection the way Zan was—Nina had touched me, while Zan couldn't—but what if she was a more advanced species? Maybe she had posed as a human and then disapparated somehow. Or beamed herself out of

MBA, like they did on *Star Trek*. Yes, it sounded crazy, but I of all people knew it wasn't impossible to encounter alien life. And Nina being from another planet would go a long way toward explaining her almost complete lack of emotion.

Only Zan had said that she sensed Nina was in trouble. If Nina was a fellow space alien, wouldn't Zan have known? Or perhaps she *had* known, but had chosen not to tell me.

"Fine," Chang said curtly. "Maybe there is a secret hatch somewhere. Frankly, I don't have any better ideas. But to find it, we'll have to measure every inch of this base and compare that to these plans. If there are any differences, then we'll have a lead as to where the secret space might be."

"That'll take a lot of time," Dad said.

"We've got a base full of people willing to help," Chang replied. "And now we finally have something productive for them to do. I'll pull everyone off their projects and get them working on this."

"We'll start with the mess hall," Dad said, putting his arm around Mom.

"Thanks," Chang told them, then turned to Daphne. "Run some security tests on your computer. If you find any evidence of tampering, let me know." He stood and headed out the door. "Dash, come with me."

I did as ordered, following him into the air-lock staging area. "Need me to help measure?"

"You and all the other kids. Go tell everyone school is canceled for the rest of the day on my orders. Why don't you guys start with the gym?"

"Sure thing." I started toward the rec room, but Chang caught my arm.

"Dash, one more thing."

"Yeah?"

Chang knelt before me so we were eye to eye. "Your parents were right about you earlier. You're a really smart kid, and you sometimes pick up on things other people don't. Even though this base is full of brilliant scientists, I trust your ideas as much as any of theirs. So if you come up with anything that you think is important—or even odd or strange—anything at all that could help us figure out where Nina is, come tell me right away, okay?"

"Okay."

"Thanks." Chang hopped to his feet and headed into the science pod. Normally, he was a proud person who walked with his head held high. Today he sagged, looking angry and frustrated.

I was flattered to hear how highly Chang thought of me—but it was disconcerting to see him so upset. After all, Chang was one of the smartest people I'd ever met. If *he* couldn't figure out where Nina had gone, what chance did the rest of us have?

Excerpt from *The Official Residents' Guide to Moon Base Alpha*,
"Appendix A: Potential Health and Safety Hazards,"
© 2040 by National Aeronautics and Space Administration

EXERCISE EQUIPMENT

It might seem counterintuitive to think that exercise equipment, which is designed to *improve* your health, could actually cause injury or harm. However, a great number of injuries on earth happen while exercising or playing sports. You will be working out at least two hours a day in order to counteract the deterioration of bone and muscle mass caused by the moon's low gravity—and any of the equipment can be dangerous if used improperly. In particular, lunarnauts are advised to utilize extreme caution when using the virtual-reality enhancements for any of these devices. Furthermore, the tension bands, while a necessary substitute for physical weights, have great potential for injury if allowed to snap back into anyone's body or face.

Lunarnauts should follow the same basic safety procedures when working out on the moon that you would on earth: Warm up before strenuous exercise, don't overexert yourself, be careful when competing in any sort of physical competition against a fellow lunarnaut—and remember to stay properly hydrated.

While all this may sound dangerous, do not be daunted. If done with proper care, exercise can be safe and great fun. In fact, the *least* safe thing you could do on the moon would be to not exercise at all!

SENTIENT NANOBOTS

Lunar day 217

T minus 37 minutes to Capsule Drop

"I know what happened to Nina!" Roddy cried suddenly.

We were with Kira in the gymnasium, taking measurements of the room for Chang. Violet, Inez, and Kamoze were there too, although they were only playing with all the exercise equipment. My parents had broken the news to them all that Nina was actually missing, not playing hide-and-seek, but none of them seemed too bothered by this. They hadn't put together how dire Nina's situation was—and no one felt any good would come of explaining it.

I fired the laser from a measuring device along the exterior wall between the emergency backup air lock and the corner. "What happened?"

"She wasn't human," Roddy said proudly.

I turned to him, startled, wondering if he also suspected she might be an alien. "She's not?"

"No," Roddy declared. "She was an amalgamation of sentient nanobots."

"You're an amalgamation of sentient nanobots," Violet repeated, and then all the little kids laughed.

"Ha, ha," Roddy sneered at them, then turned his attention back to Kira and me. "I'm serious. This is completely plausible."

I checked the measurement the laser had given me—thirty feet—and compared it against the measurement in the digital copy of the blueprints on a tablet computer. The numbers matched. So far, every measurement I'd taken had matched the blueprints perfectly.

Roddy launched into an explanation, even though Kira and I hadn't asked for one. "You know what nanobots are, right? Incredibly small robots. Well, there's a top secret project at NASA to develop nanos that can work in sync together. If you had enough of them, they could take any shape they wanted to, then form a hive mind and behave as a single unit."

Kira stared at Roddy. "You think Nina was a robot?" I would have expected her to immediately dismiss this theory as idiocy; instead she sounded surprisingly intrigued.

"No," Roddy told her. "I think she was a *billion* robots. A nanotechnology prototype. NASA sent her up here to test her out. Then she must have malfunctioned or something and all the nanobots scattered, which is why we can't find any trace of her now."

"Where'd the nanobots go, then?" I asked.

"They could be anywhere," Roddy replied. "They're so small, you wouldn't be able to see a thousand of them if they were right in front of your nose. They could even be *in* your nose and you wouldn't know."

"Eeeew!" Violet shrieked. "Snot robots!"

To my astonishment, Kira actually seemed impressed by Roddy's idea. "Wow," she gasped. "That's amazing."

Roddy seemed equally surprised that Kira had given him a compliment. He flashed her a wolfish grin. "Of course it is."

Kira said, "I know in the past I've accused you of having some really stupid theories, but this one is different."

"Really?" Roddy asked.

"Yes," Kira said. "This one is *incredibly* stupid. It's like a hundred times dumber than any of the others. I didn't even think that was possible."

Roddy's face fell as he realized Kira had only been leading him on. "It's not that stupid."

"It *is*," Kira told him. "Remember your stupid theory that aliens created spray cheese? This nanobot theory leaves that one in the dust."

Roddy sat on a rowing machine, making a point of not working anymore. Not that he'd been working much to begin with. He'd mostly been lurking near Kira and trying to impress her. "Fine," he said. "If you're so smart, why don't *you* tell me what happened to Nina?"

"Someone bumped her off," Kira said, without even thinking about it.

Roddy laughed obnoxiously. "Right. And you think my robot theory is stupid?"

"No one has ever built a cloud of sentient nanobots," Kira told him. "That's sci-fi silliness. But people kill each other all the time. In fact, it's even happened here at MBA already. So why couldn't it happen again?"

I glanced at Violet and the other little kids, worried about them overhearing this conversation. They seemed to have lost interest in us, though. Instead they were busy trying to jump rope with the elastic tension bands.

I started to argue that Kira's theory was wrong, as I knew Nina was still alive. But then I caught myself. In the first place, I couldn't explain how I knew Nina was still alive without mentioning Zan. And second, just because Nina was alive didn't mean someone hadn't at least *tried* to murder her. After all, Zan had said Nina was in desperate shape with extremely weak vital signs. That could have been the result of an attempted murder.

Roddy was shaking his head, determined to argue against Kira's theory himself. "There's only twenty-four people here. The chance of there being two murders in this small a population is infinitesimal."

"Maybe not," Kira countered. "This is a really cramped place and we're all stuck with everyone else, whether we like them or not. Everyone's getting on each other's nerves all the time here."

"That's not true," Roddy said.

"Oh, no?" Kira asked. "You and your brother can't go five minutes without fighting each other."

"That's different," Roddy sneered. "All brothers fight."

"Well, you're probably fighting ten times more here than you would back on earth," Kira told him. "Because you can't get away from each other. And that's the case with everyone else here too. There's arguments all the time."

"There are not!" Roddy argued.

"You're arguing with me right now," Kira pointed out.

"I am not!"

"Are you even listening to yourself?" Kira asked.

Roddy clammed up, trying to figure out how to argue his point without arguing.

Before he could try, I said, "Kira's right. There's been a lot of tension up here lately." I'd noticed it well before Kira had pointed it out. Even though everyone at MBA had been selected in part because they got along well with other people, we hadn't all been getting along as well as NASA had assured us we would. It seemed that everyone was always annoyed at someone else, if not two or three other people. Myself included.

Kira flashed me a smile, pleased I was backing her up. "And Nina's probably involved in more arguments than anyone else, except the Sjobergs. People actually liked Dr. Holtz, and *he* got killed. Nobody likes Nina. I'll bet half the base wanted her dead."

"Whoa," I said. "It couldn't be that many. . . ."

"The Sjobergs don't like her for sure," Kira said. "That's four right there. And she and Balnikov didn't get along either. They've been arguing ever since he got here."

"That's true," I admitted. Only a few days after Dr. Balnikov had arrived, Nina had chewed him out for how untidy he kept his workstation in the science pod. He'd responded by calling her something in Russian that my parents refused to translate for me. Things had gone downhill from there.

"That's only five," Roddy said.

"I know Dr. Kim and Dr. Alvarez were angry at her for something the other day," Kira said, ticking people off on her fingers. "And she got all over Dr. Goldstein about the greenhouse not producing enough, so Dr. Goldstein and Dr. Iwanyi were mad at her. Chang certainly has issues with her. And while I'm at it, I'm pretty sure all of our parents do too."

Roddy sat up, offended. "Are you saying you think my parents killed Nina?"

"I'm saying there's no shortage of suspects," Kira explained. "Everyone here had problems with her. Even Daphne, and she's the nicest person ever. This didn't necessarily have to be a murder that someone plotted ahead of time. Maybe Nina got on someone's case about something and they got upset, and next thing you know, Nina's dead."

I glanced back at the little kids again. They were still jumping rope, oblivious to the dark turn our conversation had taken.

"Hey," Roddy said, looking at me accusingly. "Nina got on *your* case last night. And no one ever saw her again after that."

"I thought you said this murder theory was stupid," I told him.

"Don't try to change the subject," Roddy warned me. "That's exactly what I'd expect the murderer to do."

"Dash didn't kill Nina, you nitwit," Kira said.

"How can you be so sure?" Roddy demanded.

"Because he was with me at the time she disappeared.

We were up late last night playing cards." Of course, this was a complete and total lie, but Kira probably realized it was easier than telling the truth.

"Oh," Roddy said, sounding disappointed. I couldn't tell if he was upset that I wasn't the killer or because Kira had been playing cards with me and not him. Whatever the case, he'd apparently fully bought her argument that someone might have killed Nina. "One thing, though. If someone did murder her, where's the body?"

"They got rid of it," Kira said confidently.

"How?" I asked.

"Out there." Kira pointed out the emergency air lock, toward the surface of the moon. "Think about it: If *you* killed Nina, you couldn't just leave her there, right? Because the moment anyone found the body, they'd know she'd been murdered. And they'd probably be able to figure out it was you, because there's security cameras up the wazoo here and there aren't that many possible suspects, with us being trapped here and all. But suppose you ditch the body? Then no one knows it's a murder. Instead everyone thinks it's a missing persons deal."

"Ditching the body wouldn't be that easy, though," I pointed out.

"Well, it wouldn't be that hard, either," Kira countered. "Carrying the body wouldn't be a problem, because it wouldn't weigh that much here. So the killer goes down to the control room, shuts down the security cameras . . ."

"How?" I asked again.

"Beats me. But they know how. Then they grab Nina's body, suit up, and take her out the air lock. It's no big deal if Nina goes outside without a suit, because she's dead already. Then the killer carries her off somewhere and buries her in one of the big fields of moon dust."

"Yeah!" Roddy agreed excitedly, really on board now. "There's plenty of space to do that. That's all there is out there: space. And it's not like there are millions of people around to stumble across the body. And it won't decay out there, so there won't be any smell."

"Not that we could smell it out there anyhow, because we're always wearing space suits," Kira chimed in.

"There's no buzzards or rats to sniff it out," Roddy said. "There's no police dogs to track it down. Honestly, you could probably put a body out there and it could be centuries before anyone stumbled across it. Millennia, maybe."

"And meanwhile, the killer gets away free," Kira concluded. "It's the perfect crime."

I had to admit, her theory made sense. It certainly explained Nina's absence better than anything I'd come up with. Plus, Kira was also right that, out of everyone at MBA, Nina was the person who seemed most likely to get bumped off—except for the Sjobergs. At one time or another, everyone had been angry at her for something. It gave me the willies, but I could imagine that, in a high-pressure place like MBA, someone might have snapped and killed Nina on the spur of the moment. Or at least, they'd attempted to kill her—and then left her for dead out on the lunar surface.

Even scarier, I could also imagine that someone might have plotted her murder ahead of time.

Any one of the Moonies Kira had said were upset with Nina might have felt their lives at MBA would be easier with her gone. And the Sjobergs certainly loathed her as well. I wondered if there was anyone with an even bigger grudge against Nina that I didn't know about.

"We ought to tell Chang about this!" Roddy exclaimed. "He's the second in command. If there's a killer on the loose, he should know about it."

"That's a good idea," Kira said.

For a brief moment, I wondered if it was. It suddenly occurred to me that Chang himself had a motive for wanting Nina dead: control of Moon Base Alpha. He and Nina had been the only ones who knew he was the second in command. Now, with Nina gone, he would likely end up in charge.

I didn't say anything, though, because I felt bad about even thinking that Chang might be the murderer. Although the truth was, Chang was an extremely strong man with a serious temper when pushed. I'd only seen it surface a few times, but when it did, Chang could be a very scary person.

"Okay," Roddy said, hopping off the rowing machine. "I'm gonna go find Chang!" He hurried out the door without waiting for Kira, even though the murder theory was her idea.

But then, Kira didn't make a move to follow him anyhow. Instead she turned to me and said, "Man, I thought we'd never get rid of him."

I stepped back, surprised. "You mean, that was all an act? The whole murder theory was bogus?"

"No. It's totally possible."

"Then why aren't you telling Chang about it? Roddy's going to take all the credit."

"Big deal. You really think Chang hasn't thought of this himself?"

"He didn't say anything to me about it."

"Yeah, because he didn't want to freak you out. We've already faced one psycho killer here."

I wondered if Kira was right about that. The idea of Nina being murdered didn't seem that obvious to me. Frankly, I was a little disturbed that Kira had thought of it—and worked out the details so well. It seemed she had a darker streak to her personality than I'd realized.

Kira peered out the gym door to see if anyone was

around, then signaled me to follow her. "C'mon. Let's go do some *real* investigating."

"Where?"

"Nina's room, of course." Kira gave me a devious smile, then slipped out of the gym.

Excerpt from *The Official Residents' Guide to Moon Base Alpha*,
"Appendix A: Potential Health and Safety Hazards,"
© 2040 by National Aeronautics and Space Administration

INFLATICUBES

At first glance, it might appear that InflatiCubes are as safe as a piece of furniture can get—and for good reason: They are! After all, there are no hard parts to bang yourself on, nor any sharp edges to cut yourself with. And yet, please remember that, while InflatiCubes serve the purpose of chairs, they are *not* chairs. Should you attempt to lean back or recline on one the way you might with a real chair, you could fall off the back, bang your head on the floor, and suffer harm ranging anywhere from a nasty bruise to a subdural hematoma. So please exercise caution at all times when sitting.

BREAKING AND ENTERING

Lunar day 217

T minus 22 minutes to Capsule Drop

I bounded out the gym door after Kira. "What are you doing?"

"I'm not measuring the stupid gym anymore, that's for sure." Kira made a point of shoving her laser measuring device into her pocket. "That's only busy work Chang made up to get us out of the way."

We passed the common room, which Dr. Janke and Dr. Balnikov were busily measuring.

I pointed to them. "If it was busy work, would *they* be doing it?"

Kira didn't even glance at them. "If we really want to

know where Nina went, the answer isn't out here. It's in her quarters."

"Why?"

Kira rolled her eyes. "That's the last place you saw her. And you were the last person to see her. So if somebody whacked her, they probably did it there."

"Not necessarily."

"Well, there's a better chance they did it there than anywhere else. And if they didn't, there could still be a clue to who the killer is in Nina's personal stuff."

"Nina didn't have any personal stuff."

Kira froze at the bottom of the staircase and fixed me with a withering stare, like she was getting annoyed. "Everyone has personal stuff. Nina just kept hers secret."

I knew it was pointless to argue. Once Kira made up her mind to do something, she usually did it. Plus, she had a thing about entering places that were supposed to be off-limits to her. Back on earth, she'd trespassed a lot, going behind the scenes in places like museums, zoos, and movie theaters. She claimed she did this simply out of curiosity, but my parents suspected she was really trying to get attention. After all, her mother had died of cancer when she was young and her father tended to get lost in his own thoughts for hours at a time. Causing trouble was a good way to get him to focus on her.

Given this, I wondered if Kira truly believed there were any clues in Nina's residence—or if she was merely making an excuse to sneak into it.

I followed her up the stairs to Nina's door. Normally, getting past the electronic entry system would have been impossible, but since Chang had kicked the door open earlier that day, it couldn't be locked again. When Kira pushed on it, it swung right open.

"We shouldn't be doing this," I warned.

"Who's gonna punish us?" Kira asked. "Nina's gone."

"What are you doing?" a voice behind us asked.

Kira and I spun around to find Violet peeking around the corner from the stairs. She'd apparently followed us from the gym.

"Come inside and I'll tell you," Kira said, then slipped through the door before anyone else noticed us.

Violet and I followed her into the room. Kira shut the door behind us, then explained to Violet, "We're on a top secret mission to investigate what happened to Nina."

"Okay!" Violet agreed happily. "But I thought she was made out of bananabots."

"Nanobots," I corrected. "And no, she wasn't."

"But Roddy said she was."

"Roddy was wrong," Kira told her. "As usual. Now, you can help us if you want, but I need you to be very careful.

You can touch things, but if you do, you have to put them right back where you found them. Understand?"

Violet nodded so enthusiastically it looked as though her head might come off. "What are we looking for?"

"I'm not sure," Kira admitted. "Anything unusual." She scanned the room, then frowned. "Though that might not take long. There's not much here."

"I *told* you," I said.

Kira ignored me and started poking through Nina's desk. The drawers were unlocked.

Violet picked up the InflatiCubes and searched under them, as if anything important would have been hidden that way.

I stayed by the door. I didn't feel comfortable rooting through Nina's room. Plus, I wasn't sure where else to look.

"This desk is almost empty," Kira said, sounding annoyed.

I came over to see. So did Violet.

The desk drawers had little in them, save for a few stray pencils and some other office supplies. In the right bottom drawer was a Moon Base Alpha commanders' guide. It looked very similar to the Moon Base Alpha residents' guide the rest of us had been issued, only it was a bit thicker.

In the left bottom drawer was a toolbox, which was probably more useful on a moon base than any paperwork would have been. We opened it, but found only tools inside.

"There's nothing personal in this room at all," Kira muttered. "No books. No pictures. No nothing. Maybe Nina really *is* a robot."

"You just said she wasn't," Violet pointed out.

Kira smiled at her. "What I mean is, she doesn't seem to have much of a personality."

"Sometimes Mommy says I have *too* much personality," Violet reported.

"I'm sure Nina had some books and photos and stuff," I said. "But it's probably all on her computer. I know she had a tablet, but I think Chang took it."

"Still," Kira said. "It doesn't seem she had anything in her life except running this base. Have you ever heard her talk about anyone in her family?"

"I've never heard Nina talk about anything that wasn't work," I said, then walked over to Nina's tabletop Slim-Screen. It was in dormant mode, displaying a fake marble tabletop. I tapped on it. It instantly displayed a new screen: PLEASE ENTER PASSWORD.

I frowned. My family had never enabled the password protection on the SlimScreens in our room. "Any idea what Nina's password might be?" I asked.

"Turnip!" Violet suggested.

Kira said, "Knowing Nina, it's probably a twenty-digit string of random letters and numbers she's memorized."

"Yeah," I agreed. I couldn't imagine Nina using anything personal, like a pet's name. In fact, I couldn't imagine Nina having a pet.

"Platypus!" Violet shouted, still trying to come up with the password. "Snorkel! Tiddlywinks!"

Kira got down on her back and scooted under the desk, looking up at the bottom of it.

Violet imitated her, lying down under the desk as well. "What are we doing?"

"Seeing if there's anything hidden under here."

"Is there?"

"Doesn't look like it." Kira slid back out from under the desk.

Violet did the same thing.

"Nina must have done *something* besides run this base," Kira said thoughtfully. "Everyone has a hobby, right?"

"I'll bet she liked magic," Violet suggested.

"Magic?" I repeated.

"Yes!" Violet exclaimed. "She made herself disappear."

"Music!" I said suddenly.

Kira turned to me, intrigued. "What about it?"

"Someone sent her some last night," I reported. "Someone named Charlie, only Chang says that's an alias. We figured it was some sort of cryptic message, but I'm not sure. Did Nina ever listen to music at all?"

"She did!" Violet said enthusiastically. "In the gym,

when she worked out. She listened to marching music."

"How do you know that?" I asked.

"Because I pay attention to things," Violet said pointedly. "She worked out a lot, with headphones on, but she played it so loud I could hear it anyhow."

"What do you mean by marching music?" I asked. "Like, military music?"

"Right," Violet agreed. "Like the kind soldiers march to."

"Did you ever hear her listen to anything else?" I pressed.

Violet screwed up her face in thought. "Maybe, but I don't remember."

"Were the songs that this Charlie sent her marches?" Kira asked.

"No. They were rock and roll," I reported. "One was 'Gimme Shelter' by this band called the Rolling Stones. They were pretty huge back in the old days."

"I know who the Rolling Stones are," Kira said coolly. "I know plenty about music."

"I know the Rolling Stones too!" Violet exclaimed. "Great-Grandpa used to play them for me. They did 'Jumping Jack Flash'!"

"That's right," Kira agreed, looking impressed.

Violet promptly began singing. Only, as usual, she mangled the lyrics. "But it's aaaaallllll right. Jumping Jack Flash gives me gas gas gas!"

Kira laughed. "Actually, the words are 'I'm Jumping Jack Flash. It's a gas gas gas.'"

Violet looked at her curiously. "What's that mean?"

"I have no idea," Kira admitted. "I think 'gas' was old-fashioned for something fun."

Violet giggled. "Now 'gas' means you made a toot."

"What was the other song?" Kira asked me.

"'Fifty Miles of Elbow Room' by Coronal Mass Ejection."

"Oh!" Violet cried. "I know that one! I love it!" She began to dance around the room, singing the song as she went, although it was evident that she didn't know the lyrics to this one either. For starters, she seemed to think it was called "Fifty Smiles of Elmo Bloom." Even though I'd just said the title.

"I know this one, too," Kira told me, watching Violet dance. "CME only did a cover, though. Originally, it was a gospel song."

"Really?" I asked. "Do you know what it's about?"

"Going to heaven, I think," Kira said. "Or someplace with a whole lot of space, at least."

"Like the moon?" I asked.

Kira stared at me a moment. "You think that's the message?"

I shrugged. "This Charlie's text said that he'd heard the songs and thought of Nina. Can you imagine Nina listening to rock and roll?"

Kira thought about it a moment. "Not really."

Violet was still singing, although she was now drumming her hands along the wall. "For the gates are wide on the other slide where the flowers all go boom! On the right hand and the left hand, fifty smiles of Elmo Bloom!"

"It's not 'Elmo Bloom,'" I corrected. "It's 'elbow room.'"

Violet paused for a moment, then looked at me like *I* didn't know what I was talking about. "'Fifty smiles of elbow room'? That doesn't make any sense." With that, she went right back to her drumming.

I turned to Kira and spoke under my breath. "See what I have to deal with all the time?"

"It's cute," Kira chided. "I love Violet. It's cool that she's always so happy." She then turned her attention to her smartwatch.

"What are you doing?" I asked.

"Looking up the real lyrics to both those songs. Maybe there's a clue in them somewhere. Do you have any idea who this 'Charlie' is?"

"No. Chang's working on it, but he says it might not be easy to figure out."

"You think it's a family member? Or a friend?"

I shrugged. "I don't know if Nina even had friends. I've never heard her mention one."

"Everyone has friends," Kira said.

"Nina didn't have any *here*," I pointed out. "Everyone else is friendly with each other—except the Sjobergs. I mean, we're all going to be up here for three years together. But Nina didn't even try. I never heard her talk about anything that wasn't work. Or tell a joke. I can barely remember her ever smiling."

Kira frowned. "That's pretty sad. I guess, maybe, because she came out of the military, she didn't think it was right to be friends with everyone."

"Maybe," I said. "Or maybe she just wasn't very friendly. There's only twenty-five people on this base and you came up with a pretty darn good list of folks who might have wanted her dead."

"Wait!" Kira exclaimed. "Maybe the music was supposed to be a threat of some sort. 'Fifty Miles' is about going to heaven—and then Nina ends up dead? Pretty suspicious, right?"

"We don't know that she's dead," I pointed out.

"Dead, missing, whatever. Something bad happened right after she got the song. Seems like a threat all right."

"Maybe," I admitted. "So what do you think the other song had to do with it?"

"Hmmm," Kira said thoughtfully. "I wonder if . . ." That was as far as she got. Because Violet, who was still singing about Elmo Bloom and dancing along the wall, drummed her hands along the area beneath Nina's sleep pod.

I didn't notice anything odd about it—I was doing my best to ignore Violet—but Kira did. She clammed up in midthought and came over to the wall. "Violet, stop," she said.

Violet did exactly as Kira asked. "Want me to do a different song?" she asked. "I know lots of them! 'Happy Birthday,' 'Take Me Out to the Ball Game,' 'The Star-Bangled Spammer' . . ."

"Maybe in a bit." Kira rapped her knuckles on the wall under Nina's sleep pod where Violet had just been drumming. Then she moved two feet to the left and did it again.

The sound was different.

Kira repeated the process to make sure. The spot right under the sleep pod sounded hollow, while the other spot sounded solid. "What's on the other side of this wall?" Kira asked.

"Our residence," I answered. "Our sleep pods are built into this wall too, but they're closer to the door."

Kira took a step back, staring at the wall. There were four sleep pods built into this side as well, even though only Nina used this room, because every residence had been constructed with multiple sleep pods. Someday, there might be a moon-base commander with a family.

It was obvious which pod Nina slept in, though. It was the one on the upper left, the only one with an air mattress in it. The other three were empty.

The mattress was exactly like the ones the rest of us had to use: a thin, uncomfortable rubber pad that smelled faintly like a fire at a tire factory. Her bed was made, the sheets tucked in around the edges and smoothed out with military precision.

Kira yanked the mattress out and tossed it aside. It had been designed to be as light as possible for delivery to the moon, so it wasn't hard for her to move it. Then she tossed the pillow off as well.

"Ooh!" Violet exclaimed. "Pillow fight!"

She snatched up Nina's pillow. To everyone's surprise, a teddy bear tumbled out of the pillowcase.

It was small and gray, although it was so well worn, there was a chance that it had been some other color long before. Parts of it had been rubbed bare, like it had mange, and there were a few spots that seemed to have been surgically repaired over the years, with hospital-quality sutures.

"Whoa," Violet gasped. "Nina has a teddy bear?"

"I guess," Kira said, then looked at me. "See? She *is* human after all."

I stared at the teddy bear, almost as astonished by the fact that Nina slept with it as I was by the fact that Nina had vanished. Both facts seemed equally incomprehensible to me.

Violet picked the bear up and hugged it. "Think I can keep it if Nina doesn't come back?"

"Nina's coming back," I told her. "So be careful with that. It's not yours."

"I'll be careful," Violet told me, then promptly dropped it. "Oopsy!" She picked it back up again and made a show of handling it carefully.

Kira returned her attention to the sleep pod. Now that the mattress wasn't there, she began tapping on the bottom of the pod, listening for where it sounded hollow. After thirty seconds, she'd narrowed it down to a small area. "Sounds like there's a secret compartment here," she announced.

I joined her at the sleep pod. Since it was the upper one, it was four feet off the floor, with about eight inches of space between it and the lower pod. Like the sleep pod in my room, it was cramped, dark, and claustrophobic. Kira and I both used the flashlight functions on our watches to light it up.

"Check it out," Kira said.

There was a hairline crack in the shape of a square, right above the area that had sounded hollow. It was so thin, we never would have noticed it if we hadn't known to look for it.

"What is it?" Violet asked. She wasn't quite tall enough to see into the sleep pod, so she was bouncing on the balls of her feet. "What what what?"

"Give us some room and we'll find out," I told her, then examined the crack closely.

The square panel it surrounded fit perfectly into the base

of the sleep pod. There was no handle or any other obvious way to remove it.

"Whoever made this was no slouch," I said.

"Whoever made it?" Kira repeated. "Obviously, it was Nina."

I shrugged in response, not ready to assume anything about anyone anymore.

"Can I see it?" Violet asked. In the low gravity of the moon, she was jumping high enough to peek over our shoulders.

"There's nothing to see," I told her. "Not yet."

Kira and I examined the crack more closely. There was one spot on the right side where it widened slightly. I went back to Nina's desk and dug around in the toolbox for a flathead screwdriver.

The base computer's voice came on over the intercom system. "The delivery rocket is nearing the drop zone. T minus five minutes until Capsule Drop."

On any other day, I would have been racing down to the rec room to watch the drop. But right now, there were more important things to do.

I found the screwdriver I needed and brought it back to Nina's sleep pod. Violet had now clambered up inside the pod herself to get a better view. She was curled up in the back of it, cuddling Nina's teddy bear.

"That's not yours," I told her. "It's Nina's."

"I'm only borrowing him," Violet told me. "His name is Mister Sillypants."

I jammed the blade of the screwdriver into the slight gap in the crack and used it as a lever. The square panel popped out easily. I shoved it aside and Kira aimed her light inside to see what Nina had hidden there.

"It's just a bunch of rocks," Violet said, sounding disappointed.

I looked inside. The space was six inches deep and about eighteen inches square. Sure enough, there were rocks inside. There were about a hundred, most of them on the smaller side, about the size of a tangerine, although there were a few as big as a can of beans.

Kira frowned. "Why would Nina go through so much trouble to hide a bunch of rocks?"

"I don't know," I replied. "Let's go find out."

Excerpt from *The Official Residents' Guide to Moon Base Alpha*,
"Appendix A: Potential Health and Safety Hazards,"
© 2040 by National Aeronautics and Space Administration

ROCKETS

Perhaps the most dangerous pieces of machinery at MBA are the rockets designed to deliver you there and bring you back home. While *riding* on a rocket has become hundreds of times safer in recent years, being near a rocket when it is taking off or landing is still exceptionally dangerous. This is especially the case on the moon, where the lack of atmosphere allows debris blown clear by the rockets to travel great distances at potentially deadly speeds. For this reason, no lunarnaut is to be on the surface at any time during a rocket landing or departure, including during arrivals of supply capsules and other spacecraft. Furthermore, even once the rockets have landed, lunarnauts should avoid going anywhere near the engines—which can be hot enough to melt through space suits—until said engines have had at least three hours to cool down.

ILLEGAL CONTRABAND

Lunar day 217

T minus zero to Capsule Drop

I found my parents in the common room, along with almost everyone else from MBA. They had all taken a break from searching and measuring to watch the capsule drop on the main SlimScreen. The only people who were missing were the Sjobergs, as usual.

The capsule was separating from the delivery rocket as Kira, Violet, and I entered. A camera on the rocket showed it dropping away with the moon behind it.

My parents were standing next to Kira's father. Dr. Howard was watching the capsule drop with an unusual amount of focus. Normally, his mind seemed to be a hundred other places at once. But the capsule's arrival was very important to Dr. Howard, as he was involved with the construction of Moon Base Beta. If anything went wrong, his job would become a whole lot more complicated.

My parents looked relieved to see Violet, Kira, and me, as if they'd been worried. It occurred to me only then that this probably wasn't the best day to suddenly go missing. Nina had already vanished; perhaps Mom and Dad thought it had happened to us, too.

Dr. Howard didn't even seem to notice us.

"Where have you guys been?" Dad asked. "We were looking for you."

"We found something in Nina's room," I said, keeping my voice as low as possible. "Something important."

"What were you doing in Nina's room?" Mom asked suspiciously.

"Trying to figure out what happened to her," Kira replied, before I could. "And I think we've got a clue."

"Really?" Dr. Howard asked absently. "That's nice, dear."

On the SlimScreen, the capsule was falling away from the rocket that had delivered it at thousands of miles per hour.

The view switched to a camera on the capsule itself, filming the surface of the moon as it came closer and closer.

Mom and Dad had already forgotten all about the capsule. And if they'd been annoyed at us for disappearing, they seemed to have forgotten about that, too. Now they were intrigued.

"What'd you find?" Dad asked.

"You have to come see," I told them.

"It's a bunch of rocks!" Violet exclaimed.

Kira and I had both told her to keep this a secret—or, if she couldn't do that, to at least whisper it. In her excitement, she had failed on both counts. Luckily, everyone else in the room was too riveted to the SlimScreen to notice.

The retro rockets fired on the capsule, slowing its descent.

Mom and Dad were even more intrigued after Violet's revelation. "I think we'd better see these rocks," Mom said, while Dad headed over to where Chang was watching the capsule drop. He whispered in Chang's ear. Chang's jaw immediately fell open in surprise. He forgot about the capsule drop as well and came back across the room toward us.

Kira told her father, "I'm going back up to Nina's room."

"All right," Dr. Howard replied distantly. "Have fun."

On the screen, the capsule was lowering toward the lunar surface. Someone back at NASA Mission Control in Houston was reporting that all systems looked good.

Mom, Dad, and Chang led Kira, Violet, and me out of the common room. "You guys found rocks in Nina's room?" Chang asked. He didn't sound angry at all. He sounded stunned.

"Like a thousand!" Violet reported.

"More like a hundred," I corrected.

Chang shared a surprised glance with my parents.

We all started up the stairs to the upper residences.

"What's wrong?" Kira asked.

Instead of answering the question, Chang asked his own. "Did you tell anyone else about these rocks?"

"No," Kira replied. "We only found them a few minutes ago and we came right to you."

We reached Nina's residence. Chang paused at the door, then turned back to us. "You kids are aware that all the residences here are private, right?"

"Kira made me go in!" Violet announced. "It was all her idea!"

Kira shot Violet an annoyed look. "Thanks a lot."

"You're welcome," Violet replied. She didn't really understand sarcasm yet.

Chang didn't seem very surprised that Kira had been the instigator. He didn't seem that upset, either. "Next time you want to get into someplace up here," he said, "come see me first."

"Okay," Kira said, then led the way to the secret compartment we'd found.

Chang grew annoyed at himself the moment he saw where it was. "I can't believe I missed that," he sighed. "I'm an idiot."

"We weren't looking for a space that small," Mom pointed out. "We were looking for spaces big enough to hold a person."

"Even so," Chang said, then peeked into the compartment. Mom and Dad joined him. They all reacted with astonishment.

"Those are rocks all right," Dad said.

"You didn't believe us?" Kira asked.

"It didn't seem . . ."—Dad paused to search for the right words—"in Nina's character."

"What's going on here?" I asked.

Chang fished one of the rocks out of the secret compartment. "This is a moon rock—" he began.

"We know," Violet taunted. "We're on the moon! Duh!"

Mom signaled Violet to be quiet.

Chang walked back over to the door of the room, checked the hall to see if anyone was around, then closed it. "The point is, moon rocks are extremely valuable."

"Why?" Violet asked, ignoring Mom's warning. "They're everywhere. The whole moon is made of them."

"True," Chang admitted. "They're not valuable *here*. But on earth, they'd be worth a fortune. The total amount of lunar samples that have been brought back to earth over the years is only a few thousand pounds. And those have all been supervised by NASA."

Mom said, "No one on earth has a moon rock unless NASA has given it to them, and they've limited those gifts to museums and other educational or research facilities." She took another rock out of the compartment. "If you were a private collector, no matter how rich you were, it'd be easier to get a diamond this size than a moon rock."

I asked, "You mean, that rock could be worth more than a giant diamond?"

"Exactly," Chang replied. "In fact, I can't even say what it'd be worth, because there's never been a moon rock for sale before. But I can guarantee you, there are people back home who'd be willing to spend whatever it takes to get one. Millions, certainly. If not tens of millions."

"For that?" Violet asked. "But it's ugly!"

She was right. None of the rocks in the secret compartment were pretty, especially compared to the rocks you could find on earth. On earth, there are all sorts of forces at work—like volcanoes and sedimentation and plate tectonics—that create hundreds of thousands of varieties of rock. But the rocks on the moon are exactly the same as they were a billion years ago. The ones in Nina's room were simply lumps of gray stone. They were about as bland as rocks could get.

"No rock is ugly," Mom chastened Violet. As a geologist, she couldn't help but defend her field of study. "They're all beautiful in their own way."

"Although a collector on earth wouldn't be interested in these for their looks," Dad explained. "They'd want them because they're as rare as rocks can get. And being the only person to own a moon rock has a great deal of value. But for now, the scientific community needs them all for research. Which is why possession of them has been tightly controlled. Any samples that have been collected here have been locked up in the science pod or transported back to earth under great security."

I was beginning to understand why my parents had been so shocked to discover the moon rocks. "So then . . . Nina wasn't supposed to have these?"

"No," Mom said.

"And she was going to smuggle them back down to earth?" Kira asked.

The adults all shared another look, then turned back to us.

"We can't say that for sure until we find Nina," Mom said cautiously.

"But it looks like it, right?" Kira didn't sound shocked so much as amazed to learn what Nina had been up to. "I mean, why else would they be hidden away like this? Nina the Machina wasn't so straitlaced after all."

"There are other possibilities," Mom said.

"Like what?" Kira asked.

"Er . . ." Mom stalled, trying to come up with one. "Perhaps NASA requested her to take some samples for reasons that we weren't aware of."

"Without telling *you*?" I asked. "You're the head geologist here."

"It's possible," Mom said. "NASA doesn't have to tell me everything."

"Although that brings up a point," Chang said thoughtfully. "Where did Nina get these? Are they from the samples you've collected?"

"I don't think so." Mom picked another rock out of the secret compartment and analyzed it carefully. "Like Stephen said, our samples are locked up."

"Nina probably knows the combination to the safe," Dad said.

"Maybe," Mom admitted. "But I spend a lot of time with those samples. If Nina had taken *one*, I would have noticed. Let alone this many. The only place she could have got so many would be . . ." Mom trailed off, looking out Nina's window, at the surface of the moon. "Out *there*."

Chang's eyes suddenly lit up. "That's what the text she got meant!"

We all turned to him, surprised by his outburst.

"This Charlie person must have been in cahoots with Nina," Chang explained. "I mean, why else send music from a fake account? There'd be no reason to hide your identity if you were doing something legal. And now that we know about the moon rocks, it's obvious what the message was."

"It is?" Dad asked.

"Think about the first song this Charlie sent," Chang said.

"'Gimme Shelter'?" I asked, not following.

"By the Rolling *Stones*," Chang stressed. "And the second song had the number fifty in the title: 'Fifty Miles of Elbow Room.'"

"So you think this Charlie was telling Nina to get fifty stones?" Mom asked.

"What else could it be?" Chang replied. "Nina's collecting moon rocks on the sly. Suddenly she gets this message while she's with Dashiell: Charlie wants fifty more stones. Nina immediately gets distracted by the mission, sends Dashiell packing, and the next thing you know, she's gone missing."

"That might explain the message," Mom conceded. "But we still don't know what happened to Nina."

"She must have gone outside to get the moon rocks," Chang said.

"How?" Mom asked. "Her space suit is still here."

"Maybe she didn't take her space suit," Violet suggested.

"No," I told her. "Without a space suit, she'd die in three seconds."

"Are we any closer to figuring out who Charlie might

be?" Dad asked. "Because if he's in on this plan with Nina, maybe he knows how she was getting the rocks."

"Maybe Nina went outside without her space suit," Violet said again.

Everyone ignored her this time. Chang said, "I'll have to check back in with NASA, but they probably would have alerted me if anything had come up. I'm guessing Charlie must be someone at NASA, though."

"Why's that?" I asked.

"If it was someone outside NASA, they wouldn't be able to get their hands on the moon rocks," Chang explained. "My guess is, Nina wasn't going to bring the rocks back with her own things. The plan was probably to send them down sooner, on one of the cargo rockets."

"Why?" Kira asked.

"A few reasons," Chang answered. "First of all, Nina is slated to stay here for another two and a half years. That's a long time to hoard moon rocks. Plus, NASA scrutinizes the personal belongings of everyone returning from the moon for exactly this reason."

"They think all of us might be smuggling moon rocks?" I asked.

"Not necessarily rocks," Chang said. "But anything that's been up here has value down on earth. Even a pencil that's been on the moon would be worth hundreds of dollars to a collector. NASA doesn't want people looting this place for stuff to sell on eBay, so they search our belongings as a deterrent. But suppose Nina hides the rocks in some cargo that's being returned to earth. We send plenty of stuff back with each rocket: experiments, lunar samples, garbage. . . . If this Charlie is involved in the unloading operations and knows where to find the rocks, he can get them out. Presumably, he has a line on selling them on the black market."

"There's also a chance this Charlie's a woman," Mom pointed out. "'Charlie' can be short for 'Charlotte.' Or it could be a woman who picked a masculine name to hide her identity even more."

"Right," Chang agreed. "So this Charlie, whether it's a man or a woman, sells the moon rocks and then splits the proceeds with Nina. They've got a Swiss bank account or something like that set up, and when Nina gets back to earth, there's a ton of cash waiting for her."

Mom and Dad nodded, indicating this made sense to them. It didn't make sense to *me*, though. "You really think Nina would break the law like that? *Nina?* I'll bet that when she was a kid, she never even colored outside the lines."

"It's a great front," Kira said. "No one would ever suspect her."

"I wouldn't have believed it if I hadn't seen the rocks

myself," Dad told me. "But there they are, in a secret compartment in Nina's room."

"What if the real bad guy planted them there?" I asked. "Maybe someone else was stealing moon rocks, and this message from Charlie was some kind of tip-off for Nina so she could catch the thief in action. That's why she got distracted. And when she found the bad guy, they . . ." I trailed off, not wanting to say the words in front of Violet.

"Killed her?" Violet finished, guessing them anyhow.

"Er . . . yes," I said. "And then they stuck the rocks in Nina's room to make it look like *she* was the smuggler."

My parents looked uneasy about this line of thought. Chang frowned, like he didn't buy it. "Your pal Roddy came to me with a murder theory too today."

"He's not our pal," Kira said sharply. "And that was *my* theory, not his."

"Well, I'm going to tell you the same thing I told him," Chang said. "I don't think Nina was murdered."

"No one thought Dr. Holtz had been murdered either," I countered. "And look how *that* turned out."

"And we put the person who did it on a rocket back to earth," Chang said. "Now, the chance of there being *another* murderer up here is incredibly small."

"That doesn't mean it's not possible," I told him. "A lot of people here didn't like Nina. . . ."

"That's no reason to kill someone," Mom said.

"People kill each other for dumb reasons all the time back on earth," Kira pointed out.

"This base is different," Chang told us. "Everyone here was subjected to a great series of psychological tests before coming up. If there had been any tendency toward violence in any of us, we wouldn't have been approved."

"The Sjobergs didn't have to pass any tests," Kira said. "They're total psychos."

"And maybe being up here has some kind of effect on our brains," I said. "Something that makes us go kind of crazy and be more likely to do bad things."

"I suppose that's all possible," Dad said, sounding like he was trying to get us off the subject, "though I still think it's far more likely that Nina was smuggling the rocks herself."

"Which brings us back to the same question," Mom said. "How did she get them?"

"Maybe she went outside without her suit," Violet said for the third time.

"Violet," I said, trying not to get annoyed, "I keep telling you, she couldn't survive without a suit."

"I didn't say she went outside without *a* suit," Violet retorted. "I said maybe she went outside without *her* suit. Like, maybe she took someone else's."

Everyone turned to her, surprised.

"She couldn't have taken someone else's," I pointed out. "They're all specially designed for each of us, aren't they?"

"Yes," Chang said. "But that doesn't mean that Nina *couldn't* have worn someone else's suit. She couldn't trade with someone huge like Balnikov or someone small like Dr. Kim. But if the suit belonged to someone who was the same height and build as her, it might work."

"None of the other space suits were missing, though," Mom said. "The lockers were all full." The moment the words were out of her mouth, though, she realized her mistake.

So did everyone else. "We only looked at the *adult* space suit storage," Chang groaned. "Not the kids'."

"Lily Sjoberg is about as big as Nina," Kira said.

Everyone hustled back out the door. While most of us went down the steps to the staging area, Chang simply leaped over the catwalk railing and dropped to the main floor.

He was in such a hurry, he didn't notice how crowded the hallway was. The capsule drop was over and everyone was leaving the common room. Chang almost landed right on top of Dr. Janke.

Dr. Janke wasn't upset, though. He was in such a good mood, he laughed it off. "Chang! We've been looking for you! You missed the capsule drop."

"Something came up," Chang said.

"It went perfectly!" Dr. Janke crowed. "Landed right on the spot. A hole in one!"

"Excellent." Chang slipped away from Dr. Janke. The rest of us pushed through the crowd and met him at the storage area for the kids' space suits. Since we weren't allowed out on the moon, our suits were stored in a separate area that was almost never opened. I'd only had my suit on once in the four months since I'd been at MBA, and that had been an unauthorized trip out onto the surface with Kira to find some evidence of Dr. Holtz's murder.

Chang opened the doors to the kids' space suit storage.

We all looked to where Lily Sjoberg's space suit should have been.

It was missing.

"See?" Violet asked me tauntingly. "I was right! You just didn't listen."

"None of us did," Mom said. She looked embarrassed about the whole thing.

So did Chang and Dad.

Our actions had grabbed the attention of everyone else in the area. Their celebration of the successful capsule drop instantly waned as they realized what Violet had figured out.

"Nina took Lily's suit?" Dr. Brahmaputra-Marquez asked.

"Yes," Mom said. "She's still out on the surface."

A ripple of concern went through the room.

Dr. Balnikov said, "Then she's been out there for hours! Her oxygen must be running out. If it hasn't already."

Chang pushed through the crowd and entered the control room. Everyone followed him, crowding around the door.

"Computer," Chang said, "is the GPS tracker on Lily Sjoberg's space suit functioning?"

"Yes," the base computer replied, in its usual calm voice.

"Can you give me the exact location of it?" Chang asked.

"Certainly," the base computer replied. "Lily Sjoberg's space suit is inside Moon Base Alpha."

Everyone outside the office looked to one another, unsure what this could mean.

Even Chang seemed taken aback. "Computer, to clarify, I'm not asking where Lily is herself. I want to know where her space suit is."

"I am well aware of what you are asking," the computer replied calmly. "According to my readings, the space suit is inside the base. To be more specific, it is inside the staging area."

Everyone turned around, hoping to see that Nina had somehow reappeared. As if, perhaps, she had snuck back in through the air lock while we were all busy with the computer.

She hadn't.

"You think the computer's malfunctioning?" Mom asked.

"No." Chang sighed. "More likely, Nina dismantled the GPS tracker somehow. Or reprogrammed it to give us false coordinates. Or maybe she simply ripped the dang thing off and hid it somewhere in the room."

"Why would she do that?" Dr. Janke asked.

"I don't know," Chang replied. "Maybe to cover her tracks. But whatever the case, I need all able-bodied adults to suit up. We're going out on the surface. Wherever Nina is, we need to find her. She's running out of time."

Excerpt from *The Official Residents' Guide to Moon Base Alpha*,
"Appendix A: Potential Health and Safety Hazards,"
© 2040 by National Aeronautics and Space Administration

FOOD

Surprisingly, choking is the fifth most common cause of death in the United States (approximately 2,500 people per year). And eating at MBA might be even more dangerous. Since the food on the moon is by necessity dehydrated, it is a bit thicker and harder to swallow than most earth food, even after the rehydrating process.* Thus, it may be somewhat easier to choke on than earth food. Please take extreme caution when chewing, try not to consume too much at one time, and if at all possible, avoid doing other activities while eating, such as exercising, running, or even talking.

Should choking incidents still result, it is imperative that all lunarnauts—no matter what age—be familiar with the Heimlich maneuver and its variations so that everyone can be prepared to dislodge partially masticated food from the windpipes of other people—and themselves. Please consult "Appendix B: First Aid and Safety Procedures" for this information.

---

* But still delicious and nutritious!

SPACE JERK REBELLION

Lunar day 217

Lunchtime

Almost every adult at MBA was recruited to the search party. Only three stayed behind. Lars and Sonja Sjoberg were two of them, of course; the Sjobergs never thought about anyone but themselves. They hadn't emerged from their suite since Nina's disappearance had been discovered. Either they didn't know Nina was missing, or they didn't care.

The other adult who stayed at MBA was Dr. Marquez. The official reason for this was that someone had to keep an eye on all the kids and that Dr. Marquez, as our base psychiatrist, was best equipped to help all of us deal with the potential trauma of Nina's disappearance. The unofficial reason was that Chang thought Dr. Marquez was an idiot. He believed Marquez was a lousy psychiatrist who'd only been brought to the moon because NASA wanted his wife up there and because he was famous. (Dr. Marquez had published a bestselling self-help book back on earth and was now working on one about mental health on the moon called *Lunarnauts and Lunatics*.) However, Dr. Marquez didn't seem too upset about being asked to stay behind. In fact, he seemed almost relieved. I'd heard rumors that he'd had some claustrophobia issues with his space suit on the trip up to the moon—panicking that he was running out of air and flipping out—and so he wasn't in any hurry to suit up again and go out onto the lunar surface.

The rest of the adults were all extremely competent, though. They quickly assigned themselves to teams and set out in search of Nina. There were twelve of them, so they broke up into six groups of two to cover more ground. Four adults stayed close to the base: Drs. Brahmaputra-Marquez, Janke, Goldstein, and Iwanyi. The other eight adults took moon rovers and spread out farther.

The moon rover garage had been badly damaged a month before, when Garth Grisan had tried to kill me with the base's giant robot arm. Luckily, two of the three main rovers had survived the attack, only needing minor repairs.

The third had been totaled, although the truth was, we had never needed all three big rovers at once anyhow. The rovers were going to be far more important once Moon Base Beta began construction. (NASA was working feverishly to get us a new one before then.) In the meantime, there was a smaller emergency backup rover that could fill in.

The big rovers could seat four adults at once. They weren't much different from the ones the Apollo missions had brought to the moon seventy years before. They looked like souped-up go-karts: basically a chassis, four tires, and a small engine. They weren't fancy, but they didn't have to be. All they really had to do was get everyone from place to place.

Dr. Kim and Dr. Alvarez, along with Dr. Merritt and Dr. Balnikov, set off to the north in one, planning to search Solar Arrays 1 and 2. Meanwhile, Mom and Dad and Chang and Dr. Howard went off toward the future site of Moon Base Beta. This seemed pointless to me; Nina obviously hadn't taken a rover herself, so she probably wouldn't have ranged too far away, especially when there were moon rocks all over the place. That was all the moon was, really—a massive ball of rocks. But Chang argued that there was no guessing what Nina might have done. After all, no one had figured she would ever leave the base solo to steal moon rocks. There-fore, if she *could* have gone to the Moon Base Beta site, then it was worth checking out.

In the meantime, all the kids had been assigned to go back to school.

We didn't, though. First of all, none of us could concentrate. Second, none of us wanted to do it. Having your moon-base commander disappear seemed as good an excuse as any for a holiday, and Dr. Marquez was powerless to stop us. In fact, his own children led the rebellion.

We had all gathered in the rec room for school as ordered, but Patton and Lily Sjoberg didn't even bother to show up, and once Cesar realized they were playing hooky, he decided to join them. Dr. Marquez was one of those parents who didn't really believe in discipline, so the only threat he could muster against Cesar was: "If you don't come back here, I will be very disappointed with you." "Deal," Cesar had said, and then walked out.

After that, Roddy had complained that he shouldn't have to stay in school if Cesar wasn't there, and Inez said that if Roddy didn't have to go, then she wouldn't either. The two younger Marquez kids stormed off, ignoring their father's weak warnings for them to not disobey him. After that, the rest of us went on strike as well.

In truth, Dr. Marquez didn't seem that disappointed in his children—or any of the rest of us. Instead, he seemed rather pleased to have some time to himself, and went to his residence to watch television.

Violet and Kamoze turned on the main SlimScreen in the rec room and started to watch *Squirrel Force*, their favorite TV show. I went with Kira to the mess hall to get lunch. I'd expected Roddy to go off to play veeyar games someplace, but instead he followed us. The only thing that interested Roddy more than virtual reality at MBA was girls.

Lily Sjoberg and Kira couldn't have been any more different, but Roddy didn't seem to care. His interest was constantly ping-ponging from one to the other, usually based upon whoever was closest to him. The fact that neither one liked him did nothing to deter him. He did seem to realize that Lily Sjoberg was a long shot, but he kept lurking around her anyhow, as if hoping that someday she'd see the light. As for Kira, he truly appeared to believe that her disdain for him was merely covering up her real feelings of affection. So he tried harder with her, doing everything he could to break down her resolve, unaware that this only made her dislike him even more.

On this day, as usual, he made the mistake of thinking the best way to impress her was to show how brilliant he was. He cornered us while we were rehydrating our lunches and said, "You know, statistically, the chances of them finding Nina out there are extremely slim."

Kira regarded him with her usual distaste. "No, they're not. There's twelve people looking for her."

"Twelve people can barely cover any ground at all," Roddy sniffed. "Do you have any idea how staggeringly large the search area is?"

"If I say yes, do you promise not to tell us?" I asked.

Kira giggled.

Roddy scowled at me and then turned his attention to Kira. "We're assuming that Nina left the base at around midnight last night, right? That's when she shut down the security cameras to cover her exit. . . ."

"That's only an assumption," I said, pulling my lunch out of the rehydrator.

"It's a *good* assumption," Roddy corrected. "It might as well be a fact. The cameras go down at midnight. Nina disappears out the air lock right afterwards. Obviously, she turned the cameras off."

"You really believe she went out on the surface?" Kira asked. "I thought you were sure she was a cloud of sentient nanobots."

"And *you* were sure she'd been murdered," Roddy countered. "Both were completely plausible theories. But in the light of new information, I realize that Nina was not murdered and is most likely human and left the base through the air lock."

"Is 'most likely human'?" I repeated.

"If anyone at this base is a cyborg, it's her," Roddy declared.

I groaned. "You mean, you think she's part robot?"

"It's no secret that NASA has been experimenting with cyborg technology for years," Roddy said, which was completely wrong as far as I knew.

Kira's food finished rehydrating as well. She had selected chicken enchiladas for lunch, while I'd picked shrimp cocktail. We took our plates and headed to the drink station.

Roddy stuck with us. "The point is, Nina has been out on the lunar surface for around twelve hours. Now, Nina was in excellent shape, so she could certainly cover three miles an hour, if not four. But for the sake of argument, let's say it was three. Three miles an hour for twelve hours is thirty-six miles. Which means the potential search area is a circle with a radius of thirty six miles—or approximately four thousand seventy square miles."

I paused in the midst of filling a cup with reclaimed water, alarmed by this number. "Nina probably didn't walk thirty-six miles in a straight line," I said.

"That's exactly the problem," Roddy pointed out. "If she had, we could simply search the perimeter of the circle. But instead, she's probably at some random point inside that circle. Even if she only went *three* miles out, the search area would still be over twenty-eight square miles. That's a lot of ground for twelve people to cover. It'd be like finding a needle in a haystack out there."

I shared a concerned look with Kira. We had both been

out on the surface a month before. We knew what it was like out there. The entire landscape was dull and gray. Our white space suits blended right into it. If Nina wasn't moving, it would be extremely hard to spot her out in the wasteland, if not impossible.

Before I could say anything, Zan Perfonic appeared. So as not to startle me, she projected an image of herself wandering in from the staging area and waving for my attention. In fact, she did such a good job of being unobtrusive that I almost didn't realize it was her at first.

"Can you excuse me?" I asked Kira. "I have to go to the bathroom."

Kira shot me a look of betrayal, not wanting to be left alone with Roddy. "Right now?"

"It's an emergency," I told her, then left my lunch on the counter and hurried off.

Behind me, I heard Roddy speak in what he thought was his suavest voice. "Don't worry, Kira. I'd be happy to dine with you."

As I headed to the bathroom, my watch vibrated, indicating a call was coming in. I glanced at it and saw it was Riley Bock. She'd probably just woken up back in Hawaii. Normally, I would have answered immediately, but I needed to talk to Zan and I didn't know how long she'd be around. I had no choice but to ignore the call.

Zan followed me into the bathroom. Since all the adults were out on the surface, it was unlikely anyone else was in there, but I checked the stalls anyhow out of habit. "What's up?" I asked, trying to keep the conversation in my head.

"That's what I came to ask you," Zan replied. "Any sign of Nina?"

I quickly recapped everything we'd learned since I'd seen Zan earlier that morning. She listened intently, though she was obviously thrown when I got to the part about Nina smuggling rocks. "Why would she do that?" she asked. "It seems like such a big risk to take."

"For money, I guess."

Zan frowned. Money was a concept that had caused her trouble in the past. Apparently, her planet didn't have anything like it, which had seemed odd to me until she'd pointed out that even on our own planet, money was a bizarre concept as well. After all, out of the billions of species of animal, humans were the only ones who used it. And it often seemed to cause as many problems as it solved.

"Isn't Nina being paid money for her job on the moon?" Zan asked.

"Yes."

"And she doesn't really need any of this money while she's up there, right?"

"Right. All our food and stuff up here is free. The money

would really be for when she gets back to earth."

"And it would be worth jeopardizing her life, her job, and her reputation just for more money?"

"Well, according to my parents, it'd be for a *lot* more money," I replied. "Millions of dollars, maybe."

Zan looked at me curiously, trying to comprehend this. "Why would anyone need so much money?"

"So they can buy more stuff."

"You mean, like extra food, in case of emergencies?"

"Er . . . no. Like fancy cars and mansions."

"What's a mansion?"

"It's a giant house. Like with a whole bunch of bedrooms and ten bathrooms."

"Why would Nina need a house with ten bathrooms? Does she have some sort of bowel disorder you haven't mentioned?"

"No. It's a kind of status symbol."

"Having an excess of places to expel bodily waste in your home is a sign of status on earth?"

"Er . . . yes. I guess." This conversation wasn't going quite the way I'd expected. "It's really more about the size of your house, though. Like, the Sjobergs are crazy rich, and I've heard they have one of the biggest houses in all of Europe. As well as other mansions all over the world."

"Why would one family need huge houses all over the

world? It sounds like a tremendous waste of precious resources."

"Yes," I agreed, feeling kind of ashamed about humanity. "It is. But that's how things work on earth. The more money you have, the fancier your life is."

"And the fancier your life is, the happier you are?"

"That's kind of the idea."

"But you think that might not be true."

"Well, we all definitely need to make money to live back on earth. But my family doesn't have a whole lot and we're pretty happy. While the Sjobergs have tons and they seem miserable all the time. That might only be because they're stuck here, but I'm not sure."

Zan nodded, trying to get her mind around all this. It made me wonder what life was like on her planet. How different was it from earth? How did they get by without money? Did they trade? Did they even have jobs? Hundreds more questions occurred to me, but I didn't have the time to ask a single one. Chances were, Zan wouldn't answer them anyhow.

"So," Zan said, "you believe that Nina might have taken all these risks solely to earn a great deal of money."

"That's the only explanation anyone can come up with for the moon rocks in her room."

"I always got the impression from you that Nina wasn't one to break the rules."

"That's what I thought about her. And everyone else did too. We're all pretty shocked about this."

"There's no other reason she might have taken these actions?"

"Maybe, but I don't know what it is. And neither does anyone else. Whatever the case, it seems she's definitely out on the surface somewhere."

Zan frowned again.

"What's wrong?" I asked.

"It's hard to describe. It has to do with the feeling I got from her."

"Did you sense that someone had tried to hurt her?"

Zan looked at me curiously. "You mean, like this was another murder attempt?"

I got the feeling she was judging all of humanity. "Er . . . maybe."

"I can't tell if she was hurt or not. Only in danger. And when I sensed her, it didn't seem like she was out there, on the surface."

"So where is she, then?"

"I don't know. I can't explain it, other than that it was dark."

"Like how? Did she fall into a hole or something?"

"Not exactly."

I sighed. "It'd be much more helpful if you could tell me where she *is* rather than where she's *not*."

"I'm doing my best."

"Well, try harder. Can't you try to sense her again?"

"That's much more difficult than you realize."

"Why?"

"I'm transmitting my thoughts over trillions of miles of space," Zan snapped. "Does that sound easy to you?"

"No," I conceded. "Sorry. I'm just frustrated."

"I am too."

"Is there anything else you can tell me about Nina?" I asked.

Zan sighed. She looked very sad, even a bit embarrassed about her inability to help. "Perhaps I can try once more, although I can't promise anything. . . ."

There was a sudden shout from outside the bathroom. It was Kira, and she sounded like she was upset about something.

What now? I thought. Then I told Zan, "I'll be right back," and raced out the door.

The Sjobergs had made an appearance. It was the entire family this time: Lars and Sonja had finally emerged from their suite, along with Patton and Lily. It was the first time I'd seen the adult Sjobergs in days. Like their children, they were both extremely blond and so pale-skinned, it seemed that they had never been in the sun. Lars had the build of an athlete who'd gone to seed: He was big and strong, but now he'd grown a few extra chins and his large belly strained against his shirt. Sonja had undergone so many plastic surgeries, it was hard to imagine what she'd looked like before. Her whole face appeared to be cobbled together from spare parts, some of which weren't even human. Her lips, for example, were so enormous they might have been swiped from a chimpanzee. On their own, each bit of her face— her eyes, nose, chin, and so on—might have been beautiful, but mixed together, they were unsettling. To make matters worse, the Sjobergs didn't merely *look* scary; they *were* scary. They were the meanest people I'd ever met in my life, and as usual, they were up to no good.

They had entered the greenhouse. Lars and Sonja were hungrily inspecting the ripe strawberries and tomatoes, while Patton and Lily had stationed themselves at the door to keep everyone else out.

At any other time, the Sjobergs would never have done such a thing. The other adults wouldn't have let them get away with it. But now, the Sjobergs obviously figured they could bully us kids out of the way.

Kira was taking a stand, though. "Get out of there!" she shouted. "That food is for all of us!"

"This food is a mere fraction of what we deserve," Lars snarled through the glass. "We paid a half billion dollars to come up to this horrible place. The rest of you came for free! It is only right that we are entitled to more rewards than you."

Zan had emerged from the bathroom with me. She stood beside me, staring angrily at the Sjobergs. I didn't know if she was actually feeling anger toward them or if she was merely sensing mine and reacting.

Meanwhile, Roddy was unchivalrously backing away from Kira, trying to indicate to the Sjobergs that he wanted no part of this. "You have a good point," he told them.

"Roddy," I said. "Go get your father."

"Right!" he agreed, glad for the excuse to leave the room. In his haste to go, he stumbled over his own feet and caromed off the wall.

Inside the greenhouse, Lars and Sonja were taunting us, making a show of slowly plucking the ripest strawberries. Sonja selected the biggest one, held it up to her nose, and inhaled deeply. "Oh my. It smells delicious."

Kira looked to me, expecting me to do something.

I gave it my best shot. "You know what's going to happen when the others come back and find out you've done this?" I asked. "They'll beat the crap out of you."

"I highly doubt that," Lars said. "And they couldn't possibly come up with any punishment worse than keeping us here. So we might as well take what we rightfully deserve."

Sonja bit into the strawberry, then groaned with pleasure. Juice trickled down her surgically enhanced chin. "Oh, Lars," she gasped. "It's delicious."

A nice person would have at least offered to share with her family. Instead Sonja simply wolfed the rest of the strawberry down in front of them.

"Hey!" Lily yelped. "Save some for us!"

"Don't worry, princess," Sonja cooed. "There's plenty for us all." Then she plucked a few more berries for herself.

Lily and Patton obviously didn't trust their mother to save anything for them, so they abandoned their post at the door to plunder the strawberries as well. Each grabbed a handful and gobbled them down without any self-control at all.

Meanwhile, Lars picked a strawberry for himself, looked right through the glass at us, and sank his teeth into it, the same way a shark would attack a seal.

My stomach growled in protest. It had been a month since I'd last had a piece of fresh fruit, and watching the Sjobergs devour what we'd been waiting so long for was torturous.

"Chang won't care about the rules," I said. "And Nina's not here to hold him back. When he finds out about this, he'll go ballistic on you."

"What's to say he'll even think *we* did this?" Lars asked, pointedly chewing his strawberry. "Maybe he'll think you little gremlins did it."

"No, he won't," I said. "He knows how horrible you guys are."

Saying something like that wasn't the best move around the Sjobergs. They all swung toward me, glaring angrily. Each had strawberry juice dripping from their mouth, which gave them the unsettling appearance of a group of carnivores that had been interrupted in the midst of devouring a carcass.

Patton's glare was even more devilish than the others'. I'd forgotten he had a score to settle with me. The faint outline of the Urinator suction cup could still be seen on his face.

"If anyone here deserves a pounding," he said, "it's *you*. In fact, I owe you one."

If I'd ever threatened anyone like that, my parents probably would have dressed me down. The Sjobergs seemed pleased by the idea. Sonja's eyes lit up with excitement. "That's right!" she exclaimed. "You do!"

"You swore to me you wouldn't retaliate for that!" I told him.

Patton ignored me and looked to his mother for approval. "Can I get him, Mother? Can I?"

Sonja's juice-stained chimp lips curled into a sneer. "Of course, darling. Show him that no one insults the Sjobergs and gets away with it."

"All right!" Patton crowed eagerly. "But you'd all better save me some strawberries." And then he stormed out of the greenhouse, coming for me.

Excerpt from *The Official Residents' Guide to Moon Base Alpha*,
"Appendix A: Potential Health and Safety Hazards,"
© 2040 by National Aeronautics and Space Administration

RUNNING

Given the low gravity of the moon, running can be very difficult. It is harder to control yourself, to make tight turns, or to stop your momentum should you find something in your way. In addition, MBA has many people living in a relatively contained space, not to mention various robots and other machinery moving about. Sudden contact with any of these things—or even the thick walls—could cause serious harm or injury. To that extent, it is advised that lunarnauts not run through MBA except in cases of extreme emergency. Not only is walking safer, but it doesn't even take that much more time. Since MBA is rather compact in size, running from one side to the other will only save you a few seconds, at most. Are a few seconds worth hurting yourself or someone else? Of course not. So take care . . . and slow down.

DESPERATE TIMES

Lunar day 217

High noon

"Dashiell! Run!" Kira ordered. And then, just in case I didn't understand, she grabbed my hand and yanked me down the hall.

"Go get him!" Sonja ordered Patton, while Lars and Lily cheered him on enthusiastically.

Patton obediently chased after us.

Kira and I loped through the base as quickly as we could in our bizarre, low-gravity way. On a normal day, I might have yelled for help, but all the other adults were out on the lunar surface—except Dr. Marquez, who wouldn't have been able to defend me against a butterfly. Luring Patton back into the bathroom and making another attempt to suck his face off with the Urinator didn't seem likely; the only other thing I could think of was to get to my residence, lock the door, and pray Patton wasn't strong enough to break it down.

In the meantime, while I fled, I tried to reason with the bully. "Come on!" I yelled. "I'm sorry for using the Urinator on you. I was only trying to defend myself. I never would have done it if you hadn't attacked me first!"

"Know what I'm gonna do when I catch you?" Patton roared. "I'm gonna shove your whole head down the toilet!"

So much for reason.

Kira and I bounded past the gym, the medical bay (which I hoped I wouldn't be needing soon), and the rec room. Violet and Kamoze were so riveted to *Squirrel Force*, they didn't even notice us go past. "Go SuperSquirrel!" I heard Violet cheer. "Save the day!"

I couldn't tell where Patton was behind me—I didn't want to chance looking back—but his guttural grunts and screams seemed to be getting closer. It sounded like I was being chased by an animal rather than a human.

Normally, to get to my second-floor room, I would have pulled a U-turn in the air-lock staging area and climbed the stairs to the catwalk, but today that seemed way too slow. I glanced at Kira and realized she had the same idea.

Both of us launched ourselves at the outer wall of the

rec room and sprang off it. The moon's low gravity might suck for running, but you can make some superhero-style moves in it. Kira and I both sailed up through the air across the hall and caught the catwalk rail. We were right by the doors to our rooms. Kira sprang over the rail with ease and I followed. . . .

Only, Patton lunged upward and snagged my foot right before it cleared the railing, then dragged me back down. He lost his footing, though, and fell flat on his back. I landed right on top of him. I was hoping I'd at least hit hard enough to hurt him. Instead I landed so softly, I might as well have been a bag of potato chips.

Patton clamped his meaty hand around my neck.

"No!" Kira screamed. "Let him go!"

Patton's reptile eyes flicked toward Kira, then narrowed evilly. Still looking at her, he did exactly the opposite of what she'd asked, squeezing my neck tightly.

I gasped for breath, but found none.

Above me on the catwalk, I heard Dr. Marquez emerge from his room along with Roddy.

"Dr. Marquez!" Kira cried. "Make him stop!"

For a brief moment, I wondered if maybe Dr. Marquez wasn't so useless after all.

And then, Dr. Marquez, displaying his standard inability to grasp what was going on in any situation, demanded,

"Dashiell, get off Patton right now! You're going to hurt him!"

I scrabbled at Patton's fingers, trying to pry them off my neck, but he was too strong. I began to see spots as my oxygen deprivation got worse.

Kira realized Dr. Marquez wasn't going to be any help and came to the rescue herself. She leaped back off the catwalk, landed beside Patton, and dug her nails into his scalp, yanking back hard enough to uproot tufts of his hair.

Patton howled with pain and released his grip on me. I sprang back from him, slamming into the door of Dr. Janke's residence. I knew it wasn't very cool to let Kira fight for me, but at the moment, all I could do was desperately gulp air.

Patton sprang to his feet and lashed out an arm, catching Kira in the chest. Since Patton was twice her size, he sent her flying across the hall, where she crashed into the wall of the rec room, whacked her head, and then crumpled to the floor, out cold.

The bully then spun back on me. Kira had furrowed his forehead with her fingernails, so there were now slashes of red over his eyes, making him seem even more evil than usual. He was seething with anger now, glaring at me with such hatred that I feared he might actually kill me.

I tried to back away, but there was no place to go. And I was still reeling from nearly being choked to death.

Patton lurched toward me.

"Dashiell!" Zan yelled. "Brace yourself!"

I didn't see where she was when she said this. Probably because she wasn't actually anywhere to see. She was inside my head, speaking to me without expending the energy to display an image of herself.

"I'm about to break the rules here," Zan warned. "Don't be afraid."

Patton cocked back a fist.

Something erupted through the floor between us. Cement and shards of tile spewed into the air, although I couldn't feel any of them because they didn't really exist. They were simply an image projected into my mind—and given Patton's startled reaction, his mind as well.

The creature that had burst through the floor was absolutely horrifying. It was moving so quickly, I didn't get a great view of it, but it appeared to be the worst parts of every nightmare creature combined, an unnerving combination of teeth, scales, tentacles, and slime. And I was only seeing its backside. The business end was reserved for Patton.

The creature hissed in Patton's face. A frill around its head flared out, the same way a cobra's would, only this one appeared to be lined with claws.

Patton's eyes nearly popped out of his head. His face drained of what little color it normally had. He screamed in terror and sprang so far backward, he slammed into the wall by Kira. A big wet spot blossomed in his pants as he peed himself in fear.

The alien creature slithered out of the hole toward him. It was long and snakelike, with stubby clawed legs, like an enormous, terrifying centipede.

For a moment, Patton was so discombobulated, he kept backpedaling into the wall, as if hoping to plow through it to escape. His scream became a long, high-pitched wail, and then, finally, his brain clicked into gear. He ran as fast as he could, bounding through the staging area and disappearing back around the corner toward the greenhouse, gibbering the entire way.

A moment later, the alien creature vanished. So did the hole it had come from. The floor looked exactly as it always had. There was no indication that anything had happened at all, save for Patton's whimpering in the distance and the large puddle of urine he'd left behind.

Dr. Marquez leaned over the catwalk above and stared down at me accusingly. "What did you do to him?" he demanded.

"What did *I* do to Patton?" I asked, incredulous. "Nothing! Did you see what he was about to do to *me*? He was trying to kill me!"

"You must have done something," Dr. Marquez said, sounding like he actually thought I was the troublemaker here. "He didn't run off like that for no reason."

"Maybe he ran off because he realized he shouldn't mess with me." Still feeling shaky, I wobbled across the hall to check on Kira.

She sat up as I approached, rubbing her head groggily. "What happened?" she asked. "Where's Patton?"

"He won't bother us again for a while," I told her. "Maybe forever. Are you all right?"

Kira touched the back of her head, then winced in pain. "I've got a lump. I think I blacked out for a bit."

"Only a couple seconds," I told her. "But yeah, you did." I knelt and looked into her eyes. All Moonies, even the kids, had emergency medical training on a regular basis, so I knew how to recognize the signs of a concussion. Thankfully, her eyes weren't dilated. "Do you feel dizzy or anything?"

"No," Kira replied, "I feel angry. How'd we get stuck on the moon with the biggest jerks in the universe?"

"Just lucky, I guess." I helped her to her feet.

She looked at me curiously. "What'd you do to get rid of him?"

"I fought back." I didn't know what else to say. "Though you helped. You really got him good."

Kira grinned. "Serves him right."

Dr. Marquez had come down the stairs and was now approaching, still looking peeved at me. "Dashiell, I am the adult in charge of this base while all the others are gone, so

I am going to ask you one more time: What did you do to Patton?"

I glared at Dr. Marquez so hard that his step faltered. "Patton's fine," I told him. "But Kira's not. Patton hurt her. As the adult in charge, maybe you ought to be concerned about that."

"Oh," Dr. Marquez said thoughtfully. He appeared to have forgotten that he was a doctor. "Yes. Of course. What's wrong, Kira?"

Kira didn't look pleased that I'd pawned her off on Dr. Marquez, but she seemed to understand I had a reason for it. "I banged my head on the wall when Patton threw me into it. I think I might need to have it checked out."

"Hmmm." Dr. Marquez seemed to be trying to remember basic first aid. "I suppose you're right. Come along to the medical bay with me."

Kira allowed Dr. Marquez to lead her away. I watched them go, still feeling angry. Angry at the entire Sjoberg family for raiding the greenhouse and trying to hurt me, and angry at Dr. Marquez for letting them get away with their horrid behavior.

Something flickered in my vision. For a moment, I thought it was someone coming up from behind me, but then I realized it was Zan. She was having trouble appearing to me, the same way she had after trying to find Nina—only she seemed even more exhausted this time. She was barely there at all. I could see the wall right through her.

"Are you all right?" I asked.

"I'm tired. What I just did . . . it wasn't easy." Her voice was barely a whisper.

"It was different than coming to me?"

"Your mind is open to being approached. With Patton, I had to force my way in. His mind is more closed-off than any I've ever encountered."

"I can understand why. The guy probably has moon rocks for brains."

Zan smiled, then winked out of existence for a moment. When she came back, she was even more transparent than before. "I shouldn't have done that, but . . . I didn't know what else to do. He was really going to hurt you, wasn't he?"

I felt my neck, which was sore in several places where Patton had grabbed it. "Yes."

"For no good reason?"

"Yes," I repeated, feeling even more ashamed of humanity than I had when discussing our interest in money.

Footsteps echoed in the hall behind me.

"I have to go," Zan said, and vanished for good.

Cesar Marquez peered around the corner a second later—although it was hard to tell it was him at first because he was wearing the helmet for a space suit. He cased the hallway cautiously, then asked, "Have you seen some kind of giant deadly alien snake in here?"

"No," I said, playing dumb. "Why?"

"Patton says he saw one." Cesar cautiously edged around the corner, still on the lookout. He was clutching a large serving fork for self-defense. It wasn't much of a weapon, but then there weren't many options at MBA. "Or at least, I *think* that's what he said. It was hard to understand him."

"Why's that?"

"'Cause he's curled up on the floor of the greenhouse, crying like a baby." Cesar's voice was muffled inside his helmet. "He said a giant space snake with a million teeth just came through the floor in here and tried to eat him."

I did my best to stifle a smile, then pointed to the floor to show there weren't any holes in it. "Doesn't look like anything came through here to me."

Cesar stared at the floor a bit longer than he should have needed to determine that this was true. While his mother was brilliant, Cesar had missed out in the genetic lottery for brains. He pointed to the large puddle of pee Patton had left behind. "What's that?"

"Patton wet himself."

Cesar made a face of disgust. "Oh. Gross. We don't have to recycle that, do we?"

"Maybe."

"Well, *I'm* not doing it. Patton should. It's his pee." Cesar cased the hallway one more time. "Man, *something* sure scared him. But I don't see any space snakes here."

"I guess he must have imagined it," I said.

"Yeah. I guess." Cesar tossed the serving fork aside and tried to pull the space helmet off his head. This turned out to be more difficult than he'd expected. It wouldn't come off.

"Are you okay?" I asked.

"No!" Cesar snapped. "Stupid helmet!" He yanked on it harder and harder, to no avail. One time, back on earth, Riley's dog had got her head stuck in an empty pickle jar. Cesar looked almost exactly like that now.

"Is that even your helmet?" I asked.

"No. It's Roddy's." Cesar angrily banged on the helmet with his fist, forgetting his head was inside it, and sent himself reeling into the wall.

I shook my head in dismay, glad that Zan had left before witnessing this display of human idiocy. "Well, no wonder. Roddy's a lot smaller than you."

"I didn't have time to find one that fit!" Cesar was getting angry now. "I thought there was some kind of space snake on the loose!"

I decided not to point out that if there had been some sort of deadly space alien at large in MBA, it could have easily attacked one of his many body parts not protected by the helmet. "Hold on," I said. "Let me help."

Cesar was too busy thrashing around to hear me. He apparently hadn't learned his lesson about banging on the helmet while wearing it, because he was now whacking it against the wall. With each smack, his head rattled around inside the helmet like a pinball, and yet he kept doing it, screaming a new curse word each time.

"Stop that," I said. "It's not going to work."

"It will if I hit it hard enough." Cesar reared back his head and slammed it into the wall. The helmet didn't break, although Cesar did an impressive job of stunning himself. He staggered around drunkenly for a moment.

Something occurred to me. I waited for Cesar to regain his balance, then asked, "Why didn't you just get your own helmet?"

"'Cause it's broken."

"Since when? How?"

"Since the other night. Patton and Lily and I were playing space football."

"With your space helmets on?"

"Of course," Cesar sneered, like *I* was the idiot. "You can't play football without a helmet."

"We're only supposed to use the helmets out on the surface."

"No duh. That's why we played at night when no one was

awake to bust us." With all his exertion, Cesar had fogged up the inside of his space visor. I could barely see him through the mist inside.

"And you hit your helmet hard enough to break it?" I asked.

"Yeah." Cesar laughed. "We were playing in the rec room. It was Patton versus Lily and I was the full-time quarterback. On this one play, after Lily and I scored, Patton sacked me in the end zone. I wasn't ready for it. He smashed me face-first into the corner by the door and busted the glass on my face-plate thingy."

"You mean, the visor?"

"Yeah! He cracked it pretty bad." Cesar frowned as he realized something. "You better not tell anyone about this. You rat us out and we'll come for you."

I stared at Cesar, amazed by his stupidity. And then I thought of something. "Is there any chance that you broke Lily's helmet too?"

Cesar shrugged. "Maybe. It got banged around a lot."

"Cesar!" I shouted, stunned he hadn't made the connection. "Nina went outside with Lily's helmet! If it was broken, she's probably dead!"

Understanding slowly dawned on Cesar. "Oh," he said. "Oops."

Now an even scarier thought occurred to me. "Is there any

chance you guys might have broken any of the adult helmets?"

Behind the fogged-up visor, Cesar averted his eyes. Even though he was four years older than me, he looked like Violet when she realized she'd been caught doing something wrong. "We might have."

"You *might* have?"

"Well, after I broke my helmet, we needed another, and none of the other kids' helmets would fit me. . . . so we got some adult ones."

"You got *more* than one?"

"Patton thought they fit better than ours."

"And you broke them?"

"Not necessarily. We didn't break the glass or anything. But we *did* play pretty hard with them."

"Which helmets did you use?"

"I don't remember."

I clapped my hands to the side of my head. "So they could be *anyone's* out there?"

Cesar didn't say anything, but that was as good as a response.

I raced for the control room. That's where the radio was to contact the adults on the surface. If someone out there had a damaged helmet, they needed to know fast. The glass that formed the visor was a barrier between life and instant death. Perhaps it wouldn't break right away, but if it did, the person wearing it would immediately be subjected to the extreme heat or cold of the lunar surface—not to mention being completely deprived of oxygen.

Behind me, Cesar resumed trying to get Roddy's helmet off his head by pounding it against the wall.

I entered the control room. Through the wall, I could hear Patton in the greenhouse next door. While the exterior walls of MBA were extremely thick—the better to repel meteoroids—the interior ones were paper-thin. Sound carried right through them, especially sounds as loud as Patton was making. He was still wailing, terrified. "It was trying to eat me! It was licking its lips. All six of them!"

"Stop crying this instant," his father ordered coldly, displaying the typical lack of parental kindness that had made Patton the psychotic thug he was. "You sound like an idiot."

"It's still loose in the base!" Patton cried. "If we don't defend ourselves, it will eat us!"

I couldn't help myself. I hissed as loud as I could, imitating the sound of Zan's alien creature.

Patton heard me through the wall. "That was it!" he screamed. "It's coming for us! We're all gonna die!" After that, nothing he said made sense. I couldn't understand him through his terrified sobs.

I clapped the radio headset over my ears, doing my best to drown out Patton's blubbering. It was replaced by the sound of all the other adults, out on the lunar surface, communicating with one another.

Dr. Janke: "There's no sign of Nina by the water reclamation units. Over."

Chang: "Roger that, Wilbur. Why don't you swing around toward the emergency air lock? Over."

Dr. Iwanyi: "Dr. Goldstein and I are there now. No sign of Nina here, either. Over."

The main computer was displaying a map of the surrounding area and tracking all the adults on the surface through the GPS units in their suits. There were twelve blips, each marked with the name of the person it represented.

I spoke into the microphone. There was probably some official way I was supposed to announce that I had joined the conversation, but I had no idea what it was. "Attention, everyone out on the surface. This is Dash at MBA. This is an emergency. According to Cesar Marquez, at least one of your helmets might have some damage to its visor."

There was a moment of chaos. I'd reached everyone at once and they all responded at the same time, a cacophony of fear, worry, and disbelief. Finally, Chang's voice rose above it all. "This is Base Commander Kowalski. Everyone but Dashiell, I need radio silence."

The radio waves instantly went quiet.

Chang said, "Dashiell, please elaborate."

"Cesar says that he and the Sjobergs have been playing football with the helmets at night. They cracked the visors on Cesar's and Lily's and then used some of the adult helmets, only he can't remember which ones."

There was a general murmur of anger over the radio. Everyone couldn't help themselves from calling Cesar and the Sjobergs morons—and worse—even though Cesar's mother could hear everything. In fact, I was pretty sure I heard Cesar's mother insult his intelligence as well.

"Quiet!" Chang snapped. "I need everyone to stay silent unless I request an answer. Now then, is anyone aware of any damage to their helmet?"

There was a moment of weighted silence as everyone checked. Then a voice said, "I think I see a crack in my visor."

It was my mother.

My blood instantly went cold. I fought the urge to respond, knowing it was better to let Chang handle the situation.

"How bad is it?" Chang asked.

"It only appears to be a hairline fracture," Mom replied, surprisingly calm given that her life was at stake. "But it's definitely a crack. It must have formed since we came out on the surface. I didn't notice it before we left."

I paced anxiously, silently cursing Cesar and the Sjobergs. If they'd damaged the glass, it might have looked fine until being subjected to the extreme pressure change of leaving MBA for the lunar surface.

"I think I may have a hairline fracture too," said another female voice. Daphne Merritt.

"How's yours look?" Chang asked.

"About the same as Dr. Gibson's," Daphne reported. Her voice sounded much shakier than Mom's had, as if she was trying not to panic.

"All right then," Chang said. "We can't assume that anyone's helmet is free from damage, which means we need to take emergency precautions immediately. According to my computer, some of us are too far from MBA to make heading back there a safe option." All the adults had computers built into the fabric of the arms of their suits, so they could consult them easily. I assumed Chang's was giving him the GPS coordinates for all the other adults, the same way the main computer was giving them to me. "Luckily, the operations pod for construction of Moon Base Beta is safe and the oxygen system is working. Dr. Howard and I will get the Gibsons with our rover and take them there. Everyone else, return to Moon Base Alpha immediately. Is that understood?"

There was a chorus of "affirmatives."

When Chang spoke again, his breathing was a bit more labored, as though he was hurrying across the lunar surface as he spoke. "Dashiell, inside the main storage unit for the space suits, there is a set of spare visors for each helmet, along with a repair kit. I need you to get that and find Kira, then use the small rover and bring it to us."

I tensed, startled by this order. "Me?"

Chang said, "I know it's asking a lot, pal, but we need you to do this for us."

"All right." I tried to sound calm, although my heart had begun racing.

I was going back onto the surface of the moon.

Excerpt from *The Official Residents' Guide to Moon Base Alpha*,
"Appendix A: Potential Health and Safety Hazards,"
© 2040 by National Aeronautics and Space Administration

LUNAR ROVERS

Should you absolutely have to venture onto the lunar surface and cover long distances there, chances are you will be using a lunar rover. While these can save you a great deal of time, energy, and oxygen, remember that they are vehicles and you should use the same caution when driving them that you would using any vehicle on earth. True, their maximum speed is considerably slower than that of a car, but an accident in a rover could still be extremely dangerous, especially one in which you are thrown free or the rover flips on top of you. Therefore, when driving the rover, be alert to all potential obstacles in the immediate area, such as (but not limited to) other rovers, abrupt changes in terrain, sudden slopes, sharp volcanic rocks, and robots. Do not attempt any sort of drag racing, jumps, or other trick driving on the lunar surface. And, of course, wear your restraining seat harness at all times.

MOONLIGHT RIDE

Lunar day 217

Afternoon

The last time I'd ventured onto the surface of the moon, I'd nearly died.

This was because Garth Grisan had been trying to kill me. He'd used the giant robot arm to try to swat me like a bug. In the process, the glass of my own visor had cracked, and I'd come within seconds of suffocating. The thought of going back out again had terrified me ever since. For the first few nights after my near-death experience, I'd had panic dreams where I was back on the surface, racing for safety while my air ran out, after which I'd wake screaming for help in a cold sweat. The dreams had subsided since then, but I still had them every once in a while.

My mother's life was in danger, though. So I did my best to put aside my fears, grabbed the helmet repair kit, found Kira, suited up, and headed back onto the surface.

"Can I drive?" Kira asked. Her voice came over my radio headset as we trudged toward the rover garage.

"Do you know how?" I asked. I was doing my best to remain calm, to focus on my breathing and not panic.

"Would I be asking if I didn't know how? Of course I can drive."

I glanced toward her, wondering if this was true. Since self-driving cars had come along, young people didn't need to take driving lessons. It was rare to see a car on earth that even had a steering wheel anymore. And even if that hadn't been the case, Kira was still only twelve. "Where'd you learn?"

"My cousins have some old ATVs on their farm. I've driven them before, over all kinds of terrain."

"Okay," I agreed. "Sure, you can drive."

I was glad Chang had insisted I bring Kira along with me. Even though she'd been out on the surface with me during the robot attack, she didn't seem to be suffering from any bad memories of it. (Then again, *I'd* been the one who'd almost died.) In fact, she was thrilled to be out on the surface again, freed from the confines of MBA. She was bounding along, humming cheerfully over the headset, and her high spirits lifted mine.

The sun was out, making the lunar surface glow brightly. Meanwhile, since there was no atmosphere, the sky remained jet black above, save for the stars. It was all quite beautiful, and for a few moments, I found myself thinking how lucky I was to be one of the few people who'd ever experienced this in the entire history of mankind.

The rover garage wasn't far from the main air lock, so it didn't take us long to get to it. Or at least, what was left of it.

The garage had originally been a simple white dome, but when I'd been attacked, the robot arm had torn a gaping hole in the roof. Back on earth, the government probably could have repaired it within a few days, but on the moon, where getting new parts for anything required a rocket mission, it was probably going to be years until it was fixed. In the meantime, to make sure it didn't collapse, Dad, Chang, and Dr. Balnikov had simply sliced off the top of the dome, making the whole thing look like an igloo with a sunroof.

The adults had left the garage door open when they'd taken the remaining big rovers out. Overlapping trails of moon dust led to and from the spots where the big rovers that still worked were normally parked. The wreckage of the third big rover— the one that had been destroyed by the robot—was to the side, where it could be cannibalized for spare parts. The small rover sat tucked in the back of the garage.

It was so spindly, it looked as though a kid had built it. The metal bars of the chassis were as thin as my fingers, and the motor seemed like a toy. The only part that looked sturdy was the wheels, which were quite large with extremely thick treads, designed to plow through moon dust and roll over sharp rocks.

Kira eagerly slid into the driver's seat and flipped the ignition switch. The engine shuddered to life. "C'mon!" Kira exclaimed. "Let's see how this thing handles!"

I buckled myself into the passenger seat. Kira immediately stomped her foot on the accelerator and let out a whoop. To her dismay, the little rover wasn't nearly as powerful as she'd hoped. Instead of roaring across the lunar surface like a Formula One race car, it puttered along like an anemic golf cart.

"What the . . . ?" Kira asked. "How do I make this thing go faster?"

"I think this is as fast as it goes," I told her. "Its maximum speed is eight miles an hour."

"You're kidding me." Kira steered toward the launchpad. "My grandma can walk faster than this thing."

I became aware of some movement out by the blast wall that surrounded the pad. Two of the four Moonies who'd stayed close to base to look for Nina were hurrying back toward the air lock, obviously concerned that their helmets might crack and explode at any moment.

I turned and spotted the other two adults rounding the side of the base, hurrying as well. Even though I couldn't see their faces, I could sense their fear. The harsh reality of our mission settled on me.

Despite Kira's annoyance over the rover's speed, it was still much faster than walking would have been. It wasn't long before we had cleared the launchpad and were venturing onto part of the moon I'd never laid eyes on before.

The lunar surface around Moon Base Alpha was scarred by human impact; virtually every bit of it was covered with human footprints or rover tracks, and there were piles of construction debris scattered about as well. But beyond the launchpad, most of the moon was still pristine. Except for the well-traveled road between the pad and the site of MBB—a makeshift highway of thousands of rover and robot tracks—everything still looked exactly as it had for the past hundred thousand years. There were wide seas of moon dust, a few islands of rock, and thousands of craters.

To our right, a great dune of moon dust rose, a beautiful pure white mountain two hundred feet tall. "Check that out," I said. "It's amazing, isn't it?"

"Yeah," Kira agreed. "I wish we could drive on it."

I glanced back at her. "But then we'd ruin it forever."

"So? It's gonna get ruined sooner or later. We might as well be the ones to do it. If we were the first ones up it, I'll bet we could name it after ourselves."

"We could probably name it anyhow," I pointed out.

"Mount Kiradash!" she exclaimed. "Aw, man, if this wasn't an emergency, I'd drive right up there."

"Look out!" I yelled.

Kira had been so busy looking at the mountain, she hadn't noticed the other rover coming down the road. Dr. Balnikov, Dr. Merritt, Dr. Kim, and Dr. Alvarez were racing back to the safety of MBA before their helmets failed. Kira was steering toward them, while they were all waving at us desperately, signaling us to move to the right. Kira veered out of their way so quickly I almost got whiplash.

They slipped past us, barely missing us by inches, then jounced onward toward MBA.

"Oops," Kira said.

"There's only two other vehicles on the entire moon," I pointed out. "And you almost hit one of them."

"I wasn't expecting there to be traffic," Kira explained.

I made sure there wasn't anyone else coming our way, then looked out over the endless expanse of moon. Roddy's warning came back to me: that Nina could be almost anywhere out there, and if she was, she'd be almost impossible to see. I turned back toward MBA, to find it had already disappeared from sight behind Mount Kiradash.

"Do you think Nina would have really come all the way out here?" I asked. "By herself?"

"We're not *that* far," Kira replied. "This stupid rover is so slow, I'll bet we haven't even gone a mile."

"But still, we're in a rover. It doesn't seem like Nina to come this far from the base alone on foot. It's too dangerous."

"Leaving the base at all doesn't seem like Nina," Kira told me. "Neither does stealing moon rocks. But obviously, none of us knew her as well as we thought. Everyone's been thinking she's the ultimate goody two-shoes and it turns out she's had this secret criminal life going on the whole time."

I sighed. "Well, at least now we know she wasn't murdered."

"Not necessarily. Murder's still totally possible. Maybe someone found out Nina was smuggling rocks and wanted in on it. Then Nina said no and things got out of control."

"You think she was killed because of some *rocks*?"

"They're supposed to be worth millions, right? People have killed each other for a lot less."

I stared out at the lunar surface, thinking about that. Once again, Kira was right: The fact that Nina was up to something secret didn't mean someone couldn't have murdered her. Or at least, tried to murder her. Zan had said she wasn't dead, but that was hours before. I wondered how much worse Nina's condition had grown since then. I wondered where Nina could be, period. There didn't appear to be any sign of her on the surface. But then, if Nina had been buried even a few feet off the track, I never would have seen her.

"So who's your number one suspect?" I asked.

"The Sjobergs," Kira replied.

"The Sjobergs? They don't need a couple million dollars! They've got billions."

"Maybe not. Maybe they blew all their money on stupid stuff like vacations on the moon. And now they're bankrupt and desperate. Those people are used to being rich. They wouldn't do well having to live like the rest of us, without solid-gold bathtubs and refrigerators full of caviar and pet snow leopards and stuff."

"A few million wouldn't be able to support that kind of life for them."

"It'd still be *something*. And if anyone on our base is depraved enough to kill for money, it's that family. Who knows? Maybe they're not bankrupt but they're still willing to sink this low to get more money because that's simply the kind of monsters they are."

"I don't know about that. . . ."

"Well, whatever the case, you have to admit they've been acting awfully suspicious lately."

"Yeah," I agreed, thinking of the long periods they were spending in their room and whatever Roddy had witnessed them doing the night before. "They're definitely up to something."

"Look," Kira said, pointing ahead of us. "There's the Moon Base Beta site."

It was still a good distance away from us, and it didn't look like much yet: only a few surveyor lines staked into the moon dust. MBB was going to be several times larger than MBA, but the footprint still looked awfully small compared to the amount of empty space surrounding it. Twelve space capsules were scattered about the area, each the size of a one-car garage. I couldn't tell which was the one that had come that morning, as they all looked exactly alike. None had been unloaded yet; that wouldn't happen until it was time for construction to begin.

I couldn't see the operations pod, though, as it had been built underground to protect it from meteorite impacts. It was inside a lava tube, an enormous natural tunnel of basalt that was a remnant from billions of years ago, when the moon's surface had been molten rock. The tubes had formed when the lava hardened, and they were like subway tunnels beneath the moon dust. They were pretty rare; this area was one of the few places on the moon they existed. In fact, the tubes were one of the main reasons for selecting the sites for both moon bases; the operations pods weren't sturdy enough to leave exposed on the lunar surface.

I noticed the lunar rover my parents, Chang, and Dr. Howard had taken, off to the side of the MBB site. It was parked by a dark slash of rock, the top of a lava tube, poking through the dust.

I pointed to it. "That must be where the pod is."

And then, far to my right, there was a sudden movement.

It happened quickly, at the edge of my peripheral vision. By the time I turned that way, whatever it was had vanished.

"What's wrong?" Kira asked.

"I thought I saw something," I said.

"Like Nina?"

"I don't know. Stop the rover."

Kira nailed the brakes. Even though we weren't moving all that fast, we still skidded a bit in the moon dust.

I scanned the horizon to the right, looking for more movement, hoping to spot Nina out there, alive and well. But I saw nothing.

Then, near the MBB site, there was a small puff of white. A tiny cloud of moon dust had been thrown into the air. Because of the moon's weak gravity, it drifted for a while before settling back to the surface. It looked kind of like the plume of spray a humpback whale made when it spouted.

"There!" I said, pointing.

"I saw it," Kira responded.

Another puff rose, much closer to us, off to our left.

Fear seized me as I realized what it was.

"Meteorites!" I yelled.

They were plummeting to the ground around us. Stray bits of rock that had been floating through space. Given the size of the impacts, they were certainly quite small, no bigger than pebbles. On earth, they would have burned up in the atmosphere. But on the moon, there was no atmosphere to slow them. They streaked into the surface at rocket speed, hard enough to crater the ground.

Fast enough to go straight through our space suits and kill us.

Another two puffs of dust arose, one on either side of us. More meteorites had plowed into the lunar surface. And no doubt more were coming.

We were out in the open in the middle of a meteorite shower and there was nothing to protect us.

Which meant our lives were in very serious danger.

Excerpt from *The Official Residents' Guide to Moon Base Alpha*,
"Appendix A: Potential Health and Safety Hazards,"
© 2040 by National Aeronautics and Space Administration

METEORITE IMPACTS

Perhaps the least controllable danger at MBA comes from outside the moon itself: meteorites*. Because of the lack of atmosphere, rocks that would burn up heading to earth are not slowed at all when falling to the lunar surface, impacting at extreme speeds. Therefore, even a rock the size of a pinhead can do great harm to a space suit—or a person—unlucky enough to be hit by it. (Don't worry, though: MBA has been constructed with exceptionally thick walls and windows to repel meteorites; even the skylight over the greenhouse is strong enough to withstand a major impact.) Before heading outside, check the most recent lunar atmospheric surveys to make sure there are no meteorite clouds in the area—although be aware that NASA can't track *every* rock in the solar system. Should you find yourself outside when meteorites are coming down, find shelter immediately. Where meteorites are concerned, the best protection by far is simply having a roof over your head.

---

* To clarify the difference between meteor, meteoroid, and meteorite: A meteor is the flash of light in the night sky when a piece of interplanetary debris hits the earth's atmosphere; a meteoroid is the piece of interplanetary debris itself; and a meteorite is a meteoroid that makes it through the atmosphere to the planet. Since there is no atmosphere on the moon, any meteoroid that encounters the moon's gravity will become a meteorite, and thus the terms are essentially interchangeable.

DEATH FROM ABOVE

Lunar day 217

Possibly the last few minutes of my life

"Drive!" I yelled to Kira.

"I know!" she yelled back, planting her foot on the accelerator.

The rear wheels of the rover spun wildly, kicking up their own cloud of moon dust. For a few moments, I feared that we'd sunk into the surface and were stuck, but then finally, the treads caught and we lurched forward. My helmet clanged off the back of my seat hard enough to rattle my head around like a peanut in its shell. The emergency helmet repair kit nearly slid off my lap, but I snagged the handle at the last second and kept it from tumbling into the dust.

In our hurry to rescue everyone, we had forgotten to follow official moonwalk procedures and check for any potential clouds of meteorites in the area before heading onto the
surface. Now there was nothing we could do except get to
safety as fast as humanly possible.

Three more meteorites plugged the ground in front of
us, sending up plumes of dust.

And those were merely the ones I could see. I had a limited
range of vision in my helmet, which meant there were probably other rocks streaming in from outer space all around us.

There wasn't any way to see the meteorites until they hit
the ground. There was no atmosphere for them to spark off,
and against the black sky the dark rocks were invisible. There
was no sound as they hurtled downward. Every impact was
eerily silent. We couldn't even hear the motor on the rover.
The only sound was our own frightened breathing, relayed
through our radio headsets to one another.

A minute before, when Kira had been driving like a mad-
woman, I'd been worried that the rover was going too fast.
Now it seemed terrifyingly slow. Meteorites were slamming
into the surface around us at hundreds of miles an hour, and
we were barely moving. The safety of the lava tube ahead
didn't seem to be getting any closer at all.

A new sound suddenly echoed in my helmet. My mother's voice on the radio. "Dash! Kira! Are you out there?"

"Yes!" both of us shouted back at once.

Mom gave a gasp of concern. I'm sure she hadn't meant for us to hear it, because when she spoke again, she was obviously doing her best to sound steady and reassuring. "Where are you?"

"We can see the lava tube," I reported. "It's about a hundred meters away."

Several more meteorites streaked into the ground around us. There were too many to count now. The shower was growing in intensity.

"Get here as fast as you can," Mom ordered. "We'll be waiting by the air lock. Once you're inside the tube itself, you'll be safe."

I looked to Kira helplessly.

"I'm going as fast as I can," she told me, then jammed her foot on the accelerator again, showing me she had it down as far as it could go.

Everywhere around us, there were puffs of dust. They were rising from the plain where Moon Base Beta would be built, from the dunes in the distance, and in the road around us, disturbingly close by.

Kira kept her gaze focused straight ahead and her hands locked on the steering wheel, putting us on the most direct line toward safety. Every second counted.

The tube was getting closer, though our progress still

seemed agonizingly slow. I locked my eyes on the dark slash of rock, willing it to come closer.

Suddenly a meteorite shot past me, so close I could feel it, and the right rear tire exploded. The rear axle dropped and plowed into the ground, spinning us off course. The rover leaped over a small ridge of rock and soared into the air.

On earth, we might have jumped a foot or two, but in the low gravity, the rover was airborne for a frighteningly long time.

"Hold on tight!" Kira screamed at me.

I was already doing this, clutching the chassis as hard as I could with my right hand while keeping my left arm locked around the emergency helmet repair kit.

Thankfully, we landed in a wide-open plain of dust, rather than on rock. The front of the rover plowed into the ground, kicking up a wave of dust that poured over us, turning the world blinding white. I was thrown forward from the impact, but my seat belt held, yanking me back hard into the seat. The emergency repair kit was torn from my grasp.

I'd closed my eyes to brace for the impact, and when I opened them again, I found myself plunged into darkness. For one brief, terrifying moment, I thought I might have gone blind, but then I realized that my visor had simply been covered in dust. I did my best to wipe it away, but it clung tenaciously, allowing me only a tiny smeared window to see through.

There was so much dust still flying around us, I could barely see my own feet. It was as though we'd been plunged into a snow dome and shaken. At first I thought Kira had been thrown free, but then I realized she was still in her seat beside me, only so coated with dust that she blended into the scenery.

"Are you okay?" I asked.

"Yes," she answered. "You?"

"I'm good," I said, hoping it was true. "Let's move."

Kira and I tried to unbuckle ourselves as quickly as we could. Unfortunately, the latch on my belt stayed stubbornly locked while I fumbled at it with my bulky gloved hands.

"What happened?" Mom asked over the radio.

"We wrecked the rover," I said.

"A meteorite hit it!" Kira added quickly. "It wasn't my fault!"

Unable to unlatch the buckle, I resorted to force, pounding on it angrily. It popped right open and I sprang from the rover.

A bizarrely calm computerized voice suddenly spoke in my ear. "Warning," it said. "Your oxygen levels are down to twenty percent. Please search for safety immediately." This was accompanied by a holographic display projected inside the visor, showing how low my oxygen levels were.

That seemed wrong. I hadn't been out long enough to use eighty percent of my oxygen. But maybe, in my panic, I was sucking it down much faster than I needed to. I did my best to slow my breathing.

With the cloud of dust still drifting to the ground around us, it was impossible to tell where anything was. It was hard enough to see Kira, and she was only a few feet away. I grabbed her arm and staggered forward in the direction that I *thought* the lava tube should be. A few feet on, the cloud quickly dissipated and we were back under the clear dark sky. Between the fog inside my helmet and the dust outside it, it was still hard to see much of anything, but I managed to make out the tube ahead of us.

The meteorites were still coming down. If anything, they were coming down even faster.

I spotted the emergency repair kit, half-buried in the moon dust only a few feet away, and staggered toward it.

"No time for that!" Kira yelled.

I kept going for it anyhow. If we left the kit behind and it was destroyed, our rescue mission would be a failure. Besides, it was only a few seconds' delay—although each second out there counted. I slipped my fingers under the handle and yanked it free of the dust.

"Dash! Run!" Kira yelled, as if maybe I hadn't thought of this myself.

I did my best, but unfortunately, in addition to the standard difficulties of moving fast in low gravity, we had landed in a deep field of dust, which clung to our legs like quick-sand, making our progress even more troublesome.

Everywhere I looked, clouds of dust were blooming around me. It felt like I was in one of Roddy's virtual-reality war games, with the enemy attacking from everywhere at once, only I didn't have anything to protect myself with, and should I get hit, I wouldn't be able to press the reset button.

Plus, there was the whole inability-to-run thing. Our progress felt maddeningly slow, although we were actually moving. The safety of the tube was getting closer. But time seemed to be stretching out, every second feeling like hours.

An alarm sounded inside my helmet. "Red alert," the computerized voice said. "Your oxygen levels are down to ten percent." Once again, the holographic display was projected inside the visor. It was probably supposed to be helpful, but it was blocking what little view I had left.

Something was definitely wrong with my suit. I was losing oxygen way too fast. But I couldn't take the time to breathe more slowly. Instead I kept doing my best to move fast, hoping there would be enough air left in my tank to get me to safety.

Kira stumbled beside me, but I took her arm and stead-ied her before she sprawled on the ground. A few steps later, she did the exact same thing for me.

"You're almost here!" Mom called to us. "Hurry! Only a few steps more!"

Through the dust on my visor and the display informing me I was close to suffocation, I could barely make out the entrance of the lava tube just ahead: a subterranean ring of jagged rock leading into a twelve-foot-tall, pitch-black tunnel. The area around it had been excavated so that a slope of dust angled steeply down toward the opening. The other rover was parked near the top of the slope. We staggered past it.

A meteorite ricocheted off the mouth of the tube and zinged right between Kira and me, moving so fast it might as well have been a bullet. It missed both of us by inches.

We hit the dusty entry slope and stumbled. Slopes are difficult to negotiate in low gravity, even when you're not running for your life. Kira and I both went down, tumbling through the dust toward the tube's entrance. The world seemed to flip over me several times, and then I came to a hard, painful stop, facedown on the hard rock inside the tube. Kira was right beside me.

"Warning," the computer in my helmet announced. "Oxygen levels are critically low. At current rate of respiration, you only have two minutes left."

I pulled myself to my feet and found the air lock was only a few steps away. The operations pod was essentially an enormous white balloon that had been inflated inside the tube. It was millions of times sturdier than a real balloon, of course, but the concept was the same. It looked bizarrely out of place in the tube, like a massive sausage that was jammed in a dragon's throat. The air lock sat at the end facing us. Dozens of moon-dust boot prints led along the rocky floor to it.

I hooked my hand beneath Kira's arm, hauled her to her feet, and helped her toward the air lock.

"We're here," I announced.

"I see you," Mom said, with obvious relief in her voice.

She must have flipped the switch to open the air lock automatically for us, because the door swung out as we approached. We clambered through the hole and locked the door tight behind us.

"Only one minute of oxygen remaining," the computer told me. "Hypoxia is imminent. Get to safety as quickly as possible."

Inside the air lock, a message flashed on a panel: PRES-SURIZATION IN PROGRESS.

A rush of air buffeted my suit. As the atmosphere in the air lock changed to that of earth, we could immediately hear sounds around us: the murmur of worried voices inside the operations pod, the hum of machinery, the computerized voice—now coming from outside my helmet—announcing, "Pressurization complete. It is now safe to remove your helmet."

At the exact same time, the same voice inside my helmet was saying, "Thirty seconds of oxygen remaining. If you do not reach safety immediately, you will black out and possibly die."

I yanked my gloves off, unlatched my helmet, detached it from my suit, and gulped in air.

Beside me, Kira yanked off her helmet as well, then gave me a weak smile. "Guess we made it."

"Yeah," I agreed. "We did."

We both turned to the inner air lock door, which was glass. We could see our parents gathered around it with Chang, making no attempt to hide their relief that we were alive. Even Dr. Howard was giving us his full attention for once.

"The air jets here don't have enough power to clean all that dust off those suits," Dad told us through the door. "You'll have to remove them in the air lock and leave them there. We can't have you tracking all that dust in here."

"All right," I said, and finally noticed how much dust was caking my suit. I looked like I'd been dipped in flour. Kira looked even worse. Every time she moved, cascades of dust poured from every crevice of her suit.

The two of us quickly helped each other unlatch our suits and climb out of them. Kira shrugged off hers first, then I did mine.

Kira's face suddenly went somewhat pale, like she'd had a terrible shock. When she realized I'd noticed, she tried to hide it, but it was too late.

"What's wrong?" I asked.

"This." Kira pointed to a gash in the right shoulder of my suit.

A meteorite had torn through almost every layer of it. And given the tear's location, it had come awfully close to my head as well. That explained my oxygen loss; it must have leaked out through the last remaining layer. I figured the tear was from the meteorite I'd felt pass, the one that had blown our tire and upended the rover. Though it didn't really matter *when* it had happened. The fact was, only one final membrane of fabric had remained between me and instant death. If the meteorite had been a millimeter to the left—or if I had been leaning a millimeter to the right—or if I'd torn the suit while hurrying to safety—I wouldn't have been standing there. I'd have been dead out on the surface instead.

The mere thought of it made me weak in the knees. My legs buckled and Kira had to steady me.

The inner air lock door popped open. My parents rushed through to my side. I don't know if they'd seen the gash in the suit as well, or if they simply had decided they couldn't wait anymore for me. Dr. Howard came through right behind them.

My folks hugged me while I stood there, the suit still piled on the floor around my ankles. Beside me, Dr. Howard clutched Kira tightly.

"We thought you might have . . . ," Mom began, but couldn't bring herself to finish the statement. "In our hurry to get you here, no one thought to check and see if any meteorites were in the area."

"We're so sorry," Dad said.

"It's okay," I told them.

"It's not," Mom replied. "We almost lost you two out there."

I did my best not to think too much about that statement. Instead I said, "Remember how, for the first few months after we got here, I used to complain how boring it was on the moon?"

"Yes," Dad answered.

"I really miss those days," I said, and then collapsed in his arms.

Excerpt from *The Official Residents' Guide to Moon Base Alpha*,
"Appendix A: Potential Health and Safety Hazards,"
© 2040 by National Aeronautics and Space Administration

SPACE SUITS

The potential for most danger while on the lunar surface isn't from meteorites or lunar rover accidents; it's from human error. A space suit that has been put on hastily—and thus improperly—is thousands of times more likely to result in harm than a meteorite. So before venturing onto the surface, check all your suit's life-support and safety systems several times over. Then do the same for your moonwalk partner. And while on the surface, be alert! Keep checking your systems and take care to avoid any damage. Be prepared for any emergency. Should one occur, know the ins and outs of your suit, as well as the fastest route back to base. For more on the space suits and how they operate, please consult the separate *NASA Guide to Your Space Suit*.

16

VIDEO TRANSMISSION

Lunar day 217

Post-traumatic experience recovery period

The helmet repair kit had survived the trip
through the meteor shower. Chang, Mom, and Dr. Howard
went right to work replacing their visors. Meanwhile, Dad
patched my suit the best he could. The meteor shower was
letting up—Kira and I were unlucky to have been outside for
the worst of it—and everyone wanted to resume the search
for Nina as soon as it was over.

The pod was cramped with all of us in it. It was much
smaller than I'd expected, given that four people were going
to be living there once construction for MBB was under
way. Most of the actual work would be done by robots, but

humans were still needed there. Even though the site wasn't *that* far from MBA, it still took time and energy to go from one to the other—and as Kira and I had just learned first-hand, the less time you had to spend in transit on the lunar surface, the better.

Inside the pod, there were four bunks against the side wall, four workstations, some storage areas, a tiny kitchen, and a toilet that looked even more awful than the ones we had back at MBA. This was all crammed into a tubular space smaller than my bedroom back on earth. There wasn't even a separate space for the toilet. You could draw a curtain around you, but that was it for privacy. If anyone got bad gas, they'd stink up the whole pod for days.

"This place makes Moon Base Alpha look like the Four Seasons," I told Mom.

"If you think this is bad, imagine what it was like for the crew who built MBA." Mom popped her old, cracked visor off her helmet and tossed it aside. "At least the people staying here will have the option of visiting MBA now and then for showers and time off. The MBA construction crew had to stay in a pod like this for an entire year."

"Four people? In something this small for a year?" I echoed. "I'm surprised no one went nuts."

"They might have," Dad said. "NASA was awfully secretive about the whole project."

My smartwatch suddenly vibrated on my wrist. Riley Bock was calling from Hawaii.

"It's Riley," I said. "Mind if I take it?"

"Sure," Mom told me. "We're not going anywhere until these helmets are fixed."

I accepted the call. Video of Riley sprang up on the face of my watch. She was outside my old middle school, passing from one classroom to another. As usual, it was a beautiful day in Hawaii—even though it was the middle of winter in the rest of the United States. Riley was dressed in a T-shirt and shorts, and the sun was so bright, the image was almost blinding in the darkness of the pod. "Aloha, Moonie!" she said. "Is something wrong up there?"

It took me a moment to realize she was asking this jokingly. "Why?"

"'Cause I've sent you, like, thirty texts since last night and I called once and I haven't heard boo from you today."

"Sorry. Things have been kind of hectic." I picked my words very carefully. NASA monitored all our calls, making sure that no one said anything bad about the moon program or leaked classified information. If I did that, they'd stop the conversation immediately—putting a fake "transmission failure" notice up to fool Riley—and I could lose my phone privileges completely. For example, even though there'd been a murder at MBA a month before, I and all the other Moonies had been barred from saying a single word about it to anyone on earth. The entire story had been buried by NASA.

Riley asked, "Did you watch that video I sent you last night yet?"

"Video? . . . No." It occurred to me that, in all the events of the day, I hadn't bothered reading through all the texts from Riley. "I didn't even realize you'd sent one."

"Well, you should watch it. . . ." The video feed suddenly began to cut out, reducing the image to jumbled pixels and garbled sounds for a few seconds. The decaying feed wasn't really surprising, given that I was receiving it in an underground tube 250,000 miles from earth. Frankly, it was astonishing that I'd received a clear image for as long as I had.

"Hold on," I said. "You're breaking up."

Riley seemed to still be talking, unaware that I couldn't hear or see her, but it was hard to tell for sure—because I couldn't see or hear her. And then, a single brief burst of audible speech came through: ". . . the Sjobergs . . ."

I moved toward the air lock, where I figured the reception might be slightly better. "Can you repeat that?"

Sure enough, the image cleared up a bit as I neared the air lock. For a few seconds, I could see Riley bright and clear again, as if I were right back on earth. She was standing outside the gymnasium. A lot of students had now gathered behind her, realizing she was talking to me on the moon, and were either waving hello or mugging for the camera. Riley repeated herself. "I said, I guess you're getting along better with the Sjobergs now, huh?"

While NASA would never have let me bad-mouth the space tourists, I hadn't ever made it a secret that we didn't get along. "Um . . . why would you say that?"

"Watch the video! And if they ever invite you to one of their fancy homes for vacation, tell them your best friend needs to come too!"

The picture fuzzed out again before I could respond, and was then replaced by a screen saying TRANSMISSION FAILURE. I guessed this was legit and that NASA hadn't intervened—transmitting between earth and the moon wasn't exactly easy—but the truth was, I had no idea.

Kira pointed to a computer station crammed between two storage units near the air lock. "Think we can watch the video on that?" She wasn't even trying to pretend she hadn't overheard my conversation. In the cramped pod, it would have been impossible not to.

"It might be private," Mom told her.

"I don't mind," I said. I didn't want to wait to see it. On my watch, I brought up the list of texts Riley had sent, searching for the one with the video attached. I could see why Riley had called. She'd sent the video the night before, but had then fired off plenty more texts that morning. I hadn't responded to any of them, because I'd been busy trying to not get killed by Patton Sjoberg. Or meteorites.

I located the video and transferred the file to the computer. It popped up on the screen and instantly started playing. It began with the logo of *InterNetwork News*, and then Katie Gallagher, one of their most famous anchors, appeared.

"This is an *INN* exclusive," she announced. "If you've been paying any attention to Moon Base Alpha—and honestly, who hasn't?—then you certainly know about the world's first lunar tourist family, the Sjobergs. But while the rest of the Moonies at MBA have made video logs and blog updates, we haven't heard anything from the Sjobergs at all—leading many people to speculate that perhaps their experience up there hasn't been enjoyable. Well, we are about to find out the truth. The Sjobergs have finally consented to break their silence and conduct an interview with me."

"Uh-oh," Chang said under his breath. "When did this run?"

"Last night, I guess," I told him. "I'll bet Riley sent it right after it posted."

The video shifted to a view of the Sjobergs in their room at MBA. They all sat on their InflatiCubes facing the camera, looking like a perfectly decent family for once. Lars and Sonja sat in the middle, flanked by Patton and Lily. Katie Gallagher was relegated to a tiny inset down at the bottom of the screen.

"How'd they even do this?" Kira asked. "Wouldn't NASA have blocked them?"

"Maybe they found a way to get around the NASA censors," Mom replied.

"Thanks for joining me," Katie said on the video.

"Oh, it's our pleasure," Lars replied, flashing the first smile I'd seen from him in the past few months. "We're very big fans of yours."

Katie beamed. "That's so kind of you. I hope you don't mind, but I'd like to cut to the chase. Could you address the rumors that have been swirling about your dissatisfaction with Moon Base Alpha?"

"Certainly," Lars answered. "I'd like to take this opportunity to declare that all those rumors are completely unfounded. We have no issues at all with Moon Base Alpha. In fact, we love it up here."

"What?" Kira asked, stunned. All the adults looked equally shocked.

So did Katie Gallagher. She seemed caught completely off guard—and a bit annoyed as well. As if she'd been hoping for a great exposé about Moon Base Alpha and had now been denied. "I'm sorry?" she asked. "Did you just say that you *love* it up there?"

"Yes," Sonja cooed. "It's simply wonderful. This has been

the best vacation we have ever had. Better than the French Riviera, or the Maldives, or Gstaad . . ."

"Or even the Bahamas," Lily added. "And we own a whole island there!"

"It's worth every penny we spent!" Lars proclaimed.

"Even though you spent over half a billion dollars?" Katie asked skeptically.

"Absolutely," Lars replied. "Sure, it's not the same as staying in a luxury resort on earth. There aren't any servants or fancy meals or beaches to walk on. But then, you have to ask yourself, is that really what makes a vacation great? Shouldn't it all be about the place you're going and the experience of being there? What could possibly be a more exciting place to visit than the moon? What could be a more amazing experience than taking an actual rocket into space? What could be better than spending six months in such an incredible place with my wonderful family? I wish that everyone on earth could have one fraction of the joy that we've experienced up here."

All of us looked to one another, too stunned by Lars's performance to speak.

Because there was no other word for it. It was definitely a performance. The Lars in the interview was nothing like the Lars any of us had been with for the past few months. It wasn't merely that he was spouting lies to Katie Gallagher, telling her the exact opposite of everything he'd been saying to us. It was that Lars himself seemed to be the exact opposite. The Lars in the video was gracious, kind, and well-spoken, while the real Lars was cruel and hot-tempered and rarely said anything that wasn't outright nasty. I got the distinct impression that he'd written all his answers out beforehand and memorized them.

"Is that even Lars Sjoberg?" Kira asked. "Or did they replace him with a robot?"

"Er . . . what about your relations with the other lunarnauts?" Katie asked, apparently concerned that this interview wasn't nearly as sensational as she'd hoped it was going to be. She seemed desperate to find something to provoke an angry response. "I've heard things haven't been quite so pleasant there as you're making them out to be."

Lars broke into fake laughter, as though Katie had told him the funniest joke of all time. The rest of the Sjobergs followed his lead.

"Oh, Katie," Lars chuckled, "please don't be offended, but the rumors you've heard have no foundation in reality whatsoever. Our relationships with our fellow lunarnauts have been the *best* part of this vacation. We have made so many wonderful friends here, going home is going to be extremely difficult for us."

"In fact," Sonja added, "we intend to stay friends with everyone here once we are all back on earth. We hope they'll come visit us at any of our vacation homes."

This from the woman who once announced at dinner that she wished all the rest of us would drop dead from moon disease.

While the Sjobergs all looked eerily happy, Katie Gallagher did not. She was trying to keep a smile on her face, but it was becoming hard work. She shifted her attention to the kids, hoping they'd be easier to provoke. "Patton and Lily, have you found this experience equally as wonderful as your parents have?"

"Yes," Patton said. And that was it. He wasn't nearly as adept at lying as his parents, so it seemed to be all he could manage.

However, Lily had the gift for gab, and she deftly took over. "I think that Patton and I have probably enjoyed our time here even more than our parents. I have had so much fun with the Marquez kids and the Gibson kids and Kira Howard. They really feel like family to me."

"Yes," Patton said again.

Katie Gallagher looked as though she had just sat on an entire box of thumbtacks. "So then, there hasn't been anything bad about your experience at Moon Base Alpha at all?"

"The only bad thing about this experience," Lars replied,

"is that it will have to end. Sadly, NASA tells me that it won't be possible to extend our stay, as there are many other families who have paid for the privilege of coming here after us, but perhaps we will be able to return to the moon one day. I understand there are many companies looking to build hotels here, and I think I speak for all of us when I say that another vacation here is something we'd happily sign up for."

"Absolutely," Sonja agreed. "Now that we've been here, vacations on earth will be a bore. The moon is simply the best place we've ever gone. Nothing can compare."

"Hopefully," Lars said, "in the not-so-distant future, lunar travel will be available for *everyone*, not merely the richest people. Because this is an experience everyone should have. There are simply no words to describe how amazing it has been."

"Given that," Katie said, "I suppose it's time to bring this interview to a close. Lars, Sonja, Patton, and Lily, thank you so much for taking the time to speak to me from all the way at Moon Base Alpha. It's been a pleasure."

"No," Lars corrected, "the pleasure was all ours. Thank *you*, Katie."

The video ended.

"What the heck was *that*?" Kira asked.

"Looks like NASA finally convinced them to make a statement supporting the moon base," Mom replied.

"The Sjobergs never do anything unless it benefits the Sjobergs," Chang said suspiciously. "They're not going to do some PR campaign for NASA. They *loathe* NASA. They're up to something here. I guarantee it."

The radio crackled with a new transmission. "Hey, guys!" Daphne chirped. "We haven't seen a meteorite strike in the past ten minutes and the satellite isn't picking up any incoming, so it looks like it's safe for you to come on home!"

Mom radioed back. "That's good to hear. How's Violet doing?"

"Great, as usual," Daphne replied. "In fact, she's right here and wants to say hi."

"Hi, Mommy!" Violet called. "Can I have some space ice cream?"

"Did you eat your lunch?" Mom asked.

"Um . . . yes," Violet said, in a way that indicated she hadn't. She hadn't mastered lying nearly as well as the Sjobergs had.

"We'll talk about it when we get back," Mom said, then signed off and turned to all of us. "My helmet's fixed. How's everyone else's?"

"Good as new," Dr. Howard said, tightening the final screw on his visor.

"Same goes for Dash's suit," Dad said, pointing to the patch he'd put on it. It didn't *look* good as new to me, but it looked much better than it had before. "I recharged your oxygen tanks too," Dad told me.

"All right," Chang said. "Suit up, everyone. We're going back out there."

Despite Daphne's claim that the meteorite shower was over, my heart still began racing. I stared out the window at the surface of the moon, feeling my stomach churn with anxiety.

Hopefully, for once, a trip onto the lunar surface wouldn't be a near-death experience.

Excerpt from *The Official Residents' Guide to Moon Base Alpha*,
"Appendix A: Potential Health and Safety Hazards,"
© 2040 by National Aeronautics and Space Administration

NONAPPROVED OBJECTS

To protect the delicate balance of the interior atmosphere of MBA, only sanctioned objects should be brought into the base. Any personal items you wish to bring from earth must be approved by NASA, then submitted to the Administration for proper sterilization, irradiation, and packing before delivery to the moon. Rest assured that similar steps will be taken with all equipment and foodstuffs delivered to base. Furthermore, no objects should be brought in from the lunar surface without official approval, to protect against contamination of MBA. True, the lunar surface is sterile itself, but there is always a chance that extremely hardy life forms can survive in these circumstances—and they might be dangerous to humans. Think of MBA as a bubble protecting you from an extremely harsh environment, and don't do anything to pollute the interior!

FRAYED NERVES

Lunar day 217

Afternoon

We refilled our oxygen tanks, suited up, and headed back to MBA. The rover Kira and I had wrecked was out of commission, so there was only one left—and it could only hold four people. Chang ordered Mom and Dad to drive Kira and me back in it, while he and Dr. Howard would walk. Dad protested, but Chang pulled rank as the interim base commander, and that was that.

The trip back to MBA was far less eventful than the trip out had been. But even so, it was still terrifying.

I spent the entire time worrying that a meteorite was suddenly going to plunge from the sky and kill me. Or kill one of the people I was with. I did my best to remain calm, but I wasn't fooling anybody. They could all hear me over the intercom in our helmets. I'd never realized you could tell that someone was frightened simply by their breathing, but you can.

I could hear it in Kira's sharp, ragged breaths. And I could see her nervous fidgeting. Despite all her claims that she was fine, she was just as scared as me.

So rather than make us walk from the garage to the air lock, Dad lopped a few precious minutes off the trip and dropped us off at the front of the base with Mom. Then he drove on to the garage while we all stepped into the air lock.

The other big rover was still parked by the air lock. Dr. Balnikov, Dr. Merritt, Dr. Kim, and Dr. Alvarez had been in a much bigger rush when they'd returned, fearing that their helmets might fail, so they hadn't spent a second longer outside than they needed to. The rover had been hit by a few meteorites and looked badly damaged, which made me think about what would have happened if *I* had been hit by a meteorite like that. I hurried into the air lock as quickly as I could. So did Kira and Mom.

The moment I stepped inside, where I was safe from incoming space rocks, I was finally able to relax. Less than two hours before, I hadn't been a very big fan of MBA. Now I couldn't have been happier to be back there.

The air-lock chamber repressurized and we eagerly popped off our helmets.

Through the glass of the inner air lock, we could see Violet and Daphne waiting for us. Violet had her nose mashed up against the window and was making funny faces. She also had a chocolate mustache.

"Welcome back, everyone!" she yelled.

"Thanks, sweetheart," Mom called back. "Looks like you had ice cream anyhow."

"No, I didn't!" Violet lied.

Daphne blushed, embarrassed. "I couldn't say no to her. She's too darn cute."

It took a long time to get all the moon dust off our suits, especially mine and Kira's. The air hose system wasn't very fast to begin with, and we were coated with the stuff. By the time Dad bounded up to the outer air lock door from the garage, we'd only managed to get the helmets clean.

"Let's leave the suits for now," Mom said. "Stephen needs to come in and we have other things to do."

So we passed into the staging area with our helmets, leaving the suits heaped on the floor, and then closed the inner air-lock door behind us. Now that the air-lock chamber was clear, Dad entered it from the lunar surface.

Once I was inside the base, Violet threw her arms around me and clamped on tight. "I'm so happy you're okay!"

"Thanks," I said.

"I hate those meteoroids," she told me, then turned to the window and yelled, "Stupid meteoroids! You stay away from my brother!"

"I'm happy you're okay too," Daphne said, then hugged both Kira and me at once.

"Oof!" Violet cried from in between us all. "Help! I'm being squished!"

Almost everyone else at MBA had turned out to witness our arrival as well. Now that their raid on the greenhouse was over, the Sjobergs had retreated back into their room again. But all the other Moonies were gathered to welcome us back—except Dr. Goldstein. I figured she was in the greenhouse, assessing the damage the Sjobergs had done.

Roddy stepped forward first. "Hey, guys, I'm glad you made it."

Everyone then looked to Cesar expectantly. He stayed right where he was, though, looking down at his feet, until his mother shoved him forward. "Cesar has something he'd like to say," she announced.

"Yeah." Cesar kept his gaze locked downward. "I'm sorry the Sjobergs and I broke the helmets and caused all this trouble."

"That's all right," Mom told him, though her tone indicated she was still plenty peeved at Cesar.

"How'd you finally get the helmet off?" I asked him.

"We had to use some industrial lubricant designed for the robots," Daphne explained.

"What was it like out there?" Roddy asked eagerly. "With all the meteorites coming down around you? Was it exciting?"

"*Too* exciting," I told him.

"Any sign of Nina back here?" Mom asked.

A collective sense of sadness and unease seemed to settle over everyone else.

"Nothing," Daphne admitted. "The search parties didn't find any sign of her and we haven't heard a peep since everyone came back inside."

"And you searched everywhere we planned to?" Mom asked.

"No," Dr. Balnikov admitted. "We called off the search outside when the issue of the helmets became evident, and then the meteorite shower prevented us from resuming it."

"However," Dr. Alvarez added, "we did cover a significant area and saw no sign of her."

"I got some robots going after the shower ended," Daphne reported. "They've all come up empty, but they haven't had time to range very far."

"I checked the whole base for her!" Violet said helpfully. "Even the bathrooms. But I couldn't find her."

Mom looked to me. "Any other ideas where she might be?"

It caught me by surprise that she was deferring to me on this. Then I noticed that everyone else was looking at me expectantly too. "No," I said sadly.

"Nothing?" Mom pressed.

"Come on, Dash," Violet said. "You figured out what happened to Dr. Holtz when no one else could."

A murmur of agreement rippled through the room.

Unfortunately, I couldn't come up with anything. Whether Nina had vanished on her own or someone had attacked her and then tried to hide her body, she'd still have to be *somewhere*. But I had no new ideas about where that could be.

Before I was forced to admit this, however, Dad stepped through the air lock and announced, "That wasn't a meteorite shower."

Everyone's attention now shifted to Dad.

"It was so a meteorite shower," Kira told him. "I was out in it."

"You were out in a shower," Dad corrected. "But those weren't meteorites." He held up a scrap of metal the size of a pea. "They were things like this."

Mom took the bit of metal and stared at it, aghast. "You mean that whole shower was man-made?"

"Probably not on purpose," Dad said. "But yes, it was. I

checked out a few of the other impact craters by the garage. They were all made by space junk."

I groaned. Space junk was an increasingly dangerous problem. Garbage on earth was merely ugly, but in orbit—where everything moved at seventeen thousand miles an hour—it was deadly. If a spacecraft hit something as tiny as a wing nut at that speed, it could explode and everyone on board would die. And unfortunately, if there was one thing humans excelled at, it was creating garbage. Almost every time we launched something into space, we left debris out there, ranging from little stuff like nuts and bolts that broke off rockets, to big stuff like defunct satellites. Even worse, space junk tended to multiply. If even a tiny piece slammed into a satellite, that satellite instantly became several million more pieces of space junk—each of which could destroy another satellite, creating millions of more pieces. NASA did its best to monitor and remove what it could, but it was a losing battle. Rocket launches were routinely delayed to allow clouds of space junk to pass.

However, until that moment, I had thought that space junk was a much bigger problem closer to earth than to the moon—and judging from everyone else's reactions, they were equally surprised. "Where'd it come from?" I asked.

Dad said, "Most likely, some other country had a lunar satellite blow up and neglected to inform us."

"Don't rule out the USA," Dr. Balnikov retorted. "They have more spy satellites than anyone, and I guarantee you, the CIA doesn't announce when those come apart."

"Who says it had to be a human satellite?" Roddy asked. "There are probably dozens of alien cultures monitoring us. Maybe one of their ships malfunctioned."

"Maybe your brain malfunctioned," Cesar said, smacking Roddy on the back of the head.

"It doesn't matter whose satellite it was," Mom said angrily. "What matters is that Dash and Kira could have died because of it! If there is space junk in lunar orbit, NASA needs to know about it immediately!"

There were murmurs of agreement throughout the room. "I'll notify them right now," Daphne said. "Since we know the exact time the storm hit, we ought to be able to pinpoint the cloud's location." She spun on her heel and raced toward the control room.

As she did, she almost plowed into Dr. Kim, who had just exited the science pod, carrying a small rock. Up to that point, I hadn't noticed that Dr. Kim wasn't among the crowd in the staging area. Dr. Kim was so meek that sometimes you didn't even notice her when she was the only other person in the room. "Excuse me," Dr. Kim told Daphne, even though the near collision was actually Daphne's fault, and then she froze upon seeing the size of the gathered crowd, looking like a deer caught in the headlights of an oncoming car.

Meanwhile, Roddy and Cesar's argument was escalating.

"There *are* aliens watching us," Roddy was saying. "It's been proven."

"You're such a dork," Cesar said, smacking Roddy on the back of the head again.

"Stop hitting me!" Roddy snapped.

"I'm not doing it," Cesar taunted. "Aliens have taken control of my body." He smacked Roddy once more. "There! They did it again!"

"I hate you!" Roddy screamed, then attacked his brother. The two of them crashed to the floor and rolled around, pounding on each other.

"Boys, stop it!" their mother cried. "You're embarrassing yourselves in front of the entire moon base!"

Mom wasn't paying any attention to them at all, though. Instead she was staring at the rock in Dr. Kim's hand. "Is that a moon rock, Jennifer?" she asked.

"Er . . . yes," Dr. Kim said shyly. "It's from Nina's room."

"What are you doing with it?" Mom asked.

"I . . . uh . . . I thought I'd analyze the chemical makeup of it," Dr. Kim said. "I figured that if I could determine that, then I could narrow down where the rocks had come from and pinpoint where Nina might have gone to get them."

Mom broke into a big smile. "That's a great idea!"

"Really?" Dr. Kim asked, still looking embarrassed. "Thanks."

Cesar and Roddy tumbled past them. Cesar ended up on top of Roddy and then smashed his brother's face into the floor. "Admit you're a loser and I'll let you go," he said.

Roddy yelled something in response, but with his lips planted on the floor, it sounded like "Mnewsupth."

"What was that?" Cesar released his grip, letting Roddy raise his head.

"You suck!" Roddy yelled, and Cesar promptly smashed his face back into the floor again.

Their mother looked to their father, exasperated. "Will you please do something to stop this?"

Dr. Marquez shrugged helplessly. "They're teenage boys in a confined space with limited options to exert their natural aggression. In such a scenario, conflicts are inevitable."

Dr. Brahmaputra-Marquez glared at her husband like she now wanted to hit *him* in the face.

Mom led Dr. Kim away from the Marquez family, where it was slightly quieter. I followed them, along with Dad, Violet, and Kira.

"What did you find?" Mom asked.

"Not surprisingly, it's a breccia," Dr. Kim replied.

"What's a breccia?" Violet interrupted.

"It's a rock that's composed of broken bits of other rocks,"

Mom explained to her. "Then they all get fused together by heat. Almost every rock we've found in the lunar crust is a breccia."

"And like most of the other rocks," Dr. Kim went on, "this one has high concentrations of olivine, pyroxene, and plagioclase feldspar. However, it also has significant amounts of armalcolite."

"What's armored coal light?" Violet asked.

Mom turned to her, smiling. "Armalcolite. It's a mineral that was discovered by the Apollo Eleven mission, the first time men landed on the moon. In fact, it's named after the members of that mission: *Arm*strong, *Al*drin, and *Col*lins. Armalcolite. Since then, it's been found on earth, but in only trace amounts." She turned back to Dr. Kim. "And it's somewhat rare on the moon as well, correct?"

"In many places," Dr. Kim confirmed. "But there are also occasional rock extrusions that have a good amount of it."

"Where's the closest extrusion?" Kira asked.

"Right outside the secondary air lock." Dr. Kim pointed toward the far side of the base, where the emergency backup air lock was located. "We're practically on top of it."

We couldn't see the backup air lock from where we were, so we all started walking that way, leaving the staging area and the scrapping Marquez boys behind. Roddy had managed to launch a counteroffensive, somehow wriggling out from Cesar's grasp, so now both Marquez boys were writhing around on the floor again. Dr. Brahmaputra-Marquez finally lost it and screamed at them, "I've had it, you two! Stop this foolishness right now or you're grounded!"

"Big deal," Cesar muttered. "Living here is like being permanently grounded anyhow."

"I'll take away your ComLink privileges for a month!" his mother yelled.

Cesar and Roddy instantly stopped fighting. "That's not fair!" Roddy whined. "*He* started this, not me!"

We passed the greenhouse. As I'd suspected, Dr. Goldstein was inside it, though she seemed even more distraught over her plants than I'd imagined. But then, the Sjobergs had swept through like a swarm of locusts. They'd even devoured the tomatoes and strawberries that weren't ripe yet.

My parents both paused at the sight of this. "What happened to the food?" Mom gasped.

It occurred to me that, with all the excitement of the broken helmets and the meteorite shower, I'd never had the chance to tell my parents about the Sjobergs' latest misbehavior.

"The Sjobergs ate it all!" Violet announced.

Dad immediately turned bright red with anger. "When?"

"Right after you went out on the moon," Violet told him. "They ate it all up like a bunch of jerks. And then they told Patton to beat Dash up!"

My mother turned to me, her eyes full of concern. "Did he hurt you?"

"He *tried* to," Kira said, before I could answer the question myself. "He practically strangled him."

"But Dash fought him off!" Violet announced proudly. "He scared Patton so bad he made pee in his pants!"

My father stared up at the door of the Sjobergs' residence. I'd never seen him so angry in my entire life. "Those lousy pigs," he growled. "It's time someone put them all in their place." He started toward the stairs, looking ready to pound them all into pieces.

I stepped into his path. "Dad, it's okay. I'm fine. Right now, we need to find Nina."

Dad blinked. He seemed to have forgotten all about Nina in his rage. He calmed slightly, but he was obviously still angry. "All right," he said. "But once we find her, I'm taking care of this." He kept his gaze locked on the Sjobergs' door as we headed into the gymnasium.

The emergency backup air lock was set in the gymnasium wall beyond all the workout machines. Through the windows set in the doors, we could see a lump of black rock poking up through the moon dust.

"Is that the extrusion?" I asked.

"The top of it," Dr. Kim said. "It goes far down below the dust."

"And you think all the rocks in Nina's room came from there?" Kira asked.

"I can't say that for sure." Dr. Kim lowered her eyes, as though she was ashamed. "I haven't had a chance to test all of them."

"But assuming they're all like this," Dad pressed, "it'd make sense that's where Nina would have gone for them?"

"Yes," Dr. Kim replied. "It's certainly the richest amount of armalcolite anywhere around this base."

Mom said, "And it makes sense that if Nina was collecting moon rocks to sell, she'd get ones with as much armalcolite as possible. It'd be easier to guarantee that they were from the moon rather than from earth."

"So given that," Dad said, "Nina wouldn't have had a reason to range far from the base at all. She would have only circled around the base to there."

I pressed up against the glass, looking at the lump of rock. There were thousands of boot prints all around it. "But Nina obviously didn't go there, right? I mean, she's not there now. And someone searched that area, didn't they?"

"Doctors Goldstein and Iwanyi," Dr. Kim replied. "And as far as I know, they didn't see any sign of Nina."

"I don't see any sign of her either," Violet said, pressed up against the window beside me. "Maybe she beamed up to a spaceship! Like on *Star Trek*."

"That's made up," I told her. "We can't really do it."

"Yes, we can," Violet snapped. "I saw it on TV."

I started to argue, but Mom caught my arm and signaled that this wasn't the time.

Then she looked to Dr. Kim. "Are there any other extrusions nearby that contain large amounts of armalcolite?"

"There's a few small seams north of the base," Dr. Kim replied. "But they're a good walk from here. It doesn't make sense that Nina would go all the way to them when she had so much of it so close by."

"We ought to target searches on them anyhow," Dad said. "Maybe Nina didn't know there was such a load of it right near us."

"Do you have the coordinates for the other locations?" Mom asked Dr. Kim.

"I can get them," Dr. Kim replied.

"Then let's do it," Mom said.

The adults all filed out of the gymnasium to take care of that, but Kira, Violet, and I stayed behind, looking at the lump of rock outside the air-lock windows.

"Do you think Nina really went to those other rocks?" Kira asked.

"No," I replied.

"Mom and Dad do," Violet said pointedly.

"Maybe," I said. "Or maybe they've run out of other

ideas. Not that I have any." I pressed my forehead against the glass, feeling frustrated. "Something's just not right about all of this."

"Yeah," Kira agreed. "First Nina vanishes. Then the Sjobergs start plotting something. Then we nearly get killed by satellite debris. It's like this whole place suddenly got a ton of bad karma."

"You know what you should do when you're upset?" Violet asked. "Turn that frown upside down!"

"That won't solve all these problems," I told her.

"Want to hear a joke?" Violet asked. "Knock knock!"

"Cut it out, Violet."

"You're not supposed to say, 'Cut it out.' You're supposed to say, 'Who's there?'"

"I mean it, Violet. Cut it out."

"Knock knock."

"Just quit it!" I snapped. "You can be so annoying sometimes!"

The smile faded from Violet's face. Her lower lip quivered. Then she raced out of the gymnasium, crying at the top of her lungs.

I slumped against the emergency air lock and looked to Kira. "You're so lucky you're an only child."

"You're lucky to have a little sister like that," Kira said pointedly. "She was only trying to cheer you up."

"I know, but . . . she just doesn't understand that sometimes, things can be serious. All this stuff's going wrong here and she's telling knock-knock jokes."

"Maybe she's scared and that's how she deals with it. She's only six."

I frowned, realizing Kira was probably right. Which made me feel ashamed about the way I'd treated my sister. I hadn't behaved any better than the Marquez boys. Worse, probably. "I guess I should apologize." I sighed, then headed back out of the gym, looking for Violet. Kira tailed me.

We followed the sounds of sobbing, but they didn't lead to Violet. They were coming from Dr. Goldstein, who was still sitting in the greenhouse, mourning the loss of her tomatoes. Violet was nowhere to be seen. For a moment, I worried that she had disappeared the same way Nina had, but then decided this wasn't likely. When Violet got upset, she usually found someplace to hide. She'd done it plenty of times before; once, we'd found her tucked away in the storage cabinets in the science pod.

We continued our search, rounding the greenhouse toward the air-lock staging area.

There was no longer a crowd around the air lock. Dr. Brahmaputra-Marquez had finally broken up Cesar and Roddy's fight and dragged them to their residence. I could hear her chewing them out angrily through their flimsy door, halfway across the base. "There is a crisis going on here," she was yelling, "and you two are behaving like a couple of nitwits!"

The only people in the staging area now were Chang and Dr. Howard. They'd finally made it back from MBB and were emerging from the air lock.

Kira threw her arms around her father and gave him a big hug. She'd put on a good face before, but it was now evident that she'd been worried about him being out on the surface so long. "You're back!" she exclaimed. "Are you okay?"

"We're fine," Dr. Howard replied, hugging her back. "It was actually quite pleasant."

"Pleasant?" Kira repeated.

"I've never had such a long walk on the surface," Dr. Howard explained.

"Did you see Violet come through here just now?" I asked.

"No," Chang replied. "But we've been busy unsuiting in the air lock. Do you know where Lars Sjoberg is?"

"In his suite, I think," I answered.

"Thanks." Chang started up the stairs to the upper level of residences. I now realized he looked just as angry as my father had about the Sjobergs earlier. His brow was furrowed and his muscles were tensed.

Mom raced out of the control room. "Chang! Hold on! We've made some progress on where Nina might be."

Chang didn't stop. "Great. Get to work on it. Meanwhile, I'm gonna get some answers out of Lars."

"About what?" Mom asked.

"Everything," Chang said. "Between his kids messing with our computers and this video they released, they're up to something. And for all we know, it connects to Nina. So I'm going to find out what it is."

"You're not going to hurt him, are you?" Mom asked.

"The idea had crossed my mind," Chang told her. "I talked to Daphne on the way back. She told me about the Sjobergs' run on the greenhouse."

Mom turned to Dad, who'd exited the control room behind her. "Stephen, stop him!"

"Why?" Dad asked. "I *want* him to beat the snot out of Lars Sjoberg."

Mom shot Dad an annoyed look.

"He told his son to beat up Dashiell!" Dad said defensively.

"The last thing we need right now is two idiots sending each other to the medical bay," Mom replied.

Chang was almost to the door of the Sjobergs' suite.

"Wait!" I yelled.

I was surprised that I'd done it—and done it loud enough

to stop Chang in his tracks. He paused right outside the door and asked, "What?"

"I think I know another way to find out what they're up to," I said.

Excerpt from *The Official Residents' Guide to Moon Base Alpha*,
"Appendix A: Potential Health and Safety Hazards,"
© 2040 by National Aeronautics and Space Administration

MENTAL DETERIORATION

While living at MBA will doubtlessly be an amazing experience, it may also have the potential to cause stress, depression, or other mental strain. Please be alert to your own mental condition—as well as that of those around you—for any signs of trouble. If you are experiencing any mental issues, please seek the aid of the moon-base psychiatrist immediately, and rest assured that any issues you report will be handled in secret with no social repercussions. Should you feel that the MBA psychiatrist is not fully able or capable of dealing with your needs, arrangements can be made to talk to additional mental specialists at NASA via ComLink.

Do not in any way neglect your mental health needs. There is no shame in admitting to having problems. The *real* shame is in ignoring them.

HYPOTHETICAL SPACE SNAKES

Lunar day 217

Midafternoon

The problem was, I couldn't really explain my plan to everyone else. There was no way to do it. All I could say was, "Just give me a chance to talk to the Sjobergs."

"And what if they tell Patton to hurt you again?" Chang asked.

"Then you can break down the door and beat the crap out of all of them," I replied. "And you'll be able to tell NASA that you were doing it to protect me."

Chang considered that, then nodded. "I can deal with that."

"Hold on," Mom said. "You're okay with the possibility that my son might get hurt?"

"I'm not going to get hurt," I told her.

"Right. Because I'll be there to protect him," Chang said.

"No," I corrected, "because Patton's not going to hurt me. I promise. Not after last time."

"What happened last time?" Mom asked.

"Dash scared Patton bad," Kira said. "He actually peed himself."

"How?" Dad asked.

"Sometimes bullies crack when you stand up to them," I replied.

Mom and Dad never came around to the plan, but there wasn't time to argue. Nina was still missing, and if the Sjobergs were connected to her disappearance, we had to find out. Finally, after Chang swore he would wait right outside the Sjobergs' door, ready to burst in at the slightest sign of trouble, my parents gave in. After all, there was still plenty of work to do in the search for Nina. They reluctantly returned to the control room to plot a new search grid with Daphne and Dr. Kim while Chang walked me to the Sjobergs' suite.

He pounded his huge fist on the door and demanded, "It's Chang. I need to talk to you."

"Go away," Lars said through the door. "We have nothing to say to you." He spoke in his normal, disdainful voice, rather than the pleasant one he'd used for his TV interview.

Chang's anger flared, but he did his best to keep it in

check. "Lars, I'm not *asking* you to open this door. I'm *ordering* you to do it as the interim moon-base commander. If you don't open it, I have the right to kick it open. I've already done it once today, so I know it's not that hard. And then you'll have a busted door on your suite that you can't shut or lock until NASA can send up repairs for it, which might be another few months."

There was an annoyed grunt on the other side of the door, followed by some whispered words in Swedish: the Sjobergs quietly discussing the situation with one another.

Chang pounded on the door again. "I'm losing patience out here! You've got five seconds and then I knock this thing off its hinges."

"All right," Lars grumbled. "Keep your pants on. I'm coming." A second later, he opened the door a crack and glared through it. "What is the meaning of this?"

Chang quickly shifted his weight into the door, knocking it open with such force that it clonked Lars in the forehead and sent him sailing backward into Sonja. I stepped into the room behind him.

I'd never been in the guest suite before. In fact, I'd never even had a glimpse of it until seeing the video of the Sjobergs that afternoon. Although it had been billed to them as a "luxury suite," it looked as crummy as every other room at MBA. It was merely larger, which actually made it seem worse somehow. The Sjobergs didn't have any more furnishings than we had, just the same cheap InflatiCubes to sit on and a SlimScreen table. In the big room, these few items seemed even smaller. Our room felt relatively cozy. Theirs felt like an empty storage locker.

The only thing that was nicer in their room was their wall-size SlimScreen. It was bigger than ours—as their wall was bigger—and was top-of-the-line. The resolution was amazing. They'd been watching a western on it, which was now paused. Three men were frozen in the midst of a gunfight. It felt as though we were right in the Wild West with them.

Lars, Sonja, and Lily were all staring at us angrily. Lars now had a red welt swelling on his forehead where the door had hit him. "How dare you invade our private space like this?" he spluttered.

To their side, Patton had tensed up in fear upon seeing me. Even though it had been a few hours since Zan had scared him, he still appeared disheveled and on edge.

Which was what I'd been hoping for. I turned to Chang. "I'll be okay."

He glanced at me skeptically. "You sure?"

"Yeah."

"What is going on here?" Lars demanded, then jabbed a thick finger at me. "What's he doing here?"

"Dash has to ask you guys a few questions," Chang told him. "Treat him well, okay? If you don't, I'll have to come back and teach you to play nice." With that, he slipped back out the door and closed it behind him.

The angry look on Lars Sjoberg's face suddenly turned evil. Now that Chang had left me alone with him, he looked like a cat who'd been given a mouse to play with. "You little fool," he told me. "You have made a terrible mistake coming here."

"You shouldn't threaten me," I told him, then turned to Patton. "Remember what happened when *you* threatened me today?"

Patton quivered at the memory of the alien beast he'd seen and gave a little whimper.

"Well, I can make that thing come back," I said. "It's my friend. . . ."

"That's not true," Patton said weakly, like he was trying to convince himself.

"Why do you think it showed up when it did?" I asked. "Why do you think it attacked *you* and not me? It protects me when I'm in danger. So if any of you cause any trouble for me now, all I have to do is call to it. . . ."

"No!" Patton screamed. He turned to his father, his eyes wide with fear. "Don't threaten him! Do whatever he says!"

Lars shot an annoyed glance at his son. "Patton, there was no space snake! You imagined it!"

"I didn't!" Patton screamed back. "I saw it! I swear! It was right in front of my face!"

"Then where is the hole you said it came out of?" Lars demanded. "I didn't see one! This little jerk is toying with you!"

Rather than deal with Lars anymore, I looked directly at Patton and asked, "Why are you all lying to the news about how much you like MBA?"

Patton started to answer, but before he could, Sonja shouted something at him angrily in Swedish. It sounded like a threat.

Patton clamped his mouth shut.

"Come on," I told him. "Don't make me summon the space snake."

Patton looked to his parents, then to me. He seemed to be trying to figure out which was worse to deal with, angry Sjobergs or a bloodsucking alien serpent.

Sonja kept threatening him in Swedish.

So I stepped up my game as well. "Okay," I sighed. "But when you're being eaten alive, don't say I didn't warn you." I cupped my hands over my mouth as if about to call out.

Patton cracked. "No! I'll talk! Dad and Mom secretly invested in a space travel company!"

"Patton!" his father roared. "Shut your mouth!"

Patton cringed in fear and fell silent again.

But he'd already said enough. The Sjobergs' behavior suddenly made complete sense. "So that's what this is all about?" I asked. "You're trying to make the moon sound great to trick other rich people into coming to visit?"

Lars wheeled on me. "Get out of our room! Right now!"

He was a terrifying man, but I stood my ground anyhow. If I backed out now, Patton might realize I was bluffing, and then I'd never get him to speak again. "What company did you invest in?" I asked Patton.

Sonja's barrage of Swedish threats increased.

So I leveled a threat of my own. "You should know something about that space snake you saw, Patton. It was only a baby. There are others here that are much, much bigger. There's a whole nest of them right under the base. I think I'll summon one of the adults this time. Or maybe two . . ."

"Maximum Adventure Travel!" Patton squawked. "That's the company! Please don't call the snakes on me!"

"That's enough!" Lars bellowed.

"I didn't want anything to do with any of this!" Patton blurted, then pointed at his father. "It was all his idea! If you want to sic the snake on anybody, it should be him!"

"Patton!" his mother gasped.

Patton ignored her and kept pleading his case. "He made us come up here in the first place. He made us sabotage the robots the other night. . . ."

"Why?" I asked.

"To slow construction of Moon Base Beta. He developed the program to mess up the robots and forced us to install it on the base computer. . . ."

"And that's what Roddy caught you doing?" I asked.

"Yes."

"Shut up!" Lily yelled at her brother. "You idiot! You'll ruin everything!"

Patton screamed back at her. "I'm not about to get eaten by some freaking snake-monster to protect Dad's scheme!"

"And how does Nina fit into this?" I asked. "What did you do to her?"

Patton gave me a startled look. "Nothing! We didn't touch her! All we did was mess with the robots!"

"She didn't find out what you were up to?" I asked.

"No!" Patton cried. "We never heard a thing from her! We didn't have anything to do with her disappearance, I swear!"

Given his fear of being eaten alive, his answer seemed genuine. Since he was spilling his guts about everything else, it didn't make sense that he'd lie about Nina.

Lars suddenly sprang at me. I tried to scramble back toward the door, but it was too late. Lars caught me by both arms, pinioning them to my sides, then shook me roughly and screamed in my face. "You had better keep your mouth shut about everything you have heard here!"

"No, Father!" Patton yelled. "Don't hurt him!"

I recoiled from Lars's rancid breath, then screamed, "Help!"

"Now you've done it!" Patton wailed in fear. "He's calling the snakes! We're all going to die!" A big wet spot bloomed once again in his pants.

I wasn't calling for Zan, though. I was calling for the backup I *knew* would be there.

The door tore off its hinges as Chang kicked it open. He took one look at Lars and ordered, "Let Dash go."

Lars didn't. Either he was too angry at me to pay attention, or he didn't hear Chang over the screams of the other Sjobergs. Instead he kept threatening me. "If you disobey me, I will make life very difficult for you! You and your whole family!"

"I warned you," Chang said, and then punched Lars in the face. Lars sailed across the room and bowled over his entire family, who ended up sprawled in a pile on the floor.

Chang turned his attention to me. "You okay?"

I nodded. My arms hurt from Lars grabbing them so tightly, but other than that, I was fine.

Lars was much worse. His lips were both split from Chang's punch and blood was flowing from them. "You fool!" he yelled. "You have just made the worst mistake of your life! I'll have you fired for this!"

"You were hurting a child," Chang said calmly. "Then I warned you to stop and you didn't. Therefore, my use of force on you was appropriate."

"I will destroy you!" Lars raged. "I can ruin your life, even from up here on the moon!"

"Stop it!" Patton told his father. "If you keep threatening them, they're going to call the snake!"

"No," I said. "Not this time. But you'd better keep your distance from me and all the other kids here from now on. If you bully any of us again—or even think about it—all I have to do is whistle and you'll be snake chow."

Patton whimpered. "I'll be good. I promise."

"There is no space snake!" Lars roared at him. "Stop being such an idiot!"

"If you keep treating your kids like that," I said, "I'll sic it on *you*."

Lars stopped yelling and looked at me. There was a hint of fear in his gaze, as though despite his arguments, some part of him was afraid the snake really did exist and might come for him.

I walked out of the room with Chang behind me. There were probably more questions I could have asked the Sjobergs about their involvement with Maximum Adventure, but I had enough to piece together a lot of the story.

And I'd had more than enough of the Sjobergs for one day.

"What's all this about a space snake?" Chang asked, once we were on the catwalk outside their room.

"It's just a bloodthirsty alien creature I made up to keep Patton in line."

"Nice work." Chang gave me a pat on the back, then sighed.

"What's wrong?"

"I was sure they were connected to Nina's disappearance somehow. Now we're back to grasping at straws again."

The pride I'd felt about outwitting the Sjobergs vanished. Chang was right. Nina was still missing—and we weren't any closer to figuring out where she was.

Excerpt from *The Official Residents' Guide to Moon Base Alpha*,
"Appendix A: Potential Health and Safety Hazards,"
© 2040 by National Aeronautics and Space Administration

PERSONAL HEALTH

Despite the fact that MBA is a sterile environment, there are still ways for you to get sick, so take whatever steps you can to provide for your own personal health—and that of your fellow lunarnauts:

- Clean your hands with sterilizing solution after using the bathroom or doing any other activity in which they may have been contaminated.
- Get plenty of sleep.
- Brush your teeth three times a day and floss as well.
- Report to the medical bay as soon as you feel ill, and if you are sick, please do your best to quarantine yourself away from the other lunarnauts. Unchecked sickness can spread very rapidly in an enclosed habitat such as ours.

IMAGINARY FRIENDS

Lunar day 217

Late afternoon

My parents went back out onto the surface again.
So did most of the other adults. Once Dr. Kim mapped out
the possible locations that Nina might have gone to find
armalcolite, they decided to fan out to hit all of them as
quickly as possible. Daphne's robots moved much slower
than humans could, and we were running out of time. I
think everyone suspected this might be a wild-goose chase,
but they all still felt like they had to do *something*, and searching the base for the three-hundredth time wasn't particularly
useful. Nina obviously wasn't there, so she had to be somewhere out on the surface.

This time, Chang was the only adult who stayed behind. Chang was annoyed by this, but even he realized that he needed to be around to make sure the Sjobergs didn't revolt again. "Now that you've provoked them," Mom had warned, "who knows what they'll do if we're all gone?"

"Probably eat our entire stash of chocolate bars," Dad suggested.

I was really worried about everyone going back out, but my parents did their best to reassure me that their helmets were now in perfect shape. Plus, NASA had pinpointed the location of the cloud of space junk that had rained down before and assured us it was too far away to be a problem again. So I had no choice but to let my folks go and hope for the best.

I spent the first few minutes with Chang in the control room, keeping tabs on my parents, but this turned out to be more nerve-racking than I'd expected. Their progress in the rover was agonizingly slow and I kept imagining incoming showers of space junk. Meanwhile, Chang had his hands full talking to the Johnson Space Center, asking them to look into the Sjobergs' connection to Maximum Adventure, updating them on the search for Nina, and listing what the rain of space junk had ruined so that repairs could be initiated. So I returned to my family's residence, looking for a quiet place to think.

Instead I found Zan.

She appeared to me the moment I walked through the door.

"Hey!" I said, locking it behind me. "Thanks for helping me out with Patton today."

Zan frowned. "I'll never be able to do something like that again."

"I don't think you'll have to. Patton's *still* terrified. I convinced him I can summon that snake thing whenever I want."

I'd been hoping Zan might find this amusing, but she seemed saddened by it instead. "My behavior in that instance was wrong."

"No, *his* behavior was wrong," I pointed out. "He was trying to beat me up! You saved me!"

"Even so, it violated so many rules. . . . Many of my fellow beings were not pleased."

"How did they even know you did it?" I asked. "Can they see us?"

"It's difficult to explain. But . . . there were some on my planet who felt I shouldn't be allowed to come back."

"No!" I exclaimed.

Zan smiled, seeming touched by my response. "They didn't prevail, obviously. I'm here. But I must be very careful from now on. I take it from your mental state that this has been a very difficult day."

"I'll say. Kira and I almost died in a meteoroid shower."

Now it was Zan's turn to look worried. "You went out on the surface again?"

"It was an emergency." I filled Zan in quickly on what had happened.

She listened intently to my whole story, then asked, "So everyone has gone back onto the surface to look for Nina once more?"

"Yes. They didn't get to finish the search before, with the helmets being damaged and all. . . ."

"Even so, given what I know about your species, it seems as though it would be dangerous for Nina to range very far from the base."

"It is, but she's obviously not close by."

"That may not be the case."

"Yes, it is. We've looked everywhere."

"Perhaps not."

"We *have*," I snapped. "Unless she shrank herself— which isn't possible—there's nowhere else on this base she could be!"

"Please don't get upset with me, Dashiell. I'm only trying to help."

"Well, you're not doing a very good job of it."

Zan didn't say anything for a while. Then she asked, "Why are you upset with me?"

I turned away from her, annoyed at myself for how I'd spoken to her. "I'm not. I'm upset with everything else. Nina and the Sjobergs and nearly dying because of some stupid space junk . . ."

"No, Dashiell, you're also upset with me. Remember, I'm connected to your mind. I can sense your emotions."

I realized she was right. It was disconcerting to be talking to someone who could figure out what I was feeling better than I could myself. "I guess I'm just frustrated."

"Why?"

"Because you're from this super-advanced alien race and you can't even help me. You can beam your thoughts all the way across the galaxy but you can't figure out where Nina is? You can read my emotions but you can't warn me that satellite debris is about to rain down on the moon?"

"I can't predict the future."

"Well, what *can* you do? Because all you ever seem to do is ask me questions! You don't tell me about you, or your planet, or what kind of danger humans are in. . . ."

"I never said humanity was in danger."

"But we are, aren't we? That's the whole point of this, right?"

Zan hesitated, trying to figure out how to respond. "Not exactly."

"What's going to happen?" I demanded. "Is there a giant

asteroid heading toward earth? Is the sun about to explode? Are we all going to blow ourselves up?"

"None of those things are going to happen," Zan said, so calmly that it was maddening.

"Then what is?!" I shouted. "You tell me it's incredibly important that we stay in contact, but you won't tell me why—and then you wonder why I'm frustrated with you? Do you have any idea what this is like?"

Zan locked eyes with me, and for a moment, it was almost as though I could feel her inside my head. "It appears to be very stressful for you," Zan said. "More than I realized. I am sorry, Dashiell. I wish I could be more help where Nina is concerned, but I'm not that powerful. However, you are correct that I need to be more open with you. And I will be."

"Starting when?"

Zan considered this thoughtfully. "Soon."

"How soon?"

"Who are you talking to?" Violet asked.

I spun around to find my sister poking her head out of her sleep pod behind me.

I mentally cursed myself for being careless. I hadn't checked the sleep pods to see if I was alone in the room when I'd come in—and in my frustration, I'd forgotten not to speak out loud during my conversation with Zan.

Zan seemed equally startled. Her blue eyes grew wide with concern.

"I'm not talking to anyone," I said quickly. "Just myself."

"Liar, liar, pants on fire," Violet taunted.

"I should go," Zan told me.

"Wait!" I told her. I was so flustered, I spoke out loud once more.

"There!" Violet cried. "You did it again!"

"I won't be gone long this time," Zan said. "I promise. But right now I'm a complication you don't need."

With that, she vanished.

I turned my full attention to Violet, feeling even more frustrated now. She was climbing out of her sleep pod. Her hair looked like she'd been asleep for a while; it was tousled like cotton candy. But she seemed too chipper to have woken up only a minute or two before. I wondered how much of my conversation she'd heard.

She looked around the room, searching for whoever I'd been talking to. "Where are they?" she asked.

"What were you doing in here?" I shot back, trying to change the subject.

"Hiding from you. You were mean to me before, so I came in here because I didn't want anyone to find me. But then I fell asleep. And then you came in and woke me up with your shouting." Violet picked up an InflatiCube and looked under it, as if maybe I'd been talking to a very tiny person who could hide under it. Or a hyperintelligent insect. "Where'd they go?"

"How long were you listening to me after you woke up?" I asked.

"I don't know," Violet replied. "I can't tell time. And besides, I don't even have a watch."

"Well, guess."

Violet screwed up her face in thought. "Four hours."

"You're right," I sighed. "You can't tell time."

Violet stared at me thoughtfully. "Do you have an imaginary friend?"

My gut reaction was to deny this, because it was dumb for a twelve-year-old to have an imaginary friend. But then I realized I didn't have a better explanation. "Yes. I do. I was just talking to her."

"What's her name?"

"Zan Perfonic."

Violet snorted with laughter. "That's silly."

I shrugged. "That's her name."

"Not her name! It's silly that you have an imaginary friend! You're twelve!"

"There aren't that many other kids here to hang out with."

"It's still silly. Having imaginary friends is weird."

"*You* have an imaginary friend!" I exclaimed.

Violet looked at me curiously. "No, I don't."

"Yes, you do. You were talking about her this morning!" I tried to remember the name. "DooDah? The talking manatee?"

"DeeDah," Violet corrected, like I was the crazy one. "She's a space walrus. And she's not imaginary."

I rolled my eyes. "You think there's really a space walrus living in the women's bathroom here?" I turned toward the door, done with this conversation. "And you say *I'm* silly. . . ."

"I don't really know what she is," Violet told me. "I haven't seen her. But I heard her and she *sounds* like a walrus."

I stopped by the door and spun around to face Violet again. "What do you mean, you heard her?"

"I was in the bathroom and I heard a walrus."

"When?"

"This morning. I got up early because I had to poop and when I was in the bathroom I heard her."

"Have you ever heard DeeDah before?"

"Nope. This was the first time."

I had a sudden flash of inspiration. Some things that had baffled me all day were starting to make sense. I grabbed Violet's hand and led her out the door. "What did she sound like?"

"I told you! A walrus! Where are we going?"

"To the bathroom."

"Why? Do *you* have to poop?"

"I want you to show me where you were when you heard DeeDah."

"You can't go into the girls' room! You're a boy!"

I led Violet down the staircase into the staging area. "Violet, I need you to think about this. Tell me exactly what you heard in the bathroom. Can you make the noise the walrus did?"

"I think so. It kind of went like this." Violet lowered her voice as low as she could and bellowed, "Mmmmmeeeelllllllppppp."

We were passing the control room. Chang was at the computer, keeping tabs on everyone outside. He laughed at Violet's noise and said, "What are you up to now?"

"Dash wants to go into the girls' room to talk to DeeDah!" Violet exclaimed.

Chang laughed again, not taking her seriously.

It occurred to me that this was everyone's standard reaction to things Violet said.

I shoved through the door into the girls' bathroom and led Violet inside. I probably should have sent Violet inside first to see if anyone was using it, but I was too distracted. "Was that the only noise you heard DeeDah make?" I asked.

"No," Violet said.

"Hey!" a voice shouted from one of the toilet stalls. Just my luck, it was Lily Sjoberg. "Boys aren't allowed in here!"

"That's what I told him!" Violet reported,

"It's an emergency," I explained.

"Then use the men's room!" Lily shouted. "I don't want you stinking everything up in here!"

"Calm down," I told her. "It's not that kind of emergency." Then I looked at Violet and asked, "What else did DeeDah do?"

"Well, she made the noise a lot. Mmmmeeeeeellll-llppppppp. Mmmmmeeeeeellllllppppp. And so I said, 'Who is this?' and she said, 'DeeDah.'"

"This doesn't sound like an emergency!" Lily shouted from the stall. "Get out of the girls' room, you pervert!"

"Can you just give me one minute?" I asked. "It's important."

"No!" Lily shouted back. "I don't want you lurking around in here listening to me on the toilet."

"Lily," I said, "believe me, the last thing in the world I want to do is to listen to you on the toilet."

"Me too," Violet agreed. "You toot like an elephant."

"That does it!" Lily announced. "If you don't get out of here right now, I'm going to scream!"

I lost it. I could have stepped out of the bathroom and let Lily have her peace, but it *was* an emergency. I was doing something important, and I'd had it with the Sjobergs bullying everyone on the moon base every chance they got. "No," I warned. "You're going to keep your mouth shut. If you so much as make another peep in there, I'm going to take one of the suction hoses from that toilet and cram it onto your face so hard that it sucks your brain out through your nose!"

To my surprise, I sounded pretty scary. Maybe it was because we were in the bathroom and my voice was echoing a lot. Maybe it was because I was so angry, I really *was* scary.

When Lily spoke again, she sounded pretty frightened. "You wouldn't."

"Don't test me," I growled. "It wouldn't be that hard. Your brain isn't that big. So just shut up for one minute and I'll be out of here."

"Okay," Lily said meekly.

I returned my attention to Violet once again. She was smiling at me. "Wow," she said. "You're tough."

"Where did the voice you heard come from?" I asked her.

"From the toilet," Violet said.

"Really?" I asked. "Think hard."

Violet did. She made a show of it, scrunching up her face. "It was the toilet," she said definitively.

"Show me," I said.

Violet entered the second stall and sat on the toilet there. "I was actually on *that* toilet," she informed me, pointing to the first one, "but we can't use it because Lily's pooping there."

Lily make a weak sigh in response.

"But I was sitting like this when I heard the noise, and it came from right down there." Violet pointed into the toilet bowl.

I looked at her finger, jabbing downward. "You're sure? Could it have maybe come from *under* the toilet?"

Violet scrunched up her face again. "Maybe."

"Like, from under the floor?"

"I guess."

I knelt before Violet, looking right into her eyes. "Is it possible that you might not have heard this walrus perfectly? Because she was under the floor. Do you think that maybe instead of saying 'DeeDah,' she said 'Nina'?"

Violet's mouth dropped open in understanding, which was all the answer I needed. Then she grew defensive. "It *sounded* like 'DeeDah'! And it was really hard to hear her!"

"It's okay," I said. "You're not in trouble. In fact, you may have saved the day."

Violet brightened in excitement. "Really? I'm a hero?"

"You're a hero," I agreed. "It's the rest of us who screwed up." I led her back out of the stall, racing out the door. "Thanks, Lily. We're done."

"You can go back to pooping now!" Violet informed her.

I dragged Violet right across the hall and into the control room and told Chang, "I think I know where Nina is."

Excerpt from *The Official Residents' Guide to Moon Base Alpha*,
"Appendix A: Potential Health and Safety Hazards,"
© 2040 by National Aeronautics and Space Administration

WORK AREAS

Sometimes, it may be easy to forget that MBA isn't merely a living space; it is also a working science laboratory. As such, there are many potentially dangerous items within its walls: flammable, poisonous, or unstable chemicals; potentially infectious organisms; lasers; etc. Even the telescopes can be dangerous if caution is not exercised around them. And other workspaces may have their dangers as well. To that end, all lunarnauts ought to stay clear of each other's workspaces— and everyone should take steps to ensure that their work remains at their workspace and doesn't end up in the living areas. If you encounter something that you believe belongs in one of the workstations, don't touch it. Find the proper expert and report it to them so that they, or someone else suitably trained, can handle said object.

BIG REVELATION

Lunar day 217

Late afternoon

Chang immediately stopped what he was doing and looked to me expectantly.

"Where?" he asked.

"Under the girls' bathroom!" Violet announced.

Chang frowned. "Violet, this is no time for jokes."

"She's not joking," I said. "I think she talked to Nina in there this morning. Only she didn't realize who it was."

"I thought it was a walrus in the toilet," Violet explained.

Chang looked at her quizzically. "Why would there be a walrus in the toilet in the moon base?"

"Because there's water in the toilet," Violet told him. "And walruses like the water. Duh."

"Violet heard Nina calling for help," I said. "But it was probably hard to hear her down through the floor, so it didn't sound like 'help.'"

"It sounded like 'Mmmmmmeeeeeelllllllpppppp,'" Violet added.

"And then Violet asked who it was and she said, 'Nina,'" I continued. "Only Violet misunderstood and thought she said, 'DeeDah.'"

"And then I told her who *I* was," Violet said. "And she said to tell someone she was down there."

"So why didn't you?" Chang asked.

"I *did*," Violet said pointedly. "I told lots of people there was a walrus in the bathroom. Mom and Dad and Dr. Marquez and Dr. Janke and Dr. Balnikov and Inez and Roddy." She gave me a hard stare. "I even told *you*."

"You did," I admitted, then looked to Chang. "None of us took her seriously."

"Oh," Chang said. "But how could she be under the bathroom? I've checked the blueprints a dozen times. There's nothing under the floors here. The base sits directly on the lunar surface."

"But what's under the lunar surface?" I asked.

Chang gave me a curious look. "What do you mean?"

"The blueprints only show the base itself," I explained. "They don't show what it was built on. Back when we were in the operations pod for Moon Base Beta, Mom told me that they had a similar pod for the construction of *this* base. Well, where was it?"

Chang's mouth fell open. "Oh my God," he gasped. He immediately turned to the computer screen and demanded, "Computer, do we have an image of the lunar surface here *before* MBA was built?"

"Certainly," the computer replied. "Loading it now."

A high-resolution satellite photo of the lunar surface appeared on the screen, huge swaths of gray dust marked by occasional islands of dark rock.

"Now mark the outline of where MBA is located," Chang ordered.

"It would be my pleasure," the computer said. The connected octagons of MBA appeared on the photo. At the top of the larger one, directly below where the bathrooms and the air-lock staging area were, there was a long streak of dark rock.

"Is that a lava tube?" I asked.

"It's *the* lava tube," Chang corrected. "The one where the operations pod was." He snapped to his feet and hurried out of the control room, making a beeline for the girls' room.

Violet and I followed him.

"If I recall correctly, this wasn't originally the planned site for MBA," Chang explained. "I wasn't involved at that point, so I don't know for sure, but I think it was supposed to be close by. Only once the operations team got here, they found there was some sort of problem with the original site and that it was more structurally sound to put MBA here, right above where they were living."

"So the pod itself is still down there?" I asked.

"There wouldn't be any point in removing it." Chang led us back into the girls' room.

I could still see Lily Sjoberg's ankles underneath the door of the first toilet stall.

"Hi, Lily!" Violet called. "We're back!"

"Oh no," Lily groaned.

"Are you almost done?" Violet asked. "You've been in here forever!"

I asked Chang, "Do you really think the pod's life-support systems are still working?"

"I wouldn't have expected it," Chang replied, "but they must be if Nina's down there."

"Hey!" Lily cried. "There's not supposed to be any men in the women's room! What is going on here today?"

"Sorry," Chang told her. "It's an emergency."

"Another one?" Lily grumped. "What's a girl have to do to get a little peace around here?"

"Nina!" Chang shouted at the floor. "Can you hear me? It's Chang!"

"Hi, Nina!" Violet yelled. "This is Violet! I'm here too!"

There was no response.

"Nina!" Chang yelled again. "Are you there? Please respond!"

Nothing.

"Maybe she left," Violet said.

"No," Chang said, looking worried. "There's nowhere else she could go. But whatever life-support system is down there wasn't designed to be working this long. If Nina's oxygen has run low, she might be in an unresponsive state."

"Like what?" Violet asked. "Texas?"

"Er . . . no," I explained. "Chang means that Nina might have gone to sleep."

"Oh," Violet said, seeming pleased with this answer.

I was worried, though. If Nina was running low on oxygen, she was probably unconscious. Or in a coma. Whichever one, it wasn't good.

Then suddenly, there was a noise from below us. A slow, rhythmic clanking of metal on metal. There were three clanks close together, followed by three spaced farther apart, followed by three close together again.

"Sounds like the toilet's acting up," Violet said.

"No," Chang told her happily. "That's Morse code. Three short, three long, three short. SOS! That's Nina! She's alive!" He turned back to the floor and yelled, "We hear you, Nina! Sit tight! We're coming!"

The clanking shifted and became a simple rhythm. *Bang bang bang bang bang.*

"That means she heard us," Chang reported, then led us back out of the bathroom.

"Bye-bye, Lily!" Violet called.

Once we were out the door, Chang turned to me and said, "Your suit's still in the air lock, right?"

"Yes." There had been no time to clean and remove it.

"Good," Chang said. "Get in there and suit up. I'll join you in a minute."

"Suit up for what?" I gulped.

"The rescue mission," Chang told me.

My heart began to race. It seemed as though I started sweating in an instant. "Why me?"

"Because Nina is in desperate circumstances and we need to move fast." Chang opened a storage unit and pulled out a helmet repair kit and a backup oxygen tank. "I wouldn't take you out there if I thought I didn't have to, but I have to get Nina *now*, it's too dangerous to solo, no other adults are around, and I trust you with my life. Okay?"

"Okay," I said. I wasn't in any hurry to head back outside,

but Chang's faith in me was heartening. I turned to Violet and told her, "You did good work."

"I know," she said.

"Sorry I got upset at you earlier. You were only trying to cheer me up and I was a jerk."

"You were."

"I'll be back soon," I said, hoping that was true. Then I gave her a hug and headed for the air lock.

LACK OF VIGILANCE

In the very unlikely event that something *does* go wrong at MBA, resulting in injury, problems can be compounded if other lunarnauts don't attend to the situation quickly. So be alert and vigilant at all times. Memorize the emergency drills and practice them with regularity. Familiarize yourself with basic medical procedures. And if anything strikes you as strange, unusual, or potentially dangerous, don't keep it to yourself. Report it to the moon-base commander immediately.

RACING THE CLOCK

Lunar day 217

Late afternoon

Two minutes later, I was back on the surface of the moon.

Chang had gathered the emergency equipment and rushed me through suiting up. Now we were heading clockwise around the base as quickly as we could go.

I was terrified. I feared I was going to get plugged by a falling piece of space junk, or that the patch on my space suit might fail, or that a thousand other things might go wrong.

Chang wasn't exactly being reassuring. He was so concerned about saving Nina, he wasn't very focused on me. He kept charging ahead, almost seeming to forget about me, then getting annoyed that I was slowing him down.

"Come on," he chided as we passed the rover garage. "Nina doesn't have much time."

"I'm doing my best," I told him.

"Well, we need to move faster," he said sternly. "Try to keep up."

I picked up the pace, but it was a struggle. The exertion made me use a lot more oxygen than I wanted to, which made me worried—which made me breathe even heavier, which used even more oxygen, and so on. My heart was pounding in my chest like I was running a marathon.

We rounded the science pod to the north side of the base. I had never been there before, and since there were no windows facing this direction, I'd never been able to see it. Moon Base Alpha wasn't very attractive, but this area made the rest of it look like the Garden of Eden. It was full of ugly gray machinery: the water reclamation unit, the power storage for the solar arrays, the devices that made oxygen and filtered our air, and a whole bunch of other unattractive, clanking things that did stuff I didn't understand but that probably kept all of us alive. Plus, every piece of broken machinery and unused scrap of building material had been dumped there. With no atmosphere to erode it and no wind to blow it away, it all just sat there, and would still be sitting there in ten thousand years. It was as though humans had scoured the earth for the least attractive industrial park and then rebuilt it on the moon.

A thick ridge of dark, ancient volcanic stone poked through the moon dust ahead. It ran from the solar array to underneath the moon base.

"That looks like our lava tube," Chang told me.

"It's buried," I said. "How do we get into it? How'd *Nina* get into it?"

"There, I'll bet." Chang pointed to a gap in all the machinery along the wall of the base, where a large sheet of steel lay on the ground. If we hadn't been specifically hunting for it, we might have easily overlooked it; it blended in with all the other garbage. On earth, the steel might have weighed several hundred pounds. Here, Chang lifted one end with ease.

Below it was the entrance to the lava tube.

"Looks like we found the right place," Chang said. He propped the steel sheet against the water reclamation unit.

I stared at the gap in the rock warily. It was much smaller than the entrance to the operations pod at MBB. Even though I was afraid to be out on the lunar surface, the tunnel didn't look much more inviting. It was merely a narrow, dark, jagged hole, the kind of place you could imagine dangerous things lurking inside of. I knew there weren't any such things as space snakes, but if there *were*, they would have lived in holes like this.

"Let's go," Chang ordered. "I'll lead the way."

We each had spotlights built into our helmets for getting around on the lunar surface during the long periods when the sun wasn't out. Chang flipped his on and stared into the hole. The light made it less daunting, but it was still awfully spooky.

Chang descended into the tube. He was a big guy and his suit made him even bigger, so the narrow entrance was a tight fit. He had to duck his head to get under the moon base.

"All right," he told me. "Come on down."

I flipped on my own helmet lights and edged into the hole after him. Since I was much smaller, it was easier for me to get inside, although I still took care around the jagged rocks.

We had left the sheet of steel that had concealed the hole propped against the water reclamation unit above, although there hadn't been much room between the unit and the lava tube to do this properly. I hadn't gotten far into the tube before the steel succumbed to gravity and toppled. It crashed back to the surface right above my head, making the tube even darker.

I figured the same thing must have happened when Nina had come into the tube the night before. And with the steel over it, the entrance was hidden perfectly. It made sense that the search parties that had come through earlier hadn't looked for Nina underneath a flat piece of steel on the ground. After all, Nina was a human being, not an ant. And no one had known there was a lava tube underneath the moon base.

Except Nina, apparently.

The tube descended steeply beneath the foundation of the moon base, which was three feet of solid concrete. Just below it, we came across the operations pod.

It looked almost exactly the same as the one at MBB. It was smaller and the air lock was an older model, but the basic design was the same. Chang already had the air-lock door open.

"Hurry," he told me.

I stepped inside after him. He closed the door behind us, then pressed the button to activate the repressurization.

It didn't work the way it was supposed to. The entire air lock shuddered like a balky washing machine, and then a red warning light flashed on the ceiling. I knew that at least some atmosphere had been created, because I could suddenly hear things outside my helmet, but something definitely seemed to be wrong. There was a loud, sputtering noise, like a generator struggling to provide energy.

"Warning," a pleasant computerized voice said, although it was barely a whisper, as though it was running out of power.

"Pressurization has been completed, but due to a malfunction in the oxygenation system, oxygen levels are critically low. Please exercise caution and do not mphrfllthhppp." The warning decayed into gibberish as the central computer died. The red warning lights flickered around us.

That wasn't exactly reassuring. I had to fight to keep from hyperventilating and gulping all my oxygen down at once.

"Dang it," Chang muttered. "That's not good."

This wasn't exactly reassuring either.

I checked the sensors built into the sleeve of my space suit. The carbon dioxide level around us was dangerously high, while the oxygen was barely registering.

"I guess we leave our suits on?" I asked.

"Only if you want to live," Chang replied. He pressed the red button on the side of the inner air-lock door.

Nothing happened. The door stayed locked.

"We'll have to do this manually," Chang sighed. "The pod's running out of power. It's probably shunting everything it has to the critical life-support systems." With that, he tore off the plastic covering around the air-lock door, revealing a manual release lever. "Grab on," Chang told me.

Both of us grabbed the lever and yanked it upward. It should have been easy to open, but something was wrong with this, too. It took every ounce of strength Chang and I had to swing it upright.

The inner air-lock door popped open, allowing us into the pod.

Inside, the lights had gone off to conserve power. Our headlamps fired beams through the darkness, illuminating bits and pieces. I had once scuba dived into an underwater cave off the coast of Kona with my father. I hadn't liked it very much. This looked eerily similar, but was about a thousand times scarier.

Now that we were inside, I could see this pod was significantly smaller than the one at the site for MBB. It was hard to imagine four adults being comfortable inside it for a day, let alone a few months. There was a tiny workspace, an even tinier kitchen, and four drop-down bunks at the back.

Even though it was small, I still didn't see Nina right away. But there was plenty of evidence she was there. The pod was a mess. Nina's space suit—or rather, Lily Sjoberg's— was crumpled in a wad by the wall. The helmet lay on the floor beside it. A long crack zigzagged across the visor.

The kitchen had been ransacked. Luckily for Nina, a little food had been left behind there by the original crew. Foil wrappers from emergency rations were scattered everywhere.

My immediate impression was that Nina must be in a bad state. She was normally so clean and tidy; I'd seen her flick invisible motes of dust off her clothes. She would never have left her living space in such disarray unless something was wrong.

"There!" Chang exclaimed, pointing to the rear of the pod.

I glanced the way he was looking, expecting to see something human. Instead I saw what looked like a giant foil-wrapped burrito nestled on a bunk. It took me a moment to realize it was a silver emergency blanket with Nina cocooned inside. Then it occurred to me that the heating had probably shut down in the pod. It would have been freezing without our suits on. To conserve what little heat she had, Nina had completely swaddled herself. Even her head was tucked inside the blanket.

Chang moved to the bunk. I followed him, though in my haste, I tripped over the space helmet on the floor. It spun away from me and bumped into the wall. The glass visor promptly shattered.

Apparently, Nina had made it to safety with only seconds to spare.

"Stay where you are," Chang ordered curtly. "Don't touch anything."

I froze halfway across the pod. For a moment, I was afraid there was some other danger we'd have to deal with, but then I realized why Chang wanted me to keep my distance. He was opening Nina's blanket and was worried she was dead.

Chang unfolded the blanket and I caught a glimpse of

Nina's head. Her normally perfectly gelled hair was a rat's nest, and her skin was an unhealthy grayish color. I couldn't see her face, but given the startled gasp Chang made at the sight of her, she probably didn't look good. Thank goodness he'd stopped me. If I'd been any closer, I might have puked in my space suit.

Chang leaned over Nina to examine her closely. I couldn't tell what he was doing from where I stood, but I guessed he was checking for a pulse. A few tense seconds slipped by. Then Chang gave a sigh of relief. "She's alive."

I sighed as well. "So she's okay?"

"She's not great," Chang said grimly. "I think we got here just in time. Bring me the oxygen tank."

I did as he'd ordered. The oxygen tank had a hose that was officially designed to latch onto a valve on our space suits, but there was an adapter that allowed a small clear plastic mask to be attached to it. The mask was like the emergency kind you see on airplanes, with a thin elastic strap to keep it over your head. Chang had already attached the mask to the tank, but getting the mask onto Nina's head while wearing space gloves turned out to be incredibly difficult. I ended up cradling her head while Chang fumbled with the strap.

Now I had a disturbingly close view of Nina's unconscious face. All the blood seemed to have drained from her. She looked like she'd been carved out of wood, like a ventriloquist's dummy. She didn't even flutter an eyelid while we struggled to save her.

Finally, with a triumphant cry, Chang managed to get the mask onto Nina's face and clamp the plastic part over her nose and mouth. Another few seconds ticked by.

And then, a small cloud of moisture formed inside the mask. Nina's chest rose slightly. After that, she seemed to realize—at least subconsciously—that there was suddenly much more oxygen available for her. She began to breathe regularly.

Chang heaved a huge sigh of relief. "That was close. If we'd been a few minutes later, she might have gone into a coma."

"You saved her life," I said.

"No," Chang told me. "I only brought the oxygen. You're the one who figured out where she was. *You* saved her life. Nice work, kiddo."

I smiled. Despite everything, I didn't feel scared anymore. "Thanks."

"Keep an eye on her. I'm gonna try to fix her helmet so we can get her out of here." Chang headed back across the pod to where he'd left the helmet repair kit. He picked up Lily's helmet and set about the difficult task of replacing the visor while wearing space gloves.

Something suddenly grabbed my hand.

I nearly leaped out of my space suit. I squawked in fear,

spun around—and then realized it was Nina. Her eyes were already open, although she still seemed awfully drowsy, like she was still asleep.

"Dash?" she asked. Her voice was muffled by the oxygen mask.

"Yes."

"I'm not dead?"

"No."

"That's good." Nina smiled dreamily. "I really screwed up, didn't I?"

Chang hurried back over. "Take it easy, Nina. You don't need to talk right now. You've been through a big ordeal. . . ."

"I want to talk," Nina replied. "I want to explain. . . ."

"You can do it later," Chang said.

"No. I want to do it now." Even though she was barely alive, Nina was still determined to do things her way. "You deserve to understand why I'm here. . . ."

"We know about the moon rocks you were collecting," Chang said.

Nina's eyelids lifted in surprise for a moment, then drooped again. "How?"

"Dash and Kira found them," Chang replied.

Nina's eyes flicked to me. "I should have guessed. I didn't want to take them, but I was in desperate trouble and had no other choice."

"What kind of trouble?" I asked.

Nina didn't answer. Her eyes drooped back closed. It looked as though she'd lapsed back into unconsciousness again. I felt myself tense up with concern.

"Nina?" Chang asked, worried.

"Financial trouble," Nina murmured, her eyes still closed.

I relaxed, thankful that she was still all right.

"My mother is very sick," Nina went on. It sounded like it was a struggle for her to talk, like saying each word was a strain on her, and yet she forced herself to continue. "And her insurance was canceled. I thought it had been paid, but it hadn't. . . . I needed money . . . but I didn't have many ways to get it up here."

"NASA couldn't help you?" Chang asked.

Nina shook her head very slowly. Even that slight motion seemed to be a huge effort for her. "The solutions they offered were unacceptable. . . . But then, an opportunity presented itself."

Sadly, Nina's tale of financial trouble wasn't very surprising to me. My family had experienced our own problems. It was tough to take care of things when you weren't on earth. And when you were gone for three years, unexpected problems tended to pop up. We'd been renting our house to some people, but they'd trashed the kitchen and skipped out without paying after a few months. Arranging repairs from space and dealing with all the payments had been almost impossible. When we'd been recruited, NASA had insisted that they had people who would be able to help us Moonies in cases like this. Unfortunately, those people hadn't been much help at all.

To make things worse, everyone back on earth generally assumed we were all getting rich being Moonies. After all, we were famous. But all the adults were NASA employees and had signed contracts saying they wouldn't cash in on their fame while at MBA. That meant no charging people for interviews or selling memoirs for millions of dollars. It made sense, really. NASA wanted to recruit people to the moon who were interested in the science, not in making money. But that wasn't common knowledge. Mom and Dad were pretty sure that every contractor they reached out to to fix our kitchen was jacking up the price because they thought we were loaded.

So it wasn't like someone like Nina would have a ton of money in the bank, and her options to get more would have been limited. She couldn't simply quit working at MBA and get a better-paying job. There weren't any other jobs on the moon—and Nina wasn't scheduled to return to earth for another two and a half years. I wouldn't have expected her to turn to crime, but I could understand why she had done it. And as crimes went, stealing moon rocks was awfully harmless. No one would get hurt, and frankly, the moon could use a few less rocks.

"What kind of opportunity?" Chang asked. "You mean Charlie? The one who texted you the music?"

Nina looked a tiny bit surprised that we'd figured this out, but then nodded. "Yes."

"The music was a code, right?" Chang pressed. "'Fifty Miles of Elbow Room' and a song by the Rolling Stones were an order to get fifty stones."

"That's right," Nina replied, and then started singing in her dreamy state. "'The gates are wide on the other side, where the flowers ever bloom. . . .'"

Chang interrupted her. "What's Charlie's real name?"

"I don't know," Nina said.

"Really?"

"Really. I know he works in cargo and that's it." Nina paused for a few seconds to breathe deeply. "The idea was for me to send the rocks back down on the next rocket."

"And since he's in cargo, he can unload them before anyone else notices them," Chang concluded.

"Yes," Nina said. "I got the first batch without any trouble, but then last night, he sent another message asking me to increase the shipment. . . . It should have been easy. But it wasn't. . . ." In Nina's delicate state, it seemed as though even merely speaking was taking a lot out of her.

Chang placed a hand on her shoulder, signaling he could do the talking. "Let me guess what happened. You shut down the security systems around the main air lock so you wouldn't be recorded leaving. You left your watch behind so you couldn't be tracked—and you took Lily Sjoberg's suit because all the suits have transmitters and you didn't want yours to record you'd left the base. Probably, no one would have ever checked, but if they did, you'd be in the clear."

"I thought she dismantled the transmitter," I said. "Or messed with it somehow to get it to say she was inside the base when she wasn't."

"No, the transmitter worked fine," Chang told me. "It gave us Nina's exact coordinates. We just didn't understand it. We thought it was telling us that Nina was *inside* the base. It never occurred to anyone that Nina might be *under* the base."

"Oh," I said. If I hadn't been wearing a space suit, I would have smacked my forehead.

Chang returned his attention to Nina. "Anyhow, you took Lily's suit. And most likely, you would have been out and back without anyone ever noticing. Only something was wrong with Lily's helmet. The visor was cracked."

Nina's eyes opened in surprise. "How did you know?"

"Cesar and Patton broke it," I explained. "They were wearing them to play football at night and broke a bunch of the visors."

Even in her exhausted state, Nina's eyes flashed with anger. "Those morons. I almost died because of them."

"A lot of us almost died because of them," Chang said pointedly. "While looking for *you*."

Nina bit her lip. It was as close as she'd ever come to appearing embarrassed. "I didn't mean for any of this to happen. . . . If it hadn't been for the helmet, everything would have been fine. But I didn't notice the visor was damaged until I was over here."

"You were heading to the rocks with armalcolite?" I asked.

Nina's eyes flicked to me, surprised. Then she nodded. "Yes. And then the crack appeared and my suit computer said the situation was critical. I only had a minute or two. There wasn't enough time to get back to the main air lock, but I knew the pod here was still operational. Or I hoped it was. It wasn't until I got in here that I realized all the communications gear had been removed. The radio in Lily's helmet couldn't get any reception down here and I didn't have my watch. So there was no way to contact you back in the base."

"So you tried yelling through the floor," I said.

"Yes. I yelled for hours, until I was hoarse. Violet was the only one who heard me. I asked her to get help, but she must not have passed my message along."

"She did," Chang said. "But we didn't realize what she was talking about."

Nina sighed tiredly. Admitting to all her mistakes appeared to have drained her. "I didn't have the strength to keep shouting. The oxygen system in here wasn't working properly. I had to conserve my breath. And my strength."

"Good thing you did," Chang told her. "The carbon dioxide level in here is toxic."

Nina's eyes began to flutter closed. "Now what do we do?"

"Wait for you to get your strength back," Chang answered. "I'll fix your helmet and then we'll get you back to base."

"I mean, what do we do about me?" Nina asked. "What I did is a criminal offense. I should be court-martialed."

"That's NASA's call." Chang shot me a conspiratorial glance. "And NASA won't know what happened up here unless we tell them."

"You *have* to tell them," Nina said. "As acting commander, it's your job."

"I'm not acting commander anymore," Chang replied. "You're alive."

"I don't deserve my position. . . ."

"Everybody makes mistakes," Chang said.

Nina sighed again, but seemed too tired to argue the point. Her eyelids slid closed and she drifted back to sleep again, snoring softly.

As she did, something occurred to me. Chang was right that everyone made mistakes, but Nina made them less than most people. In fact, besides getting stranded on the moon,

I couldn't think of any mistake Nina had ever made before. And frankly, Cesar, Patton, and Lily were the ones who'd really screwed up: They'd broken the helmet; Nina simply hadn't noticed. Nina was cold and robotic and she could be a real jerk, but there was always a reason for everything she did. At heart, she was doing her best to run a moon base, which wasn't easy. Given all the things that could go wrong and all the people she had to deal with, she did an amazing job most of the time. Most people probably would have screwed up one thing after another, but Nina hadn't.

So if anyone had ever wanted to catch Nina doing something wrong, they would have had to wait a very long time.

Unless they tricked her into it.

Chang was watching Nina, making sure she was all right. Then he returned his attention to repairing Lily's helmet.

"How long have you known you were the temporary second in command?" I asked.

"About four weeks, I guess. NASA made the decision shortly after Dr. Holtz died."

"And you didn't tell *anyone* at the base?"

"No. Like I said, Nina figured it was better to keep things quiet until NASA made it official."

"So you've never talked about it since?"

"No."

"Where were you when she told you the news?"

"The control room." Chang looked at me curiously. "What's all this have to do with anything?"

"Nothing," I said, though it was a lie. In fact, what Chang had told me was extremely important.

I had a very good idea who Charlie was.

Excerpt from *The Official Residents' Guide to Moon Base Alpha,*
"Appendix A: Potential Health and Safety Hazards,"
© 2040 by National Aeronautics and Space Administration

OTHER HAZARDS

This list is not intended to be comprehensive. There may be other potential hazards to life and limb that have been overlooked. It is quite likely that, even at a lunar outpost such as MBA, most injuries will not be caused by meteoroids or rocket explosions, but by the same innocuous things that cause injury on earth: tripping over objects carelessly left on the ground, banging one's head on a cabinet door, slipping and falling in the shower, etc. While the medical bay is equipped to handle these types of injuries, it is certainly better to simply try to avoid them in the first place. So please exercise caution at all times.

SECRET IDENTITY

Lunar day 217

Dinner time

It was an hour before Chang felt Nina had recov-
ered enough to get her back to the base. During that time,
Chang left me with her briefly to go to the surface and call
everyone else on his radio. He announced that we'd found
Nina and that all search parties could return to base, then
came back down to the pod and repaired Nina's helmet.
Nina slept the whole time. When we finally woke her back
up, she seemed to have completely recovered her strength. I
had expected that we'd have to help her return to the base,
but she wouldn't hear of it. She suited up and walked back
all by herself.

By the time we returned, all the other adults were back from the search. Everyone was gathered in the staging area and cheered Nina's arrival as we came through the air lock.

"Welcome home!" they all whooped.

"Congratulations on not being dead!" Roddy said.

"This calls for a celebration!" Dr. Marquez exclaimed.

"No," Nina said sharply. "There's no need for that. I haven't done anything worth celebrating. Now if you'll excuse me, I have a great amount of work to catch up on." With that, she slipped through the crowd and headed up the stairs toward her residence.

"Work?" Mom asked. "Nina, if anything, you need time to recover."

"And you should eat something," Daphne added. "I whipped up a special welcome-back dinner for you! I rehydrated all of your favorite foods!"

"That was a waste of resources," Nina told her. "I had plenty of emergency rations in the pod. Now, I'm retiring to my quarters for the night—and I'd recommend that the rest of you do the same. Due to today's events, I assume that many of you have fallen behind on your projects, so tomorrow we're all going to have a great deal of work to catch up on. Good night." With that, she slipped into her residence and shut the door behind her.

"Boy," Kira said, "talk about your party poopers."

"Yeah," Violet agreed. "She really pooped this party good."

"She's upset that we're behind schedule?" Dr. Alvarez muttered. "We're behind schedule because of *her*!"

"Maybe we should have just left her out there," someone muttered, though I didn't see who it was.

With the celebration dead, everyone began to drift back to their rooms. It had been a long, stressful day, and Nina was right that tomorrow would be busy too. I was pretty sure I was going to have extra schoolwork to catch up on.

I was still hungry, though. *I* hadn't eaten any emergency rations. In fact, I hadn't eaten much of anything since breakfast. So I took some of the food Daphne had rehydrated for Nina and scarfed it down in the mess hall. It tasted like damp cardboard, but for once, I didn't care. Mom sat with me, while Dad hustled Violet off to bed.

"Nina didn't even thank everyone for helping look for her," I said, once I'd polished off my dinner.

"I think she was embarrassed by all the attention," Mom told me. "And by the fact that she had to be rescued at all. By a twelve-year-old boy, no less."

"I guess," I agreed.

"Ready for bed?" Mom asked. "You must be exhausted."

"Actually, I feel grimy," I told her. "Do you think I could have a shower tonight?"

"Yeah, I think you've earned yourself a shower." Mom proudly tousled my hair, then grabbed my dirty plates. "I'll take care of these. See you back in the room."

That's life on the moon. The biggest reward you can get is a shower.

It wasn't even a good shower. It was merely standing under a trickle of lukewarm water. But I wasn't really sticking around to shower anyhow.

"Charlie" was still near the mess as well.

I cleaned myself off anyhow. It might have been lame compared to an earth shower, but it was better than nothing.

Then I toweled off, dressed, brushed my teeth, checked to make sure no one was inside the control room or the mess hall—and headed into the greenhouse.

I wasn't supposed to go into the greenhouse without permission. No kids were. But I figured it would be all right because Dr. Goldstein was in there.

She was leaning against a table full of potted seedlings, staring at her ruined tomato plants. She wasn't crying anymore, but she still seemed kind of sad. There was a faraway look in her eyes, and she didn't even hear me come in.

"Dr. Goldstein?" I asked.

She turned, noticed me for the first time, and started in surprise. I wondered if I looked that way every time Zan appeared to me. Then she forced a smile onto her face.

"Hello, Dashiell," she said. "What brings you in here?"

"Are you Charlie?" I asked.

Her smile faded. Then she seemed to realize this was a mistake and tried to cover. She didn't do a very good job of it. It took her a few moments to figure out what the right response might be. She finally put on her best blank look and said, "What are you talking about?"

I'd already seen enough to know I was right, though. "I won't tell anyone," I said. "I only want to know why you did it."

Dr. Goldstein simply stared at me now, seeming unsure what to do.

"Was it to get Nina demoted?" I asked. "So that Chang would become the base commander?"

Dr. Goldstein's eyes widened in surprise. She seemed to forget all about faking innocence. Or maybe she was tired from hiding what she'd done and ready to own up to it. "How did you ever figure that out?"

"Well, Chang and Nina said they were the only ones who knew that Chang was the temporary second in command. They never discussed it with anyone else, and the only place they ever talked about it was in the control room. But when I was in the control room earlier today, I realized you can hear anything in this greenhouse through the wall. So I figured if you're in here, you can probably hear everything in the control room, too. And you're in here all the time, while no one else is supposed to be."

Dr. Goldstein looked at me curiously. "And that was all the evidence you had?"

"No. I also know you had some problems with Nina. She was riding you pretty hard about how the greenhouse wasn't working. So I figured, maybe you wanted to get her out of power. . . ."

"I wasn't trying to kill her," Dr. Goldstein said quickly. "I was only trying to get her in trouble with NASA so she'd be demoted."

"I know," I told her. "Stealing moon rocks is a serious crime. Chang said it wouldn't be that hard to create a fake alias like Charlie. In fact, he said practically anyone here could do it if they put their mind to it. I checked your bio at dinner. Before you switched to horticulture, you were a computer science major."

Dr. Goldstein turned away from me, and it seemed she might start crying again. "You're right about everything. I really didn't think Nina would accept, but I figured it was still worth a try. There'd been a rumor she needed money. . . ."

"Her mother is sick," I said. "And something went wrong with the insurance."

"Oh my." Dr. Goldstein put her hand to her mouth, looking horrified. "I had no idea. I thought she'd made a bad investment or something. Her mother . . . ? Oh, what have I done?" Tears started to flow down her cheeks. "I didn't think anyone would get hurt. It seemed so simple. The first time she went out to get the rocks, I watched her to see how she'd do it, and she was only gone fifteen minutes. Last night, I figured it'd be the same, only when she came back in, I'd pretend like I was passing by and catch her in the act. Then I'd report her to NASA. But she didn't come back and I . . . I didn't know what to do. . . ." Dr. Goldstein put her face in her hands and broke down, sobbing.

That was the other piece of evidence I'd had against her. The crying. Dr. Goldstein had been distraught all day. I had assumed it was about her plants at first, but in retrospect, it seemed like an awfully extreme reaction, even after her precious tomatoes had been devoured by the Sjobergs. Instead Dr. Goldstein had been acting like she was really devastated about something—like putting someone's life in danger, maybe. And most importantly, she'd been upset that morning, *before* anyone else had discovered Nina was missing. The way I figured, she'd known something had gone wrong and was very upset that she'd caused it, but didn't know what to do without revealing her involvement. Thus all the tears. Only it didn't seem like the best time to bring all that up.

Instead I said, "It wasn't your fault. Cesar and Patton are the ones who broke the helmets. . . ."

"But I made her go out there," Dr. Goldstein cried.

"No, you didn't. She went by herself."

"Because I promised her money. Money I wasn't ever going to deliver. Money she needed for her sick mother. And then, when I realized something was wrong, I didn't alert anyone because I didn't want to get in trouble." Dr. Goldstein pulled a handkerchief from her pocket and blew her nose loudly. "Oh, I'm such a horrible person!"

I hadn't expected this to happen, so I wasn't quite sure what to do, except to say, "No, you're not."

"If I'd only busted her the first time she went out, this never would have happened," Dr. Goldstein sobbed.

"Why didn't you?"

"Because I thought Nina might be able to talk her way out of it. She'd claim she was gathering rocks for scientific reasons or something. But if I could prove she'd done it twice . . . show that she'd already stashed some moon rocks in her room . . . then the evidence would be stacked against her." Dr. Goldstein blew her nose again and started blubbering into her hankie.

"Oh." I didn't know what else to say. I'd never had an adult cry like this in front of me before.

Dr. Goldstein seemed to be getting embarrassed about it herself. She did her best to control her crying and looked at me with red-rimmed eyes. "I know, I'm a wreck," she admitted. "I've been a wreck all day. Nina isn't the only one who nearly died because of what I did. You and Kira nearly got killed looking for her. And so many other people ended up in danger. I never expected things to spiral out of control like this. If I had, I never would have done it."

"I know."

"I'd just had it with Nina. She didn't seem to have any idea how hard this all was." Dr. Goldstein waved an arm around the greenhouse. "She acted like growing plants on the moon should have been *easy*. Like all I'd have to do was stick them in the dirt and water them. But it's not easy at all. In fact, it was far more difficult than anyone had realized, and I was doing my best, but she was still treating me like I was a failure. Like the plants weren't growing because I was slacking off. And even when I *did* finally get some things to grow, that still wasn't good enough for her." The sadness had vanished and anger now flared in Dr. Goldstein's eyes. "She kept riding me and riding me. Insulting my intelligence. Implying it had been a mistake to bring me up here. And I thought, Chang *had* to be a better leader than her. Plus, he's a scientist like me. He'd understand what I was going through. That things don't always work out the way everyone predicts they will. I tried to find another way to get rid of Nina. I filed complaints with her superiors. And you know what happened?"

"They ignored them?" I guessed.

"Worse. They chastised me for insubordination, rather than getting on Nina's case. And then they told Nina about it and she got upset and started treating me even worse. So I'd had it. I figured something had to be done. So I created Charlie and reached out to Nina and she actually accepted. At first, it worked out better than I could have imagined. And then . . . it didn't. I'm so sorry."

"It's okay," I said, and I meant it. Even though Dr. Goldstein was right—my life had been put in danger because of her—I didn't feel angry at her. In fact, I understood exactly why she'd done the things she'd done. Frankly, I had my own issues with Nina and wouldn't have minded Chang running MBA instead. And everything that had gone wrong that day hadn't really been solely Dr. Goldstein's fault. Cesar Marquez and the Sjobergs had also been responsible.

Now the anger faded from Dr. Goldstein's eyes and a kind of resolve set in. Like she had made an important decision. "Thank you for coming to me this way, Dashiell. For giving me the chance to explain myself, rather than going right to Nina or Chang. It was very . . . helpful."

"Sure."

"I think I'm going to have to turn myself in, though. Admit to NASA what I've done and suffer the consequences."

"I think Nina's going to do the same thing," I said.

Dr. Goldstein nodded. "Sounds like Nina. Always following the rules."

"Well," I said. "Not *always*."

Dr. Goldstein laughed, then seemed surprised she'd done it. "It's not like NASA can fire me anyway," she said. "There's no other horticulturalist for a quarter million miles." She started toward the door, then paused by one of the denuded strawberry plants. "Those lousy Sjobergs," she muttered. "As if this day hadn't been terrible enough."

As if on cue, the shouts of Lars Sjoberg rang through the base. As usual, he sounded angry and abusive.

Dr. Goldstein and I hurried out of the greenhouse to see what was happening.

We weren't the only ones alerted by the commotion. Everyone else was flooding out of their rooms as well.

Nina and Chang stood on the catwalk outside the Sjobergs' door. Despite the tirade of insults Lars was hurling, Nina remained perfectly cool and calm. Despite everything she had been through that day, she already seemed back to her old self.

"I have been brought up to speed on your behavior of the past few days," she was saying. "In light of the fact that you have secretly invested in a rival space tourism business, sabotaged our robotics systems, and stolen food that was communal property, NASA has decided to revoke your

ComLink privileges. All your access to the Link is hereby canceled."

"You can't do that!" Lars roared. "I have paid a great sum of money for those privileges."

"And you abused them," Nina pointed out. "Therefore, to prevent any more abuse, you will be allowed no further contact with anyone on earth for the remainder of your stay here."

"What?" the rest of the Sjobergs gasped. Then they all started arguing at once how horrible their lives there would be without access to television, Internet, and friends.

"You ought to count your blessings," Nina said. "You're getting off easy. If I could, I'd lock every one of you up in this room for the next two months with nothing but dehydrated food and a bucket to poop in. But NASA rejected that. They will, however, be filing charges against you all for collusion with Maximum Adventure and for sabotage of federal property."

"You're making a big mistake," Sonja threatened. "Start trouble with us now, and when we get back to earth, we will ruin this place. We'll launch a smear campaign to say such terrible things about it that even your own astronauts won't want to come here."

"NASA has already released details of the crimes you have committed to the press," Nina stated. "They'll be sharing further details of your misbehavior here in the days to come. Your eating all our fresh food today, for example. By the time you get back to earth, the entire planet will know you as the liars, cheats, and thieves that you really are. So anything you say about this base will be suspect."

Sonja recoiled as though Nina had slapped her, horrified by the idea of anything happening to her precious image. The rest of the family seemed equally upset.

"You can't treat us this way!" Lars bellowed.

"Yes, we can," Nina said. "It's in your contract with us." She started to leave, then turned back and said, "Oh, and one more thing. I may not be able to lock you up, but I *can* institute stricter controls over you. If you, or any of your family members, try to retaliate with physical aggression against anyone on this base, I have given Chang here full authority to beat you senseless. Is that understood?"

Lars actually fell silent for a moment. Then he growled, "This is a terrible mistake you are making. Do you have any idea who you're dealing with here?"

"Yeah," Chang said. "You're the four biggest jerks in the universe."

With that, he and Nina turned away and walked down the catwalk. Lars started screaming again, issuing threats and curses, but everyone simply ignored him and returned to their rooms, letting him know they weren't afraid of him anymore.

Which was probably the most devastating thing we could have ever done to Lars Sjoberg.

"My, my," Dr. Goldstein said. She was actually smiling now, looking happier than I'd seen her in weeks. "I guess one good thing has come out of this day after all."

ONE LAST THING

The greatest key to your safety at MBA is . . . you! A careful and alert lunarnaut is a safe lunarnaut. So take great care to keep yourself—and others—safe and secure. Watch where you're walking. Take care on the stairs. Don't leave things lying where other people can stumble over them. Don't exit the air lock until you are absolutely sure it has pressurized. Make sure your space suit is on properly before heading out onto the lunar surface. Don't leave flammable or explosive substances out in the open. In short, exercise good old-fashioned common sense. Let's keep MBA as safe and injury-free as possible!

THE ASTEROID

Lunar day 218
Well after bedtime

"Hello, Dashiell," Zan said.

I pried my eyes open to find her peering into my sleep pod. Or at least, projecting the image of herself doing that into my brain.

I checked my watch. It was midnight. But even though Zan was waking me from much-needed sleep, I found myself happy to see her. "Hi," I replied, reminding myself to keep the conversation in my head. My family was asleep in their pods around me.

My watch also indicated I'd received a great number of text messages since I'd last checked it. Most of them were from Riley, wanting to know what I'd thought of the Sjobergs' video. With all the excitement, I'd forgotten to text her that I'd seen it.

"I'm sorry to disturb you like this," Zan said.

"It's all right." Although I could have remained in my pod, talking to Zan in my head, it seemed weird to have a conversation that way. So I kicked my covers aside and slipped out into the room.

"It's not all right," Zan countered. "You had an extremely stressful day—partly due to my behavior."

I gave her a confused look. "You didn't stress me out. If anything, you helped. You let me know Nina was still alive—and then you saved me from Patton. In fact, you scared him so badly, I don't think he's going to be bullying anyone anymore."

"I'm glad I could be of help. But as you pointed out, my behavior has also been frustrating. There are some things I've kept secret that have been bothering you."

I paused in the middle of pulling on a T-shirt. "Well, yes . . ."

"I'd like to tell you the truth."

"Right now?"

"Yes."

I glanced around the residence. My family was sound asleep, but I still didn't feel like having such an important conversation in the room with them. If I got excited and started talking out loud again, they'd wake up and think I was losing my mind. I'd already dodged a bullet with Violet once that day. "Can we go somewhere else to talk? Somewhere private?"

"Sure. As long as it isn't the bathrooms."

"I was thinking of the medical bay. No one's in there right now."

"Fine."

I headed for the door, taking care not to wake my family. My parents, who'd had an extremely long day themselves, were out cold. Violet was shifting around in the midst of what seemed to be a very vivid dream. "Wow," she murmured in her sleep. "That's a big penguin!"

I opened the door and peeked into the hall. No one was about. Zan and I slipped out onto the catwalk, passing Nina's room on the way to the stairs.

Despite the late hour, not everyone was sleeping. In the stillness of the base, I could hear a few voices coming through the doors of the residences.

Kira and her father were the easiest to hear. They were both laughing a lot. It sounded like they were playing a game, and Kira was creaming her father, but he was taking it in stride. I wondered if they did this often at night, if this was when he engaged with her, rather than during the day, when there were too many other things to distract him.

Nina was also awake. It sounded as though she was filing a report with NASA. "I believe, as the MBC of Moon Base Alpha, it is my duty to be completely open about the events of lunar day 217 and my role in them . . . ," she said flatly, sounding as robotic as usual.

Voices also came from the residence of Dr. Goldstein and Dr. Iwanyi. They were having a hushed but intense discussion, trying not to wake Kamoze.

"There's no point in turning yourself in," Dr. Iwanyi was saying. "Ultimately, no one got hurt. Nothing that happened was really your fault."

"I still did something wrong," Dr. Goldstein was saying. "At the very least, I led Nina to believe I could help her with her mother, and that's not going to happen."

"Well, maybe there's a way we can fix that," Dr. Iwanyi said. "We have plenty of connections in the medical community back on earth. I'm sure something can be done. . . ."

Roddy was up too. He was in the rec room with his hologoggles on. It appeared he'd reached the finale of Romeo and Juliet; he was now kissing the virtual heroine again. Evidently, the game ended much more happily than the actual play. "Oh, Juliet," Roddy sighed to the invisible girl. "I think I love you."

"What's going on there?" Zan asked me.

"You don't want to know," I told her.

We reached the medical bay, went inside, and locked the door. Then we found two InflatiCubes and sat across from each other.

"You have been asking why it is so important that I talk to you," Zan said. "Wondering if mankind is in trouble. I told you it wasn't . . . but that was not completely honest of me."

My skin suddenly felt cold, as though I'd stepped outside the moon base entirely. "So . . . humans *are* in danger?"

"In a sense."

"From what?"

"Yourselves. Surely you are aware that nature is a delicate balance on every planet, and yours is in trouble."

"Yes," I said. This wasn't a secret. The news from earth was always filled with stories of mass extinctions, choking clouds of pollution, islands and coastal cities inundated by floodwaters from rising seas, and other such environmental disasters.

"Humanity is running out of time to confront these problems," Zan said. "Faster than you realize. Earlier today, you asked me if there was an asteroid heading toward earth. Well, there is, in a sense. Humanity is the asteroid. You're doing as much damage to earth as an asteroid would. The only difference is, an asteroid would destroy life on your planet immediately, while humanity is going to take a few centuries."

I realized I was gripping the examining table tightly. Apparently, I'd needed to steady myself after hearing Zan's news. "How much time do we have?"

"I can't predict the future. After all, the course you are on is not necessarily guaranteed."

I looked at Zan, intrigued. "You mean, humanity could still survive?"

"That's correct."

I began to understand what Zan was getting at. "Because of you?"

"Perhaps." Zan fixed her gaze on me, staring at me so intently that I could feel her inside my head. "Yours would not be the first species to encounter problems like this. They are, in a sense, a sort of growing pain. There are ways to harness the power of the universe that you have not discovered yet, ones that could solve many of the problems you have created for yourselves."

"Really?" I exclaimed. "So can you tell us what to do?"

Zan didn't answer right away, which was an answer in itself.

"You're not going to give us this information, are you?" I asked.

"That is still being decided."

"Why? Is it some sort of galactic test? Like, if we can't figure it out for ourselves, we don't deserve to survive?"

Zan laughed. "No, it's nothing like that. This information has been passed from many species to others. In fact, that is how my own species received it. It was a gift."

"So why won't you give it to us?"

"Because we're not sure you can be trusted with it. Humanity has some unusual characteristics that greatly concern us. In particular, your way of taking new technology and trying to destroy each other with it."

"Oh," I said sadly.

"When mankind invented steel, practically the first thing you did was make swords from it," Zan explained. "Within only a few years of inventing airplanes, you were using them to drop bombs on each other. And when you finally figured out how to split the atom, which could have done so much good, you immediately used it to build bombs, wiping out millions of people—and ultimately threatening the lives of every being on your planet."

I nodded, feeling ashamed on behalf of humanity. "But if we're going to die anyhow, why not take a chance on us? Maybe we *won't* make weapons with this new technology."

"But you might. And the problem is that such weapons wouldn't only be dangerous to *you*. They'd also be dangerous to civilizations on other planets. Once you start dealing with the sort of power we're talking about, it can have effects far beyond your own tiny world."

"Even though those other planets are light-years away from us?"

"Did you know that if a star even a few light-years away from the earth were to explode, the radiation from it could ultimately shred the delicate atmosphere of your planet, killing almost everything?"

"Yes." When you lived in a small base with some of earth's most renowned astrophysicists, this sort of thing tended to come up at dinner. I also knew that, luckily, there were no stars anywhere near earth that close to exploding.

"Well," Zan said, "imagine a power even bigger and more destructive than that. A power that can travel much faster than light speed. In the wrong hands, it wouldn't simply destroy your earth and every living thing on it; it could destroy innocent lives on planets all through the galaxy."

I sagged, daunted by the thought. "So how do I fit into all of this?"

"As I have told you, we have been observing your species for some time now. However, observations can only tell us so much. They allow us to suspect *why* you might behave the way you do, but they don't tell us for sure. Now, there are some among my species—and those on other planets— who believe they have seen enough. They say your behavior has already proven you unworthy of our help. But there are others—myself included—who feel we may not fully understand all there is to humanity."

"So you came to me to explain it to you? To see if we can be trusted?"

"Yes."

It seemed that I should have been flattered by this, but instead I felt uneasy. Like an enormous burden had been placed on my shoulders. "Why me? Out of all the people in the world . . . ? Why not somebody smarter than me? There's a dozen geniuses on this base alone."

"Who's to say that you aren't as smart as they are?"

"Well, they're older than me. I'm only a kid!"

"That's not necessarily a bad thing. After all, who builds the weapons and then uses them in your society, adults or children?"

I bit my lip, trying to stay calm. The idea that I was standing as a representative for the future of all humanity was almost as unsettling as the idea that humanity was in jeopardy.

"I know this is all a lot to deal with," Zan said, sensing my feelings. "It is why I tried to keep things secret as long as I could."

"So what is it that I'm supposed to explain?" I asked. "What do you need to know about us?"

"They're not the sort of things you can simply tell me. It's more like I need to experience them *through* you."

I looked at Zan, concerned. "You mean, when you're in my head, you're not just talking to me? You're . . . *being* me?"

"I suppose you could say that. But that's not exactly it either. Have you ever asked someone a question and known that they're not giving you the full answer?"

"Of course."

"Well, suppose you could know the full answer every time you asked the question. And more."

"I see. I think."

"There are many things that concern us about humanity," Zan said. "I know I do not have to go into them with you. Many have been on display here at this very base: brutality, greed, jealousy, pride, cruelty. . . ."

"And that's just Lars Sjoberg," I muttered.

Zan laughed. "Yes. And many of these things are unusual—if not unique—to your species. However, I have also learned that there are many good things about humanity. Things that are not quite as common in the galaxy as you might think."

"Like what?"

"Music, for one."

"You don't have music on your planet?"

"We didn't until we encountered humanity. It never

occurred to anyone to make it. And even now that we know about it, we don't seem to have the gift for it that you do. We have never made anything as beautiful as Mozart did. Or the Beatles. Or Coronal Mass Ejection."

"You like CME?"

"Very much so. And there are other wonderful things you have developed besides music. Painting. Theater. Sculpture. Poetry. The amazing things you can do with food. Empathy. Love."

Everything on the list was shocking. But the last one blew me away. "You don't have love?"

"We have something like it, I suppose, but what you experience is far more powerful. With my own kind, I have never felt anything like what you feel for your parents. Or Violet. . . . Or me."

I locked eyes with her, surprised by this last revelation. Because up until that point, I hadn't realized it myself. But now, there was no denying that I had a massive crush on Zan.

"Is that why you chose me?" I asked. "Because I like you?"

"It didn't hurt," Zan said with a smile.

I realized I was blushing and turned away.

"It's nothing to be embarrassed about," Zan said quickly. "Really, you ought to be proud of these feelings. In fact, you ought to be thrilled that you have them. I am only experiencing a tiny fraction of what you experience, but this love is an amazing thing."

"It isn't always," I said.

"Maybe not. It seems quite complicated at times. Which is part of what I am trying to understand. The potential of this—and of all the good things in humans—is amazing. If you were to harness all this, rather than your destructive instincts, you might be able to do more incredible things than any other civilization we've encountered."

"Really?"

"I believe so."

"So why don't you all come to us, then? Make contact. Help us do good instead of bad."

"That isn't my decision to make. But what I learn from you will hopefully go a long way to influencing that decision."

"Hopefully?"

"There's one last thing you should know. In truth, most intelligent life in the universe has written you off already. They did it long ago, when they first observed you. They haven't seen what I have. They haven't tried to. In fact, they are unaware of this mission at all. Because it shouldn't be happening."

I swallowed hard, growing worried. "You mean, you don't have permission to be here?"

"Not exactly. I am not working alone, but . . . the group I'm with is only a small faction, fighting for what we believe is right."

"Like the rebels from *Star Wars*?"

Zan smiled. "I suppose you could say that."

"Are you fighting some sort of evil empire?"

"No. Evil is one of those things that seems to be uniquely human. We don't have anything like Darth Vader. Or Adolf Hitler. Or Lars Sjoberg. But we do have a sense of right and wrong. And there are many who would say that what I am doing right now is wrong."

"Why?"

"Because humanity is thought to be beyond saving—and any attempt to help you will only result in the disaster I mentioned before."

I closed my eyes, trying to make sense of everything. The idea that humanity's fate was hanging in the balance—and that I was possibly the only thing that might tip the scale in our favor—was overwhelming. I immediately regretted hounding Zan to tell me the truth—or that I'd ever met her in the first place. I wished that she'd chosen someone besides me, that I was freed from any responsibility, that I had never been selected to come to Moon Base Alpha at all.

"Dashiell?" Zan asked. "Are you okay?"

I didn't answer her. In fact, I was quite sure I didn't have to. I could feel her inside my brain, pushing against my thoughts, trying to make sense of things. But I could barely make sense of things myself; I was confused by a dozen different emotions. The only thing I knew for sure was that I missed earth terribly. I wanted to be off the moon, back home, breathing fresh air under a bright blue sky. I wanted to be on a beach in Hawaii, feeling the sand between my toes and the cool rush of water as it came in from the sea. I wanted to see animals. I wanted to smell flowers. I wanted to be surrounded by life. I wanted to see my friends.

"Dashiell?" Zan asked. It felt like she was forcing herself into my mind harder now.

And then, suddenly, all the emotions I was feeling combined into a sensation I'd never experienced before. For a moment, it felt like I was being pulled through something, although I couldn't say what, and I had the sense that I had suddenly traveled very far, very fast, in a mere fraction of a second.

And then I felt an honest-to-God breeze on my face.

I opened my eyes.

I was on Hapuna Beach in Hawaii, with the water lapping around my feet. The sun was close to setting, making the ocean shimmer and turning the clouds pink.

Riley Bock was standing right in front of me, holding a surfboard and staring at me with complete and total astonishment. "Dash?" she gasped. "How'd you get back here?"

I tried to answer, but couldn't. Something was tugging me back. There was a blinding flash of light that forced me to close my eyes again.

When I opened them once more, I was right back in the medical bay on Moon Base Alpha. Hawaii—and the rest of earth—was 238,000 miles away.

I felt completely exhausted, and yet exhilarated, too.

"What happened?" I asked.

"You know how I travel here from my planet by thinking myself here?" Zan asked.

"Yes."

Zan smiled, her blue eyes gleaming with excitement, and said, "I think you just did it."

Future site of
Moon Base
Beta

Lava Tubes

MBB
Operations Pod
(subterranean; see inset)

Joel
Crater

Mount
Kiradash

Holtz
Crater

Route to
MBB Site

Reisman
Crater

Chanda
Hill